"Dan." It was a whisper,
blown away by a gust of wind swirling
around the lighthouse. "Kiss me."

"I am." His teeth closed tighter, not hard enough to cause pain, but enough to make Savannah's breath tangle in her throat.

"No. I mean, *really* kiss me."

He smiled again. With his mouth and with his eyes. "I am." He soothed the pink mark his teeth had made with the tip of his tongue. "I will."

FAR HARBOR

"The talent for storytelling is obviously embedded deep in Ms. Ross's bones."

—*Romantic Times*

Also by JoAnn Ross

JoAnn Ross

Far Harbor

POCKET BOOKS
New York   London   Toronto   Sydney

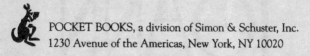 POCKET BOOKS, a division of Simon & Schuster, Inc.
1230 Avenue of the Americas, New York, NY 10020

This book is a work of fiction. Names, characters, places and incidents are products of the author's imagination or are used fictitiously. Any resemblance to actual events or locales or persons, living or dead, is entirely coincidental.

Copyright © 2000 by The Ross Family Trust created 10/23/97

Originally published in hardcover in 2000 by Pocket Books

ISBN-13: 978-1-4165-2350-5
ISBN-10:   1-4165-2350-2

This Pocket Books paperback edition November 2006

10 9 8 7 6 5 4 3 2 1

POCKET and colophon are registered trademarks of Simon & Schuster, Inc.

Cover art by Ben Perini
Cover design by Rod Hernandez

Manufactured in the United States of America

For information regarding special discounts for bulk purchases, please contact Simon & Schuster Special Sales at 1-800-456-6798 or business@simonandschuster.com.

To my outstanding editor,
Caroline Tolley, who, in the beginning,
knew my story better than I did

FAR HARBOR

1

~~~

She was not running away. Savannah Townsend might not have a firm grasp on every little aspect of her life these days, but about this she was perfectly clear.

She may have walked away from her marriage, the career she'd worked hard to achieve, and a spectacular Malibu home with floor-to-ceiling windows that overlooked the vast blue Pacific Ocean. But what was a woman to do when her seemingly idyllic existence turned out to be little more than a pretty illusion, as ephemeral as the morning fog curling around her ankles?

"Well?" Lilith Lindstrom Ryan's smile was brimming with self-satisfaction. "Isn't it perfect?"

"For Norman Bates, perhaps," Savannah murmured as she eyed the Far Harbor lighthouse with misgiving.

Savannah remembered the lighthouse standing regally at the edge of the cliff like an empress above a forest of dark green conifers. Now it had the look of a dowager who, through no fault of her own, had somehow found herself on skid row.

Graffiti covered the graceful tower that had once gleamed like sunshine on snow; the glass of the lantern room had been broken, and the railings that had been painted to match the red top cap were not only rusted, they looked downright dangerous.

The two houses on the cliff-side property were in even worse shape. Paint was peeling off the once white clapboards, and curling red shingles suggested that the roofs would leak.

Surprisingly, the grounds hadn't been entirely ignored since the lighthouse duties had been taken over by an automated light housed in an unattractive but utilitarian concrete tower a mile away. Someone had planted the most amazing garden Savannah had ever seen. A dazzling mix of tall, stunningly beautiful lilies, irises, Shasta daisies, and spiky bright snapdragons in primary colors were bordered by snowy white clouds of baby's breath.

"It was beautiful once," Savannah's mother reminded her. "And could be again. You just need to use your imagination, darling."

"I am. I'm imagining spiders the size of my fist and the hordes of mice that are undoubtedly living in the place." Savannah really hated rodents. Especially these days, when they reminded her so much of her rat of an ex-husband. "It's a good thing we're here in the daylight, because if we'd come at night, I just might start believing in the ghost."

The lighthouse was rumored to be haunted. By whom was a matter of speculation that had kept the good citizens of Coldwater Cove, Washington, arguing for nearly a century, but the most popular notion was that the ghost was a former lighthouse keeper's pregnant wife, Lucy Hyatt.

"A ghost would be wonderful publicity," Lilith said enthusiastically. "But even without it, lighthouses are incredibly romantic. And that sweet little assistant lighthouse keeper's cottage will make a perfect honeymoon getaway."

"Good idea. Are you going to call Frankenstein and his bride for the booking, or shall I?" Savannah asked dryly.

"You were always such an optimistic little girl." The silver crescent moons hanging from Savannah's mother's ears caught the stuttering morning sunlight as she shook her head. "So open to new things. Your aura used to be as bright as a morning star. These days it's distressingly muddy. . . .

"Why, if I weren't a white witch, I'd put a spell on your horrid ex-husband for hurting you so badly. At least you had the foresight not to take his name."

"Savannah Fantana would have sounded like something from an old Gilda Radner *Saturday Night Live* skit." Savannah wished the subject hadn't come up. Talking about her unfaithful, amoral ex-husband definitely wasn't on today's to-do list.

Today was about finding a suitable bed-and-breakfast location. Having spent weeks searching Washington's Olympic Peninsula, Savannah had begun to despair of ever finding a suitable candidate for her post-divorce venture.

"Besides," she said, "as I told Raine when I first came home, I think my pride was a lot more wounded than my heart."

"That's why you spent all those days hiding in bed and the nights crying into your pillow."

"All right, perhaps I was more upset than I let on," Savannah reluctantly allowed. "But I've put my marriage behind me." Didn't she have the papers, stamped with the official seal of the state of California to prove it? "In fact, I honestly believe Kevin might have actually done me a favor."

Lilith arched a perfectly formed brow. "And I suppose his restraining order trying to prevent you from using any recipes you came up with while working at Las Casitas Resort was yet another favor?" Sarcasm was not her mother's usual tone. But when necessary, Lilith could wield it like a rapier. "Not to mention stealing half the equity in your beautiful house."

"Raine forced him to drop that restraining order." While Savannah had always been proud of her sister, she'd never imagined needing her legal skills. "As for the house, California's a community property state. Kevin was entitled to half the proceeds."

"By law, perhaps," Lilith allowed grudgingly. "Common decency is another matter altogether and something the man was definitely lacking.

I'm still tempted to turn him into a toad. The only problem is, some other witch has obviously already done it."

Savannah certainly couldn't argue with that. She wondered how many women grew up believing in Prince Charming, only to wake up one morning to discover they'd ended up with the frog instead.

"I thought you'd given up paganism in order to sell real estate."

"A person can be both Wiccan and Realtor, dear."

While she tried to be tolerant of her mother's lifelong flighty behavior, Savannah hadn't been at all pleased to learn, upon returning home to Coldwater Cove, that Lilith had been arrested for setting illegal fires and dancing nude in Olympic National Park during Beltane. With her usual flair for making the best of a bad situation, her mother had recently married the arresting officer.

"I wonder who planted the flowers," she murmured, deciding that the time had come to change the subject.

Whoever had chosen the landscape design definitely had an artist's eye. The varying hues of the flowers swirled together like ornate patterns in a priceless Oriental carpet. Unfortunately, the riot of color and lush, shiny green leaves only made the buildings look more ramshackle by comparison.

"Oh, that'd be John."

"John?"

"John Martin. He's Daniel O'Halloran's nephew.

He has a bit of a mental disability, I believe, but he's never let it get in his way. He's also the sweetest boy you'd ever want to meet and the reason Daniel came back to Coldwater Cove last year."

"Why is that?" Since her sister had become a partner in Dan O'Halloran's law practice this past spring, as well as marrying his cousin, Jack, and Dan had done some legal work for the family, Savannah had heard bits and pieces of the story. But she wasn't aware of the details.

"Oh, it's the most tragic story," Lilith said with another shake of her head. "John's parents were killed when a log truck hit their car on the coast road near Moclips. John survived the crash, but he spent months in intensive care. Worse yet, since John's grandparents on his paternal side were no longer living and the elder Mr. and Mrs. O'Halloran couldn't give up the income from their fishing charter business to care for the boy, Daniel took a leave of absence from his prosecutor's job in San Francisco and returned to Coldwater Cove so John wouldn't have to recover in some rehabilitation center among strangers.

"Needless to say, Dan's wife, who they say is from a wealthy old Bay area family, wasn't thrilled with the idea of leaving her Pacific Heights mansion to play nurse to a mentally handicapped thirteen-year-old boy in the little house in the woods, so she remained behind in California.

"By the time John was finally released from the hospital, Dan must have come to appreciate the slower-paced lifestyle of our little burg,"

Lilith wrapped up her story, "because he bought a lovely home on the water. In fact, you can see it from here." She pointed toward a house, constructed of native cedar logs, that overlooked the Strait of Juan de Fuca.

"It's spectacular." The two-story glass wall thrusting out from beneath the wood shake roof reminded Savannah of the prow of an ancient sailing ship. All that was missing was a painted figurehead.

"Isn't it stunning? Unfortunately, by the time it closed escrow, his high-society wife had already divorced him."

"Seems to be a lot of that going around," Savannah said dryly.

"Sad, but true," Lilith agreed. "However, in your case, you're right about it being for the best. . . . Well, what do you think about refurbishing this place?"

Savannah had confidence in her ability to run a small inn, but she'd never considered herself a miracle worker. "Didn't you say something about a Victorian in Port Townsend that's just gone on the market?"

"Yes, but Victorian bed-and-breakfasts are so common these days. And you couldn't ask for a better location than this."

Good point. The lighthouse had, admittedly, been built on one of the most stunning sites on the peninsula. "I'm surprised a developer hasn't bought the property for a resort."

"Oh, I can't imagine the owner allowing that. Having grown up on the grounds, he's very sentimental about the lighthouse. Didn't I tell you his name?"

"No. It didn't come up."

"He's Henry Hyatt."

"Hyatt? Surely not Lucy's son?"

"The very same. He was five years old when Lucy drowned. In fact, there are some who insist that Lucy's spirit refused to leave the lighthouse as long as her child still lived there."

Although she'd never believed any of the ghost stories, Savannah couldn't resist a glance upward toward the railing surrounding the lantern room where, according to local legend, Lucy could often have been seen, weeping as she stared out toward her watery grave. Although the August sun had burned off the last of the morning fog, Savannah shivered.

After spending another three days visiting countless houses from Port Angeles to Port Gamble, Savannah found herself back at the Far Harbor lighthouse. Ever since she was a little girl, she'd been drawn to this special, romantic place.

Savannah's mother had been a flower child, a war protester, an actress usually cast as the soon-to-be-dead bimbo in low-budget horror films, and a singer with a frail but pretty voice who'd managed to stay in the business mostly because of her looks, which were still stunning. Whenever Lilith Lindstrom Cantrell Townsend Ryan's life had spun out of control, which it did with an almost predictable regularity, she'd bring her two daughters back to Coldwater Cove to live with their grandmother, Ida.

On every one of those occasions, the moment Savannah would catch sight of the tomato red cap of the lighthouse in the distance as the ferry approached the small town, she'd feel as if she was coming home. Or at least to the closest thing she'd known to a real home during her unstable childhood years.

She had to agree with Lilith that the Victorian in Port Townsend wasn't what she was looking for, yet she had seen others that had possibility.

"A lot more possibility than this place," she murmured as she walked along the path between the houses and the lighthouse. Fragrance from the remarkable garden floated on the evening breeze.

The sun was setting over the Olympic Mountains like a brilliant fan, turning the water to molten copper and gold. Savannah sat down on a bench in the garden and thought that Lilith was certainly right about one thing: this would make a perfect honeymoon location. That idea brought to mind the first bride who'd come to this lighthouse.

No one had ever known why Lucy Hyatt had been a passenger on the *Annabelle Lee*, a passenger ship bound for San Francisco that had foundered during a winter squall. There were as many stories as there were people who could still remember that so-called storm of the century, but the most popular and prevailing theory continued to be that she'd abandoned her husband and five-year-old child and was running away with her big-city lover, the dashing scion of a Bay area family who'd made their fortune in imported sugar and California land speculation.

Lucy and the sugar heir had been seen talking at the railing shortly before the ship's departure from its Seattle port, and although more than eighty decades had passed since the tragedy, rumors continued to persist that he'd paid for Lucy's ticket.

Whatever the reason for her having been aboard in the first place, survivors at the time had all agreed that Lucy had been washed overboard by the violent, storm-tossed waves. The following morning her broken body was found on the rocks below her husband's lighthouse.

When that tragic tale proved depressing, Savannah rubbed her arms to ease the goosebumps, took the heavy brass key her mother had given her from her purse, and went inside.

She strolled through the rooms, stepping over fast-food bags and empty beer bottles she suspected had been left behind by vagrants and partying teenagers and imagined lace Priscilla curtains framing sparkling windows that looked out over the water.

"Candles in the windows would be a nice touch," she decided out loud. Her voice echoed in the empty, high-ceilinged room. "But electric ones." She certainly wouldn't want to accidentally burn the historic building down.

An odd sensation teased at her mind, like the

misty-edged remnants of a dream after awakening. A warmth began to flow through her blood, easing the tensions of the past months, and while she suspected her New Age mother would ascribe her feelings to some sort of fanciful past life *déjà vu*, Savannah couldn't quite ignore the feeling that the lighthouse was once again welcoming her home.

Instead of the odor of damp wallpaper and mold that hung on the musty air, she breathed in the imagined scent of lemon oil and pictured how the scarred heart-of-pine floor would gleam once it had been sanded and stained.

"I hope the fireplace works."

She ran her fingers over stones that didn't appear to be crumbling too badly. A crackling blaze would certainly warm rainy winter evenings. She'd recently seen a pair of andirons in Granny's Attic, an antique shop on Harbor Street across from the ferry terminal, that would prove the crowning touch.

"It really is perfect," she assured herself as she tried to decide between a seascape or a mirror over the hand-carved cedar mantel.

She crossed the floor and looked up the spiral staircase leading to the lantern room.

"Are you there, Lucy?" she called out. She didn't really expect an answer, and if Henry Hyatt's mother's ghost *was* actually haunting the lighthouse, she was keeping silent. "You're not going to be alone anymore, because I'm going to buy your home and clean it up."

Her words echoed around her. "It's going to

be lovely again," she promised, undaunted by the lack of ghostly response. "A place you—and I—can be proud of."

Outside, the sun was sinking ever lower in the late summer sky; inside, dust motes danced in the slanting sunbeams like ballerinas wearing gilt tutus. Giddy with anticipation, Savannah began dancing herself, spinning across the scuffed and scarred floor in time to the swelling music playing inside her head as the shadows darkened and draped the Far Harbor lighthouse in a deep purple veil.

2

"So, what do you think, Uncle Dan?"

"I think you're terrific." Daniel O'Halloran reached over and ruffled his nephew's hair.

"That's what you always say." John Martin grinned and ducked his head. "I meant about the flowers."

"Hey, you're the designer. I'm just the manual labor guy." He turned the Tahoe onto the gravel road that led up to the Far Harbor lighthouse. "But I think using these branch berries as a groundcover is a great idea."

"They're bunchberry."

"Right. Yet another reason why you're the gardener." Dan paused, deciding that the time had come to break the news he'd been withholding for the past week since the lighthouse had gone on the market. "There's something we need to talk about, Sport."

"What?"

Since subtlety had never been John's strong suit, Dan decided to just dive straight into the dangerous conversational waters. "Henry Hyatt's put the lighthouse up for sale."

"The lighthouse?" The color drained from John's face. "*My* lighthouse?"

"Technically it's Mr. Hyatt's," Dan reminded him carefully.

"But he doesn't care about it. He let it get all run down so that kids would write on it and throw rocks. If it wasn't for me, it'd be really ugly."

"I know." Dan sighed, thinking of all John had overcome in his life already and wishing he could spare him this. "But to be perfectly fair to Mr. Hyatt, he hasn't exactly been in the best of health the past few years."

"He moved out before that. And never came back."

"He moved out because the place was too much for him to handle after he fell and broke his hip. And we really don't know for certain that he never came back." Dan decided to try a different tack. "Besides, I have the feeling that after his wife died, it got to be a little hard emotionally on him to live there alone."

"Because of his mother. Because she drowned."

"That'd be my guess."

"But he was just a little boy when that happened. Now he's old. He should have gotten over that hurting by now."

"I'm not sure anyone can ever get over the loss of a loved one," Dan said quietly. "Not completely."

There was a moment's silence. Dan could practically hear the gears cranking away in John's head. "Now you're talking about my mom and dad."

"You, of all people, should understand that sometimes people feel a lot of stuff deep down inside that they're not real comfortable sharing with strangers."

"Yeah. Sometimes, when I think about the accident, I feel like crying. But I don't, at least not when anybody can see me, because I don't want them to think I'm a dummy."

"No one could ever think that."

"Sometimes people do," John said matter-of-factly. "But Mom always said that I just need to work harder to change their minds."

"Your mom was a wise woman."

"I know." John sighed. "Sometimes I miss her a lot."

"Me, too, Sport." It had been more than a year, and the loss of his older sister still hurt. Dan figured it always would.

After having made the decision to buy the Far Harbor lighthouse, Savannah was back on the grounds, the inspection report in hand. It wasn't as bad as she'd feared. The roofs would need replacing, there was a little dry rot in the basement of the larger of the two houses, and the wiring would have to be brought up to code in all three buildings, but at least they remained structurally sound.

Mostly all that was needed was a lot of hard

work and elbow grease. After these past months of feeling like a ship adrift at sea without a rudder, Savannah found herself looking forward to having her sights set on a new goal.

When she'd caught her husband having sex with the relentlessly ambitious, take-no-prisoners attorney from the resort's legal department, right in his office, on the glove-soft Italian leather couch she'd bought Kevin for an anniversary present, Savannah had discovered that the old saying was true—fury really did cause you to see red.

As a scarlet flame blazed before her eyes, she'd been sorely tempted to commit castration with her new filet knife. Fortunately, common sense kicked in, and after deciding that the unfaithful, lying, narcissistic husband she'd once adored wasn't worth going to prison for, she moved into the Beverly Wilshire hotel, arranged to have all her calls—except those from her adulterous spouse—forwarded, ordered a ridiculously expensive bottle of champagne from room service, and then proceeded, for the first time in her life, to get rip-roaring drunk.

The following morning the phone had jarred through her skull like a Klaxon. It had been Raine, calling with the news that their grandmother had been taken to the hospital after a fall and now the courts were demanding that an adult other than Lilith take over the care of Ida's pregnant teenage foster child.

Nursing the mother of all hangovers, bolstered with a Thermos of strong coffee and a large bottle of extra-strength pain reliever, Savannah had left California that day. As soon as she'd arrived back in Coldwater Cove, she'd immediately been swept up into a series of family emergencies. Once those crises had been taken care of, her own problems had belatedly come crashing down on her like a blow from behind.

She still wasn't certain exactly how long she'd spent curled in a fetal position beneath her covers, wrapped in an aimless lassitude. Finally, when she'd just about decided that she was destined to spend the rest of her life in bed, she'd awakened one sunny August morning feeling as if she'd survived a coma. Thinking back on those weeks, Savannah realized that she'd been behaving much the same way she had during childhood when, terrified by the violent thunderstorms that rumbled and crashed over the mountaintops, she'd cower in the closet beneath the stairs. The only difference was that this time she'd been hiding from life.

Determined to create a new identity, she'd called her mother, who'd recently gotten her Realtor's license, and began searching for the perfect property to turn a lifelong dream into reality. And now she'd found it.

Immersed in chipping away at the paint that was flaking off the window shutters like cheap fingernail polish, Savannah wasn't aware of the truck coming up the hill. It was only when she heard first one, then a second metal door close, that she realized she was not alone. A moment later a teenager in a T-shirt that read He Who Plants a Garden, Plants Hope appeared from behind the lighthouse carrying a black plastic flat of bedding plants.

"Hello." She gave him her friendliest smile. "I'm Savannah Townsend. And you must be John Martin."

"That's my name, all right." His eyes narrowed ever so slightly. "Are you the lady who's going to buy the lighthouse?"

"I'm thinking about it. But to be perfectly honest, the only thing going for it is your garden."

"How did you know I planted the flowers?" His cautious expression turned panicky.

"Well, the fact that you're carrying a flat of plants was my first clue. Also, my mother told me when we were here a few days ago. It's absolutely stunning. You're definitely an artist."

"People say that a lot," he agreed guilelessly. "They say, John Martin, you were born with the greenest thumb in the entire Pacific Northwest."

"They're probably right. So, does Mr. Hyatt pay you to do his gardening?" Savannah couldn't understand why, if Henry Hyatt cared so much about the grounds, he'd let the rest of the lighthouse fall into disrepair.

"No." The strange, edgy panic was back. He reminded her vaguely of a wild rabbit about to bolt. "Nobody's ever paid me. It was all my idea. But I didn't mean to do anything bad."

"Oh, I wasn't implying you did," Savannah said quickly. "I mean, I wasn't suggesting—"

"He understands the word *imply*," Dan, who'd appeared carrying a second flat of plants, offered.

"I do understand *imply*," John seconded his uncle. "I have a disability," he explained. "But I'm not stupid."

"Of course you're not," she agreed.

"How do you know that? Since you don't know me?" John asked.

She exchanged a brief look with Dan, who seemed to be watching her carefully. "You just told me."

"Oh." He appeared to accept that. "This is my uncle Dan. He's my best friend."

"Isn't that nice?" She turned her smile toward Dan. "Hello."

"Savannah." Little lines crinkled outward from morning glory blue eyes when he smiled, reminding her of a bittersweet secret crush she'd had on him the summer she'd turned twelve. "You're looking well—as always."

"She looks beautiful," John corrected. "Like a movie star. And the sun makes her long hair look like it's on fire."

Savannah laughed. "I can tell you've got O'Halloran genes, John." During their high school days, Dan and his cousin Jack had certainly charmed more than their share of Coldwater Cove's female population. "You must have kissed the Blarney stone."

The boy's freckled forehead furrowed. "I don't remember doing that."

"Well, perhaps I'm mistaken."

"Or I was too young to remember," he said helpfully.

"That could be."

"But usually I have a real good memory. Better than people without a disability, even. Huh, Uncle Dan?"

"Absolutely."

"Like I said, I'm just slow. When I was a little kid, my mom read me the story of the tortoise and the hare. About how the hare did things a lot faster, but in the end the tortoise finally won the race. I'm like the tortoise. Slow and steady."

"That certainly makes sense to me." Savannah exchanged another brief look with Dan. "So, if you don't work for Mr. Hyatt, how did you come to plant this garden?"

"Sometimes other kids take advantage of me. One Halloween, right after I got mainstreamed into public middle school, some boys talked me into throwing rocks to try to break the lantern room glass. I threw a lot, but only a couple hit.

"The sheriff caught us. After he explained that what we did was vandalism, I felt real bad. I thought and thought how I could make things better, but I didn't know how to fix the broken glass. And that's when I decided that I could plant some flowers and make it look prettier. So I did. And it really did look prettier, didn't it, Uncle Dan?"

"You bet." His grin was quick and warm and obviously genuine.

"The next spring I planted some more. Then some more after that. And pretty soon everyone started calling me the flower kid. I'm saving my money so some day I can start my own landscaping business. My mom used to say that everyone should have a dream. I figure a garden is about as nice a thing to dream about as anything else."

"You're right. I've always had a fantasy of starting my own inn, where people could come and relax and forget all about the outside world."

"And dream?"

"Definitely dream, and I can't think of a better place to do that than right here. But since I've been known to kill plants as easily as look at them, I hope I can hire you to keep up this magical garden."

"It's not magic. But I will keep it up, if you want."

"Then it's a deal." She held out her hand. "Partners?"

His grin was as wide as a Cheshire cat's. "Partners."

"Hey, John," Dan said after Savannah and John had shaken hands, "why don't you go get started planting and I'll be right along."

"Okay."

When he was out of earshot, Dan put the flat down on the bench. "So, you're really going to stay?"

"Absolutely."

He didn't answer for a moment. Instead, he skimmed a look over her, from the top of her head to her feet, clad in expensive designer sneakers that were one of the few reminders of her past life. Savannah had the impression that after the years she'd spent in Paris, Atlantic

City, New Orleans, and Los Angeles, he didn't think she'd still fit into Coldwater Cove.

"It isn't going to be easy."

"That's okay." She lifted her chin and did her best to pull off at least a bit of her sister Raine's Xena-the-warrior-princess impression. "I'm tougher than I look."

"You're going to have to be, if you're planning to tackle this place. Because it's definitely a wreck."

"A challenge," she corrected.

He chuckled. "You and John should get together and open a Coldwater Cove chapter of Optimists Anonymous."

His words rubbed at some still-raw wounds and had her feeling perversely annoyed. Savannah seriously doubted that he would have questioned Raine taking on such a challenge. Then again, Raine had always had the reputation of being the "smart, sassy" sister, while Savannah was known throughout Coldwater Cove as the "sweet, pretty one."

Well, she was going to change that. There was nothing she could do about pretty since she'd been gifted—or cursed, she sometimes thought—with the best of her parents' looks. Her mother might be fifty, her rock-star father five years older, yet both had remained stunningly attractive individuals. Nevertheless, when Savannah had finally quit hiding beneath the covers, she'd vowed to abandon her lifelong habit of avoiding unwanted conflict by abandoning her own wishes. No longer would she be so damn accommodating, especially when such knee-jerk submission wasn't in her best interests.

"Do you have something against optimism, counselor?" Her back stiffened along with her resolve even as she secretly wondered which of them she was trying to convince, Dan or herself.

"Not at all."

"Good. Because I'm going to make this lighthouse beautiful again, and when it's done I'm going to throw the biggest blowout grand opening party Coldwater Cove has ever seen."

"Sounds like a plan."

He made another of those long, silent assessments that made her feel as if he were evaluating her for jury duty, then, just when her nerves were on the edge of screeching like banshees, he picked up the flat of glossy-leaved, dark green plants. "Guess I'll be seeing you tomorrow, then."

"Tomorrow?"

"I handle all of Henry Hyatt's legal affairs, including property sales, and while I don't want to scare you off, if you happen to have a suit of armor in your closet, you might think about wearing it for your meeting with the guy."

Dan's tone suggested that negotiating with Henry may prove nearly as difficult as refurbishing the buildings. Before she could respond that she was certainly capable of doing business with a frail old man, he flashed a quick grin that was even more charming than it had been back in those long-ago days of her adolescent crush, then sauntered away, his cheerful, off-key whistling drifting back on the fir-scented breeze.

The following morning Savannah lay in bed, futilely chasing sleep. She'd left the shade up so the stars that she'd never been able to see while living in California could shine into the room. A full white moon floated in the center of the darkened rectangle of the dormer window. The ring around the moon meant something, but she couldn't remember exactly what. Magic, perhaps? Or trouble?

The moon drifted by, eventually slipping out of sight as she struggled with her churning thoughts. By the time a shimmering lavender predawn glow revealed the violets that blossomed on the wallpaper she and Raine had compromised on so many years ago, she surrendered to the inevitable. There'd be no more sleep tonight.

Untangling herself from the twisted sheets, she pulled on a robe, went into the adjoining bathroom, splashed cold water on her face, brushed her teeth, and clipped her unruly red-gold hair into a quick twist. Then, not wanting to wake her grandmother, who was sleeping across the hall, she crept down the stairs to the kitchen, where she made coffee in the snazzy red coffeemaker she'd sent Ida last Christmas.

Drawn by the lure of birdsong, she went out on the front porch and sat down on the swing where she'd spent so many lazy summer afternoons daydreaming. Cradling the earthenware mug in her hands, Savannah breathed in the fragrant steam. As she thought back on those days, she decided that despite her mother's marital instability and gypsy lifestyle, her own life had certainly seemed a great deal simpler back then.

A few stars still shone on the horizon. After an early sprinkle that was more mist than rain, the day was dawning a gloriously bright one. Despite the popular stereotype of gray clouds, sunny skies weren't that uncommon during late summer. Since the Puget Sound cities of Seattle, Tacoma, and Olympia were being flooded with new residents, content with their remote peninsula town just the way it was, Coldwater Cove's residents tended to pray for rain whenever tourists were in town.

Ida Lindstrom's Victorian home was set atop a hill overlooking the town that could have washed off an American primitive painting of New England. The flagpole in the grassy green town square at the end of Harbor Street was surrounded by a blaze of color Savannah guessed was another example of John Martin's green thumb.

Those same vibrant blooms encircled the clock tower, which was made of a red brick that had weathered to a dusty pink over the century and could be seen for miles. Its four sides had each told a different time for as long as Savannah could remember, which didn't prove any real hardship, since things—and people—tended to move at their own pace in Coldwater Cove.

As she watched a white ferry chug across the sound, which was as smooth as sapphire glass this morning, her mind flashed back to a long-ago evening when choppy waters had caused her to throw up the hot dog, barbecue potato chips, and Dr. Pepper Lilith had fed her for dinner shortly before they'd all boarded the ferry that would take them from Seattle to Coldwater Cove.

She couldn't remember what, exactly, her mother had been doing during the short trip, but the memory of Raine dragging her out of the glassed-in observation desk into the fresh air, pushing her onto a wooden bench, and wiping her face with a wet paper towel was as vivid as if it had occurred only yesterday.

Her four-years-older half sister had always been there for her, hovering over her like an anxious mother bird, taking on the role of surrogate mother. Fate may have given them different fathers, but love had made them sisters of the heart.

Savannah couldn't count the number of times Raine had come to her rescue, banners flying, like bold, brave Joan of Arc riding into battle. Now, despite being grateful for her sister's unwavering support, she'd begun to suspect that perhaps she'd been overprotected.

Perhaps, she thought as she sipped her cooling coffee, if she'd been forced to fight a few more of her own battles, she wouldn't have so blithely ignored marital warning signs that only a very blind—or naive—woman could have missed.

"Stupid, stupid, stupid," she said into the still air perfumed with late summer roses. The scarlet blossoms drooping with the weight of diamond-bright dew were as large as a child's fist and as velvety as the formal gown she'd worn to the Coldwater Cove high school's winter festival.

She'd made the dress herself, laboring over the rented sewing machine late into the night for two weeks, buried in a pile of velvet and white satin trim that took up the kitchen table and had all of them eating on TV trays for the duration of the project.

Listening to Ida's grumbling and giving up sleep to baste and hem had proven worth it; when Savannah entered the gym that had been decked out in white and silver crepe paper for the occasion, with the crinolines that showcased her legs rustling seductively and her long hair, which she'd managed to tame with a curling iron, bouncing on her bare shoulders, she'd felt exactly like a fairy-tale princess.

The velvet fantasy of a gown was gone, but not forgotten, turned into pieces of a memory quilt she'd hung over the tester bed a Melrose antique dealer had assured her had once belonged to Lilian Gish. The quilt, which had also incorporated white lace squares from her high school graduation dress, a piece of shiny black silk from a negligee her mother had worn in a movie about female vampires that had opened on Savannah's tenth birthday, and ivory satin ribbons from her wedding bouquet, was currently packed away with other sentimental items in a cedar trunk at Jack Conway's U-Store-It on Spruce Street.

Fat black-and-yellow bees droned lazily around the roses. Next door the neighbor's cat was returning from his nightly rounds of the town. Ignoring Savannah, the fat old tom curled up into a ball in a slanting sunbeam on his owner's front porch and began washing his marmalade fur.

A familiar car turned onto the road leading up the hill. A minute later, it pulled to a stop in front of the house; the driver's door opened, and Lilith emerged in a graceful swirl of skirt the hue of crushed blueberries. Along with the silk skirt and tunic she also wore a necklace of hand-strung crystals, a pair of lacy webbed dream-catcher earrings and a frown that made Savannah's stomach knot.

Having already pinned her hopes on her admittedly ambitious project as a means of reinventing herself, Savannah didn't know what she'd do if her mother had come bearing bad news about the lighthouse she'd already come to think of as hers.

3

"You're certainly **up** and about early," Savannah greeted her mother with far more aplomb than she felt. "I thought we weren't scheduled to meet with Mr. Hyatt until late this afternoon."

"Your grandmother's on the committee for this year's Sawdust Festival," Lilith divulged as she climbed the front steps, bringing with her the exotic scent of custom-blended perfume that always made Savannah think of gypsies dancing around blazing campfires.

"She roped me into helping with entertainment, so we're going to Port Angeles this morning to check out a couple bands and have our fortunes told by Raven Moonsilver. Raven's a friend of mine, and since the committee's split on whether or not to hire her to read palms, as chairman, Ida gets to cast the deciding vote."

Her mother's gaze took in Savannah's blue mug. "Thank God you've made coffee. While I try to stick to herbal teas these days, my system definitely needs a jump start at this ungodly hour of the morning." She disappeared into the house.

The thought of the always practical Ida Lindstrom having her palm read was nearly as difficult to accept as the idea of this glamorous creature, who'd periodically blazed through Raine's and Savannah's lives like a comet, turning her creative talents toward something as prosaic as a small-town logging festival.

Lilith returned with a mug of steaming coffee liberally laced with cream and sat down on the top step.

"I ran into Dan yesterday at the lighthouse," Savannah divulged. "He'd come with John Martin to plant flowers. He mentioned something that's been worrying me." She paused, hoping as she had all night that she was making too much of Dan's remarks regarding the lighthouse owner.

"What's that, darling?"

"That Henry Hyatt might prove a problem."

Lilith took a careful sip of coffee before answering. "I'm not certain *problem* is precisely the word I'd use."

Concern stirred again, along with a niggling suspicion. "What are you holding back?"

"Absolutely nothing." Lilith toyed with her necklace. "The Board of Realtors would take away my license if I failed to give full disclosure on a property."

"Okay. Perhaps you're not hiding anything about the lighthouse. What about the owner?"

"You always were my more intuitive child."

Lilith's pansy blue eyes gleamed with affection. "I believe you take after the same Celts who gifted you with all that lovely Titian hair. After all, it's common knowledge that the women from that branch of the family all possess second sight, and—"

"Mother." Savannah cut Lilith off and looked her directly in the eye. "We're not talking second sight here. It's merely the process of elimination. If there's some impediment to my buying the lighthouse, and it doesn't involve the property itself, then it would stand to reason the problem is with the owner."

Lilith slid her veiled gaze out over the sparkling bay. "I don't believe Henry really wants to sell the lighthouse."

There had been several times over the past days when Savannah had questioned the practicality of attempting to refurbish such a ramshackle property. Still, her heart sank at this news.

"Then why on earth would he list it in the first place?"

"Because he doesn't want it any longer."

"I don't understand."

Another sigh. "The problem is, he doesn't want anyone else to own it, either. Not so long as his mother's spirit is still there."

"I should have known you'd believe in the ghost."

"I've never seen her. But that doesn't mean she doesn't exist."

"Well, if she does, I certainly hope she knows

how to use a paint brush, because her former home is in definite need of a new coat of paint."

Lilith waved the comment away with a graceful, beringed hand; her recently acquired wedding band—engraved with wolves because they mate for life, she'd explained—gleamed in the morning light. "Well, whatever Henry's feelings, you shouldn't have any problem convincing him to sell. He may be getting up in years, but he's still a man."

"A bitter, dried-up old man," a voice offered from the doorway. Ida Lindstrom's head was barely visible over the huge cardboard box she was holding. "He was never all that much of a charmer, but after his wife died, he turned downright ornery."

Savannah's grandmother was a small, wiry woman known throughout the county for her seemingly endless trove of energy, her dedication to her former patients, and her strong, often controversial opinions.

In contrast to her glamorous daughter, she was wearing baggy jeans and a T-shirt that read Of Course I Believe You, But Can I Get It in Writing? The message was pure Ida, which Savannah feared didn't exactly bode well for Lilith's palm reader friend.

"It must be eight years since Ruth passed on," Lilith reminded her mother. "Which means that Henry's been without female companionship for a very long time. I can't believe that he wouldn't jump at the chance to spend the afternoon with our Savannah."

"I refuse to stoop to using feminine wiles to talk Henry Hyatt into selling me his lighthouse," Savannah insisted.

"Of course you wouldn't," Ida agreed briskly. "You're my granddaughter, after all, and everyone knows that rolling stones don't fall far from the trees." Along with her bumper-sticker T-shirts, the retired general practitioner had long been Coldwater Cove's queen of malapropisms.

Lilith rolled her expressive eyes as she rose from the step, handed Savannah her empty mug and took the box from Ida's arms. "This weighs a ton," she complained. "What do you have in it, rocks?"

"Of course not. Why would I want to be mailing rocks to anyone?" Ida was looking at the box as if seeing it for the first time. "Who's it for, anyway?"

Lilith exchanged a brief, puzzled look with Savannah. "Since it's addressed to Gwen, I assume it's for her."

"Well, of course it is." Ida's brow cleared. The momentary confusion in her eyes was replaced by the usual bright intelligence that reminded Savannah of a curious bird. "When she called last night from science camp, I could tell she was homesick, so I'm sending her a bunch of her favorite things. Wouldn't want the girl to get so upset she starts shoplifting again."

Knowing that they were the first reasonably stable family Gwen had experienced during her rocky sixteen years, Savannah could understand how hard it must be for her to be away from Coldwater Cove for any length of time, even if the teenager who dreamed of following in Ida's physician footsteps was doing something she loved—something Savannah dearly hoped would help keep her mind off the baby she'd recently given up for adoption.

"Well, the day's not getting any younger, and neither am I," Ida announced suddenly. "If we're going to get our futures told, we might as well get going."

"Please promise that you'll keep an open mind," Lilith asked her mother with a deep, exaggerated sigh.

"Does this palm reader friend of yours wear a turban?"

"No."

"How about talking to the dead?"

"That's not her field of psychic expertise."

"Then we'll probably get on well enough." The pewter bird nest of hair piled precariously atop Ida's head wobbled as she nodded with her typical decisiveness that eased any lingering concern Savannah might have had about her earlier confusion. "So long as you girls both keep your clothes on."

With that pointed reference to Lilith's nude Beltane dancing, she marched toward the car, leaving her daughter to follow.

"Wish me luck," Lilith murmured as she bent to kiss Savannah's cheek. "After this outing, the meeting with Henry this afternoon should be a piece of cake."

Eight hours later, Savannah discovered that her mother's prediction had been optimistic.

The Evergreen Care Center was a redbrick building nestled in a grove of fir trees at the far end of town. The designers had done their best to make the center appealing, with outdoor patios, a sunroom, bright colors, and framed paintings designed to stimulate both the eye and the mind. A bulletin board, covered in grass green burlap, announced a crowded activity schedule that included wheelchair bowling, a morning newspaper group, and the monthly visit of Pet Partners, an organization of dog owners who'd bring their pets to visit the residents.

"Can you imagine ever putting your grandmother in a place like this?" Lilith murmured as they entered the lobby furnished with tasteful antique reproductions.

"Not in a million years."

Savannah thought that there must be a better way than to warehouse people at the end of their lives. Not that Ida was at the end of her life. She may have edged into her late seventies during Savannah's time away from Coldwater Cove, yet except for that little unexplained dizzy spell that had landed her in the hospital a few months ago, her grandmother was as energetic and strong-willed as ever.

Despite the fact that Savannah and Lilith had arrived at the care center ten minutes early, Henry Hyatt was already waiting for them in the sunroom.

"Oh, dear," Lilith said under her breath. "That's

him, in that chair upholstered in the bright nautical-theme sailcloth."

The elderly man's back was to the glass wall, which, Savannah noted with a grudging respect for his negotiating tactics, would force her to look directly into the setting sun. The scowl on his face could have withered a less determined woman.

Refusing to be intimidated, Savannah reminded herself that getting into a power contest with this frail, elderly man was no way to achieve her goal.

"Good afternoon, Mr. Hyatt." Her brilliant smile, an unconscious replica of her mother's, revealed not an iota of her churning emotions. An emerald ring once given to her by a Saudi prince who'd hired her to cook his fiftieth birthday dinner flashed like green fire in the slanting rays of tawny light streaming into the room.

"It's a pleasure to finally meet you." When his talon-like hand stayed right where it was atop the carved wooden cane, Savannah slowly lowered hers. "I've admired the Far Harbor lighthouse for years."

"You and all those other tourists who keep coming around, pestering a man, wanting to take pictures and have themselves a tour, never once thinking that a lighthouse isn't some new attraction at Disneyland."

Acid sharpened a scornful tone that wavered ever so slightly with age. Or emotion? Savannah wondered. In either case, it was not a propitious beginning.

"Now, Henry," Lilith soothed as she gracefully settled into a chair across from him. "You know very well that Savannah's not a tourist. Why, she spent practically her entire life growing up on the peninsula."

"Because her scatterbrained gadfly of a mother didn't see fit to take care of her," he snapped querulously.

Savannah heard Lilith draw in a breath at the sharp accusation, but outwardly her mother appeared unscathed. "You're right. I'll always regret not having been a better mother, but we all make mistakes." Lilith's voice was as warm and throaty as ever, but Savannah noticed that her hands trembled ever so slightly as her fingers creased the broomstick pleats of her skirt. "Sometimes all we can do is move on."

"You've always been good at that," he grumbled. "Moving on."

Savannah had humored him enough. Henry Hyatt may hold the keys to her future in his age-spotted hands, but that didn't give him the right to intrude on her admittedly complex relationship with Lilith.

"I came here today to discuss a business proposition with you, Mr. Hyatt, not to stand by and listen to you insult my mother."

An errant thought occurred to her. Could Henry possibly be comparing Lilith's behavior to the way his own mother had abandoned him at such a tender age? Was it even possible to harbor a hurt or hold a grudge for so many years?

He tilted his head and looked up at her.

"Didn't anyone ever teach you, when you were down in California"—he spat out the name of her former home as if it had a bad taste—"that sassin' a man who has something you seem to want so damn bad is a piss-poor way of doin' business?"

"The Far Harbor lighthouse is not the only piece of property for sale on the peninsula, Mr. Hyatt." She sat down in a wing chair beside her mother and crossed her legs. Proving that Lilith wasn't the only actress in the family, she kept her smile cucumber cool and just the slightest bit condescending. "Merely the most run-down."

Before Henry could respond to that, the door opened and Dan walked in, bringing with him a distant scent of the sea. "Sorry I'm late." His face was tanned from the sun, his hair windblown. "My meeting ran late."

"Meeting, hell." Henry focused his ill humor on his attorney. "Anyone with two eyes and half a brain can see you've been out sailing."

"Got me there," Dan replied equably. "As it happens, my meeting took place on a yacht."

"Ha! That's a likely story."

"It's true. My client's a software mogul who, like so many of his breed, tends to be a bit paranoid. He prefers doing business where there's less likelihood of conversations being overheard—such as out in the middle of the sound."

"You always were quick with the excuses," Henry shot back. "Like that time you broke the window on my Olds."

"When I fouled off my cousin Caine's curveball through your windshield." Dan glanced over at Savannah and winked. "I spent the rest of the summer paying it off by painting the lighthouse."

"Wouldn't have taken you so long if you hadn't been so damn slow."

"If I was slow it was because I spent the first two weeks shaking like a leaf from my newly discovered fear of heights. I got more paint on me than I managed to get on the lighthouse."

"Mebbe I should have you paint it again." Henry waved a faintly palsied hand toward Savannah. "Since this little gal thinks it's a bit rundown."

"More than a bit," Savannah corrected.

The way she tossed up her chin and stood up to a man who'd elevated the knack of being irritating to an art form had Dan suspecting that Savannah may have toughened up a bit since having been elected Miss Congeniality of her senior class.

"Girl's got a funny way of charming me into selling the place," Henry complained. Having come to know his irascible client well, Dan realized that the old codger was actually enjoying himself.

"I'm making you an offer for the lighthouse." Savannah's clipped tone revealed her growing frustration. "I'm not asking to become your new best friend."

He cackled at that. "Gal's got spunk, O'Halloran."

"Seems to." Dan nodded. "Perhaps even

enough to save the place from a wrecking ball."

Henry's pale blue eyes narrowed. "That's your job."

"Fending off developers is my job. Replacing the wiring, reglazing the windows, sweeping spiders out of the corners, and chasing bats out of the attic is beyond the call of lawyerly duty."

"Bats?" Savannah's incredible green eyes widened. "Please tell me you're not serious."

"Now you've done it, O'Halloran," Henry spat out. "Probably caused the price to drop another ten thousand bucks. Ten thousand I should take out of your fee."

Dan refrained from responding that Henry would have to pay him first before he could go deducting anything. Old man Hyatt was not only Dan's most irascible client, he was also the most time-consuming of his pro bono cases.

"Now there's an idea," he murmured.

"Actually, bats may be a plus," Lilith offered in her usual blithe way. "Since they eat insects."

"Anyone knows about bats, it should be you," Henry barked on a laugh roughened by old age and years of tobacco smoke. "Seein' how your own mother has a few in her belfry these days."

"My grandmother served this community for fifty years," Savannah reminded Henry in a flash of very un-Savannah-like anger. Dan resisted the urge to applaud. "Which undoubtedly means that she's treated you."

"From time to time, mebbe," Henry muttered. "It's hard to recollect."

"I seem to recall Mother mentioning a case of pneumonia that nearly proved fatal because you were too stubborn to seek medical help," Lilith interjected. "Why, if Gerald Lawson hadn't stopped by that day to collect for the newspaper and called Mother, who, by the way, came out in a blizzard to care for you, you might not be here today, Henry."

Lilith's own flare of heat suggested she was on the verge of losing her temper. A woman of strong emotions, she'd advised Dan after his sister's funeral that holding in one's feelings was unhealthy for mind, spirit, and body. Months later, apparently practicing what she preached, she'd been arresting for dancing nude in Olympic National Park and ripping up Cooper Ryan's citation book.

That little display of unbridled emotion had gotten her hauled into the park jail, but displaying a seemingly lifelong ability to land on her feet, a month later she'd become Mrs. Cooper Ryan. If there was any more nude dancing going on, Lilith was staying out of public parks and restricting her audience to her new husband.

"Only God can decide whether or not a body's gonna live or die," Henry argued. He raked his fingers through snow white hair as wispy as dandelion fluff. "Though I reckon Ida may have had a hand in the outcome," he tacked on reluctantly.

Dan decided that it was time to move things along. "Well, now that we've got all that settled, what would everyone say to getting down to discussing what brought us here today?" he asked with forced enthusiasm.

"Might as well," Henry muttered in a way that suggested since neither Lindstrom woman had turned out to be a pushover, there was no point in baiting them any further. He hooked his cane over the wooden arm of his chair, folded his arms, set his face, and looked straight at Savannah. "You want the place, here's what you'd better be prepared to pay."

The price was at least twice what the property was worth.

"That's a bit more than I'd planned." Dan admired the way Savannah kept her voice calm even as the outrageously inflated price caused the color to drain from her face.

"After all," she said, obviously mustering strength, "as I mentioned before, according to the inspector who examined the property, there's a great deal of work to be done to even bring the lighthouse up to code."

She opened a manila envelope, pulled out some papers, and held them toward Henry. When he refused to take them, she placed the papers on the pine coffee table between them.

"That cost doesn't even factor in what it will take to make it livable." She countered with a price half what he'd stated.

"Some high-flying resort company from down in your old neck of the woods offered a helluva lot more than that."

"I have no doubt they did. Having worked for a number of resorts, and knowing how they operate, I also suspect that the first thing they'd do is raze the house."

Henry held his ground. "Can't see why they'd want to do that. Wouldn't be much market for a Far Harbor lighthouse resort without the keeper's house."

"It's not that large," she pointed out. "If the new owners tore it down, they could construct one of those huge redwood and cedar resorts that are springing up all along the coast."

She'd obviously done her homework; as Henry's attorney, Dan knew that International Timeshare Resorts had indeed suggested a plan to tear down both houses.

"Of course, they might decide to keep the lighthouse," she allowed. "After all, they could always use it to sell fake scrimshaw, miniature totem poles, and CDs of whale songs to tourists."

"No jackass is going to be selling fake scrimshaw made in Taiwan or Tijuana outta my lighthouse," Henry warned.

"I'd hate to see that as well," Savannah replied smoothly. "But if you sell it to ITR, it won't be your lighthouse any longer, will it?"

Henry harrumphed. "Won't be my lighthouse if I sell it to you, either."

"I was thinking about that on the drive over here." Savannah reached into the folder again and pulled out a sheet of handwritten figures. "I believe I may have a solution that would suit both our purposes."

He gave her the long, unblinking stare that

Dan had gotten used to. If she was even slightly intimidated, Savannah didn't show it.

"Well," Henry demanded crankily, "you gonna share this idea or keep it all to yourself? I'm not a damn mind reader."

"I was thinking we could become partners."

"Partners?"

Savannah nodded. "That's right."

"Why in sam hill would I want to be partners with you?"

"Perhaps because it would allow you to retain part ownership of a home that's been in your family for three generations. At the same time, you'll be making a profit from the property."

"What makes you think you can even turn a profit from that ramshackle old place?"

Dan flashed Savannah a discreet thumbs-up for having gotten Henry to agree that the property was far from livable. The only indication that she'd seen the gesture was a fleeting glint of satisfaction in her eyes—a glint that came and went so fast, Dan would have missed it if he hadn't been watching her carefully.

"I'm very good at what I do, Mr. Hyatt. I know the hospitality business and I've been preparing for this all my life." Her expression and her voice softened. "Also, quite frankly, I can't afford not to, either financially or emotionally. . . .

"There's one more thing," Savannah offered. "If we're partners, you'll always have a home at Far Harbor." She glanced around the plant-filled room that, despite the staff's attempts at cheeriness, couldn't overcome the odor of illness and despair. "You could move out of here."

Henry blinked. Once. Twice. A third time, reminding Dan of an old owl that used to live in the rafters of his grandparents' barn when he was a kid.

"Place won't be ready any time soon," Henry pointed out. His voice had lost its usual sardonic edge. It now sounded faint and frail.

"That shouldn't prove a problem." The way Lilith slipped so smoothly back into the conversation made Dan realize that she and Savannah had planned this tag-team approach ahead of time. "Mother only has one foster child living with her at the moment, and as it happens, Gwen is away at science camp. Of course I've moved out since my marriage, which means there's more than enough room for you at the house."

A three-generational female tag team, Dan thought with admiration. There was no way either Savannah or Lilith would have dared volunteer such a thing without first getting Ida's okay.

"House?" Shaggy white brows flew upward like startled pigeons. "You suggesting I stay at that crazy old woman's house?"

"I'm going to say this one more time, Henry," Lilith said with a swish of silk as she crossed her legs. "I do hope you'll listen. My mother is not crazy. She can, admittedly, be eccentric. However, since it appears that your life has settled into the doldrums these days, perhaps having it shaken up a bit might not be such a bad thing."

Henry rapped the cane on the Berber carpeting with scant, muffled effect. "My life's just dandy the way it is, damn it."

Not a single person in the room challenged the obvious lie.

"All right," he surrendered finally on a wheezing huff of breath. "Since you seem so determined to buy the place, but can't meet my asking price, I reckon I don't have much choice but to give you a break."

"Thank you, Mr. Hyatt." Her eyes swimming, Savannah stood up and took both his hands in hers. "I promise you won't regret this."

"I'm already regretting it." He tugged his hands free, pushed himself out of the chair with a mighty effort, and looked up at Dan. "It's time for *Wheel of Fortune*. You take care of the paperwork, then bring it to me to sign when it's done."

"No problem."

"Better not be." Warning stated, he shuffled away.

The three of them watched him go. Finally, Savannah sighed. "I hope I never become that dried up and bitter."

"Of course you won't." Lilith's full sleeve fluttered like a brilliant butterfly's wing as she put her arm around her daughter's shoulder. "Despite that horrid man you made the mistake of marrying, you're still my sweet, open-hearted little girl who used to bring home stray kittens."

Savannah was watching Henry make his slow, painful way down the hallway. "I seem to recall you saying something about my aura being muddy these days."

"So I did," Lilith agreed blithely. "But it seems to be glowing again." She looked at her younger daughter with approval. "It does my heart good to see things finally working out for you, darling. And now that we've got this little transaction settled, I must run."

"I thought we'd go out and celebrate," Savannah said.

"Oh, sweetheart, I'd dearly love to, but I only have an hour to get ready for the dance at the VFW."

"The VFW?" Savannah was clearly surprised. And no wonder. Dan was also having trouble envisioning this former Vietnam War protestor—who'd been arrested back in the late sixties for throwing red paint on army recruiters—doing the two-step at a hangout for former military personnel. "You do realize that those initials stand for Veterans of Foreign Wars?" she asked. "Which you're not."

"Well, of course I'm not." Lilith combed a slender hand through her long slide of silver hair. "But Cooper is. Since my behavior after he shipped out to Vietnam all those years ago was admittedly less than admirable, I feel I owe him this one."

Savannah's smile was soft and fond. "Better watch it, Mom. You're entering the danger zone. Any moment now you might discover maturity."

"Wouldn't that set tongues wagging?" Lilith's laugh reminded Dan of the silver wind chimes his mother had given him for a housewarming gift. She kissed Savannah's cheek, then Dan's. "Have fun, you two."

She left in a fragrant cloud, her skirt swirling

around her still-shapely calves and her hips swaying in a way that caused a host of masculine eyes to watch her leave. Dan couldn't help chuckling when one elderly man, apparently enthralled with this voluptuous goddess who'd suddenly appeared in their midst, actually ran his wheelchair into the wall.

He exchanged a look with Savannah, who burst out laughing. Enjoying the sound that was half honey, half smoke, Dan realized that it was the first time he'd heard her reveal an iota of humor since she'd returned home.

Savannah Townsend had been the quintessential small-town girl most likely to cause boys to hold their notebooks in front of their jeans: prom queen two years in a row, pep squad all four years, yell queen her senior year. The male membership of the senior class had voted her the girl they'd most like to be stranded on a deserted island with, and she'd been equally popular with the girls. The fact that her father had been world-famous bad-boy rock guitarist Reggie Townsend hadn't hurt her reputation, either.

Dan had recently represented Savannah's grandmother Ida's pregnant teenage foster child in an adoption case. When he'd met the family at the winery of the adoptive parents, he'd taken one look at Savannah, recently returned from LA, and decided that she was even more beautiful than he'd remembered.

With her wild clouds of fiery hair, golden California tan, and emerald eyes, she'd resembled a member of some mythical race of women, forged in fire by a master alchemist. Yet, although she'd grown up to be dazzling, he'd sensed a sadness in her that had nothing to do with the solemnity of the occasion.

They'd been thrown together again a few weeks later at his cousin's wedding, where Savannah, wearing a dress that shimmered like moonlight on sea foam, had provided a dazzling contrast to the bride's cooler, luminous beauty.

Watching her closely, Dan had noted that even as her lush ruby lips had curved often, befitting the joy of this family event, the smiles had never quite touched her eyes. As the wedding festivities went on into the night, she'd grown more and more emotionally distant—almost ethereal, like the ghost of Lucy Hyatt, rumored to still reside in the lighthouse.

But now, as she laughed, she reminded him of the Savannah he'd once known, the glowing girl who could make a guy renowned for his hit-and-run dating style think terrifying, forever-after thoughts.

When her floral perfume slipped beneath his skin, creating an inner tug more complex than mere sexual attraction, Dan reminded himself that after a tumultuous and exhausting eighteen months, his life was finally getting back on track. The last thing he needed right now was a romance with a woman on the rebound. Especially one who, despite her apparent whim to settle down in Coldwater Cove, would undoubtedly soon find small-town life too confining for her big-city tastes.

4

Ida Lindstrom sat at the old oak rolltop desk she'd bought when she'd first begun her medical practice, right here in this very house, and stared down at a leather-bound address book stuffed with pieces of paper. The book, along with the telephone that was now buzzing with that annoying off-the-hook sound, was a sign that she'd been about to make a call. But to whom?

"Think, damn it!" She pressed her fingers against her temple and forced her mind to focus on the clues at hand. She had, after all, become very good at following clues since her once razor-sharp mind had turned so uncooperative.

"A waist is a terrible thing to mind," she muttered, unwittingly falling back into her unconscious habit of malapropisms.

Frustrated, she pulled one of the pieces of paper from the flap on the inside front cover of the address book and read through the list she'd made the morning she'd returned home from the hospital after that stupid fall that had gotten everyone so excited.

"Number one. Does recent memory loss affect job performance? Ha! It can't affect my job performance because I'm retired."

All right, so she may have gotten a bit more absentminded, but that was only natural, especially in this hurry-up world when so many outside things demanded immediate attention, all at the same time. It was perfectly understandable that she'd occasionally forget things, such as her reason for having come into her former examining-room-turned-den in the first place.

"It'll come," she reassured herself as she rubbed her uncharacteristically icy hands together. The trick was to remain patient and not panic. *Concentrate.*

"Number two. Does patient have difficulty performing familiar tasks?"

No problem there. Relief came in such a cooling wave, she decided that boiling all the water out of the teakettle this morning didn't really count. That, after all, could happen to anyone.

She also didn't have any problems with language. Perhaps she mixed up her words from time to time, but if her family and friends were to be believed, and she had no reason to doubt them, she'd been doing that all her life. Nor had she suffered any disorientation of time and place, problems with abstract thinking, or decreased judgment.

"Does patient misplace things?" She frowned.

"Stupid question. Name me one person who doesn't lose their car keys from time to time." Hadn't Raine, whom everyone knew was smart as a tack, done the same thing when she'd dropped by to visit last Saturday? They'd practically turned the house upside down before finding them behind a sofa cushion.

Number eight regarding mood swings didn't count, nor did nine: changes in personality. She'd never been a moody person, had never suffered PMS, and had breezed through menopause with hardly a ripple even without the hormone replacement that was so readily available for women these days.

Why, she was the same person she'd been at thirty. "Better," she decided.

Ida had to laugh out loud at the final "warning sign" on her diagnostic list. If there was one thing she wasn't suffering from, it was loss of initiative. Hadn't she managed to take care of three delinquent teenagers when the entire social system of the state of Washington had given up on them?

Two of the girls were now safely placed with relatives, and while Gwen, admittedly, might have gone through a rough patch, she certainly seemed on the straight and narrow. Her therapist had assured the family that the girl was coming through the separation from her infant daughter as well as could be expected.

When she heard a car engine outside the house and saw Savannah's red convertible pulling into the driveway, Ida folded the piece of paper and slipped it back into the front of the address book, hiding it behind a checklist of things she should make certain she did before leaving the house. Not that she'd ever leave the shower running or the stove turned on, but it never hurt to be cautious.

"I'm a doctor. I've been diagnosing people's illnesses for fifty years. I should certainly know whether or not I have Alzheimer's," she muttered. "And I don't."

The front door opened. "I'm in here, darling," she called out to her younger granddaughter with feigned cheeriness. Today had been important for Savannah, she remembered, frustrated anew when she was unable to recall exactly why.

"I got it!" Savannah breezed into the den, her smile as bright and happy as it had been back when she'd cheered the Coldwater Cove High School Loggers to victory.

"That's wonderful!" *Got what?* Ida sneaked a quick glance at her checklist, hoping for some small assistance. "I'm so pleased for you."

"Of course now the work begins." Savannah crossed the room and picked up the phone receiver that was still lying on the desktop. "I'm sorry. Did I interrupt you making a call?"

"It's not important." So that's what that annoying sound was. Ida forced a smile that wobbled only slightly as Savannah replaced the receiver in its cradle. "Tell me all about your day. I want to hear everything."

"You were right, as usual." Savannah settled down on the sofa, kicked off her shoes, and tucked her legs beneath her.

"Of course. Grandmothers are always right." In contrast to her icy hands, Ida felt a bead of sweat form above her upper lip. Her mind turned with the heavy, slogging effort of truck tires stuck in a mud bog.

"Offering Henry Hyatt a chance to move in here clinched the deal."

Henry Hyatt. . . . She'd treated him for prostate trouble ten years ago. It had been a cold wet June during a spring of record rains that had made it seem as if summer would never come. Ida recalled the case, as she did that of all her other patients, with crystal clarity. But surely that wasn't what Savannah had been concerned about?

"I've always loved that lighthouse, but I have to admit, Gram, I'm still having a little trouble believing that it's actually mine."

Ida latched onto the clue like a drowning woman reaching for a piece of driftwood in a storm-tossed sea. The lighthouse! Savannah was buying the Far Harbor lighthouse to turn into a bed-and-breakfast. How had she forgotten such an important thing?

"You'll make a grand success of it," she assured her granddaughter with renewed vigor born of her relief at having finally sorted out the puzzle. "And I'm pleased as peanuts that my offer of hospitality to Henry helped clinch the deal. But I have to warn you, Savannah dear, if that cranky old man expects breakfast in bed, like they undoubtedly do for invalids over at Evergreen, he's going to have to sleep in the kitchen."

When Savannah laughed richly at that suggestion, Ida's clenched shoulders relaxed and the blood flowed warmly back into her hands.

"I'm so proud of you," she said as her mind cleared and her heart lifted. "Not that I ever had any doubts. In fact, anticipating your success, I bought you a little present." She reached into a desk drawer and pulled out a tapestry lighthouse tote bag.

"Oh, I love it!"

"There's something inside," Ida remembered.

Savannah laughed again as she pulled out the message T-shirt. "Behind every successful woman is herself," she read aloud.

"And don't you forget it," Ida said briskly, pleased with the way Savannah was coming out of her recent divorce funk. "We Lindstrom women are tough cookies." Although she was still furious at that shifty-eyed weasel her granddaughter had made the mistake of marrying, at least his behavior had brought Savannah home again, proving that every silver lining had a cloud around it. "They may be able to chew us up from time to time, but they can't swallow. . . .

"We'll have to call Raine right away," Ida said decisively after grandmother and granddaughter had hugged. "And, of course, Gwen. So you can tell them the good news."

Everything was going to be fine. Her girls were back home again. All except Gwen, who would soon be back from science camp in time to start her senior year of high school. Even Lilith, after a lifetime of rebellion, appeared to be on the straight and narrow, happily married to Cooper Ryan and working at something she seemed to enjoy.

Despite those recent annoying little memory glitches, life had never been better. Fretting about things she couldn't control—such as getting older—was a waste of time and would accomplish nothing.

As she found Gwen's number in her address book and picked up the receiver, Ida put her concerns away and decided to let sleeping ducks lie.

Five very long days later, Savannah sat on the bench in the lighthouse garden, running through the numbers again. She'd borrowed Raine's laptop computer, hoping the fancy money-management program would make her prospects look more encouraging. It didn't.

"It doesn't help that I keep expanding the original concept," she muttered as she glared at the flashing cursor.

John, who rode his bike to the lighthouse every day, was weeding nearby. His sunflower yellow T-shirt read Cultivate the Garden Within. Every time she'd seen Dan's nephew he'd been wearing another message shirt, which had Savannah thinking that he and her grandmother would undoubtedly get along like gangbusters.

"You're unhappy," he diagnosed.

"Not unhappy." Savannah sighed. "Just frustrated."

She took in the sight of the bunchberry he'd planted as a groundcover the first day she'd met him here at the lighthouse. The white blossoms looked like tiny umbrellas amidst the dark green foliage he'd promised would eventually spread all the way along the cliff.

"That's lovely." There was something vastly soothing about the garden, which was why she'd chosen to work here today.

"It's going to be even better," he assured her with the enviable confidence he seemed to possess regarding his horticultural work. "When summer ends, the flowers will turn to bright red berries that'll attract more birds to your lighthouse."

If it *was* her lighthouse by then. Savannah shook her head to rid it of that depressing thought. Henry had begun to waffle about signing the final sales agreement, but she refused to consider the possibility of failure.

"I like the idea of attracting birds," she said as she watched a fat red-breasted robin energetically tug a worm from the moist ground.

John rocked back on his heels. "Sometimes when I get worried and need to figure out an answer to a problem, I work in the garden and my brain works better," he offered. "Even when I don't get any answers, I don't feel so bad." He paused. "I have an extra pair of gloves."

Savannah immediately turned off the computer. "You're on." She spent the next hour attacking weeds, and while she didn't come any closer to solving her financial problems, she discovered John was right: she did feel better.

Despite her new-found garden therapy, Savannah's stress level escalated as she continued to juggle figures and go around and around with Henry, who appeared to believe that his role in life was to make people—and her in particular—as miserable as possible. Whenever she could steal a free moment, she worked off her frustration in John's garden. He seemed to enjoy her company, even after she'd mistaken a bed of newly sprouted seedlings for dandelions.

"That's okay," he assured her easily, revealing no irritation that she'd destroyed an entire day's work. "I can plant more."

She'd shown up the next morning with a Thermos of cold milk and a tin of crumbly, home-baked chocolate chunk cookies as an apology. John had taken one bite, then rolled his eyes.

"These are the very best cookies I've ever tasted." He flashed her a grin that reminded her of his uncle. "Any time you want to dig up more flowers, I won't mind—so long as you keep bringing more cookies."

Savannah laughed and promised the cookies without the destruction. But the incident did give her an idea. After checking with the charge nurse at Evergreen to make sure Henry wasn't on a restricted diet, she showed up at the nursing home with a tin of cookies still hot from the oven. It may just have been a coincidence, but that was the evening he finally agreed to her terms.

Wanting to get the deal locked up before Henry changed his mind again, Savannah was at the legal offices of O'Halloran and O'Halloran first thing the next morning.

The offices her sister shared with Dan were housed in a century-old building next to the ferry dock. The brick had been painted a soft gray-blue that reflected the water, and beneath the front windows scarlet geraniums cascaded from flower boxes she suspected were John's contribution.

A brass bell tied to the inside of the door jangled as she entered. Apparently the receptionist hadn't arrived yet, because Raine came out of her office to greet Savannah.

"Congratulations. I hear you're now a lady of property."

"I will be as soon as I sign the final papers. I thought I'd go crazy when it looked as if Henry was going to back out."

"Henry's an ornery old bird." Raine shrugged. "I think he was really just trying to make you squirm. He's an expert at that, of course. Hopefully getting out of that nursing home will give him a new lease on life."

"At least living with Gram won't be boring."

"She'll whip him into shape, all right," Raine agreed. "I'll go tell Dan you're here."

"No need." Dan appeared from the hallway around the corner. "I was on the phone, but I knew the minute Savannah walked in the door."

Since the offices faced the bay, Savannah knew he couldn't have seen her walking across the street from where she'd parked her car in front of the Dancing Deer Dress Shoppe. "I hadn't realized you were psychic."

"I'm not. I smelled the flowers and decided that either John's expanded into indoor gardens or the most gorgeous lady in Coldwater Cove has decided to grace me with her presence." He glanced over at Raine. "Present company excepted, of course."

"Of course," Raine said with easy good humor. She'd never resented her sister's beauty. To do so would be like the cool silver moon resenting the bolder, brighter sun for rising in a blaze of glory each morning. "Well, I've got some partnership papers for that software firm to write and a brief on Japanese timber sales to polish up, so I'd best get back to the salt mines. Congratulations, baby sister."

She hugged Savannah, then scooped up the yellow legal pad she'd carried into the reception area with her.

"Congratulations," Dan said. "I ran by Evergreen before breakfast this morning and got my client's signature on the sales agreement."

"Thank you." He'd promised to expedite matters when she'd called him at home last night with the news that his client had finally agreed to her terms, but she'd still worried that any delay might allow Henry to change his mind.

"That's my job," he reminded her. "I'm sorry Henry gave you so many headaches. I tried to hurry him along, but I think the problem was that he was enjoying having you visit every day."

"If that's his idea of enjoyment, he undoubtedly spends the morning craft hour pulling wings off butterflies."

"The old guy can be a bit of a challenge on occasion."

"Spoken exactly like a lawyer. Talk about mincing words," she muttered.

"I suppose we can all be accused of attorney-speak from time to time," he admitted. "Speaking of which, do you know what you get when you cross the Godfather with a lawyer?"

"No, but I'm afraid you're going to tell me."

"An offer you can't understand."

"That's terrible."

"But true," he said good-naturedly. "Let me try another one," he suggested as they passed Raine's office. "Did you hear about the lady lawyer who dropped her briefs and became a solicitor?" He'd raised his voice just loud enough to ensure that his partner heard him.

"Better be careful, Counselor," Raine called out. "You're skating perilously close to a charge of sexual harassment in the workplace."

Dan paused and stuck his head in her open doorway. "Hey, you know very well that we're an equal opportunity law firm. Which means you're welcome to take your best shot."

Knowing her sister, Savannah was not at all surprised when Raine proved ready for him. "Okay." She folded her arms across the front of her charcoal gray blazer. "What do a male lawyer and a sperm have in common?"

Dan rubbed his square chin. "I'll bite."

A familiar competitive glint shone in Raine's hazel eyes. Her smile was smug and claimed early victory. "Both have a one-in-three-million chance of becoming a human being."

"Bull's-eye." Dan clutched his heart and staggered against the wall. He glanced over at Savannah, who was beginning to enjoy herself. "Your sister is a cruel-hearted woman. I have no idea why my cousin seems so taken with her."

"Because Jack has very good taste," Raine countered. "Which, if that atrocious tie is any example, is a great deal more than I can say for you."

"Hey, this tie makes a statement." He turned toward Savannah. "What do you think?"

Savannah chewed on a thumbnail lacquered in Sunset Coral as she studied him. What did she think? That the man was drop-dead gorgeous, with that thick chestnut hair that seemed perpetually tousled and blue eyes enlivened by dancing flecks that flashed like mica in the sunlight. His complexion was tanned a rich, burnished gold from days spent sailing on the sound, his skin taut over strong, masculine bones.

His mouth was full, but roughly sculpted in a way that made it very much a man's. When an errant, distant memory of long, slow, sensuous kisses stirred in some dark corner of her mind, Savannah's hormones spiked.

"I'm not sure I get the message," she said as she took in the cartoon marsupials wearing somber black judicial robes.

"I thought it'd be obvious. Maybe it's a lawyer thing." He sighed heavily. "It's supposed to represent a kangaroo court."

Since the ridiculous tie was just about the single amusing thing about her life these days,

Savannah didn't censure her smile. "I think I like it."

"See?" He shot Raine a triumphant look. "Your sister approves of my sartorial taste. And she should know about style, having spent so many years in the playgrounds of the rich and famous."

"Last time I checked, money didn't buy taste," Raine argued.

"And I wasn't the one playing," Savannah pointed out.

"All the more reason to make up for lost time." He winked at Raine, then they continued down the hall. "It's a gorgeous day. After you sign the last of the papers, how about we pick up some lunch and go sailing?"

"Perhaps your life has become so laid-back you can take a day off, but I've got work to do. I was intending to wade through paint chips and wallpaper samples during lunch."

"You have to eat."

"I packed a salad in an ice chest in the back of my car before I left the house this morning." Raine wasn't the only sister who could prepare ahead.

"Rabbit food," Dan scoffed dismissively. "You need red meat to keep your strength up, Savannah. I was thinking we might stop by Oley's and pick up an order of ribs."

Savannah assured herself that it was only the mention of Oley Swenson's barbecue—not the prospect of an afternoon sailing with Dan—that was proving unreasonably tempting. "Thanks anyway, but I think I'll pass."

"Have you ever seen your lighthouse from the water?"

Her lighthouse. Those were, Savannah thought, the most beautiful words in the English language. "I've seen it from the ferry lots of times."

"That's only one view, coming across from Seattle. You really should see it from the strait as well. It gives you an entirely different perspective.

"When I was a kid, overdosing on Horatio Hornblower novels, I used to imagine how relieved sailors coming in from the sea must have felt when they saw the light flashing, guiding them safely into the shallows of the cove. I also thought how exciting—and frightening—it must have been to sail back past it toward dangerous, open waters again."

"I've thought the same thing," Savannah allowed as they entered an office papered in a cobalt blue that echoed the water outside the tall windows. The furniture was upholstered in a gray leather the color of a storm-tossed sea. "But as much as I'd enjoy seeing the lighthouse from that vantage point, I really can't take the time. At least not now."

"You've got a rain check," Dan said equably as he gestured her to a chair on the visitor's side of an antique partner's desk.

While he opened a scuffed leather barrister's bag to get the contract, Savannah took the opportunity to study the room in greater detail. One wall was taken up by bookshelves. A quick glance revealed several legal thrillers lurking among the leather-bound law books.

Calligraphically prepared diplomas displayed in simple wood frames hung on another wall, along with lithographed copies of the Declaration of Independence and the Magna Carta. Keeping company with the august legal documents was a needlepoint sampler that read Please Don't Tell My Mother I'm a Lawyer. She Thinks I Play the Piano in the Local Bordello.

"My sister made that for me when I passed the bar," he said when he saw her looking at it.

Savannah would have had to be deaf not to hear the lingering pain in his voice. "You must miss her terribly." She couldn't imagine losing Raine. It would be easier to have her heart ripped out.

"Every day." Dan sighed, picked up a pen and began switching it from hand to hand. The light was gone from his eyes, almost, she thought, as if someone had pulled down a dark shade. "When I first came back home, right after the accident, I wasn't sure I could take care of John. Not just physically, which, in the beginning, was difficult enough, but emotionally.

"Never having been a parent myself, I worried that I might not have the instincts. Fortunately, Karyn and Richard did a great job of grounding their son, so mostly all I've had to do is sort of follow along and keep an eye out for the pitfalls."

"I have a feeling that you're glossing over your efforts just a bit."

Savannah considered how, if Kevin had been in a similar situation, he would have been quick to take credit for John's obvious sense of stability. Just as he'd taken credit for all her hard work and innovation in each of the resorts where they'd worked together, he in a series of upwardly mobile managerial positions, while she'd always been more than content to stay in the kitchen.

"It couldn't have been easy," she said. "John's a very intuitive, open-hearted person. If he hadn't known he could trust you to be there for him, he could have been devastated."

She knew, firsthand, how important it was during those tender growing-up years to have someone you could count on. Fortunately, while Lilith had proven all too fallible, Savannah had been doubly blessed in her sister and grandmother.

"Things were admittedly a bit rocky in the beginning," Dan allowed with what Savannah was beginning to realize was characteristic understatement. "But, as I said, his parents built a strong foundation and John's a great kid. I only wish his mom could be here to see how well he's doing."

"I'm certain she knows."

"I sure hope so." The shutters lifted; a brief pain flashed in his eyes.

"Well, whether he got it from his parents, or whether it's inborn, his never-say-die mentality is definitely contagious," Savannah said. "I don't know what I would have done if he hadn't let me attack weeds instead of your client this past week."

"Ah, yes." The harsh lines bracketing either side of Dan's mouth softened. "He mentioned something about you having developed a real knack for gardening."

"Since I don't want to accuse your nephew of being a liar, I'll just say that he's overly optimistic. My weeding talents leave a great deal to be desired."

"Join the club. While I'm still permitted, with supervision, to do some planting, after I created a horticultural miracle last fall he took my hoe away from me."

"A miracle?"

"See these hands?" He held them up for her perusal.

"Yes." When her unruly mind threw up a quick, hot fantasy of those long dark fingers, which could have belonged to a pianist, playing over her flesh, Savannah had to remind herself to breathe.

"They single-handedly turned an entire bed of perennials into annuals."

Their shared laughter lightened the mood that had been threatening to turn gloomy. Dan exhaled another brief sigh, then, squaring his shoulders, slid the document across the desk toward her.

"You need to initial here"—he pointed toward the line accentuated with a flourescent red Post-it flag—"and here." He tapped the pen point on another line on the second page, then flipped to the last page. "Last chance to change your mind."

Undaunted by the herculean task ahead of her, Savannah ignored his warning.

This morning, when she'd been sitting at the kitchen table, fretting over a proposed con-

struction schedule that dragged into late fall,
her grandmother had briskly pointed out in her
no-nonsense way that "even Rome wasn't
burned in a day."

The Ida-mangled advice had reminded Savannah of what she'd suspected when she'd
packed up her belongings and walked away
from her former comfortable California existence. Rebuilding an entire life from scratch
would undoubtedly not be easy.

Knowing she'd suffer setbacks, she wrote her
name with a flourish on the final page of the
contract to purchase the Far Harbor lighthouse,
and for the first time in a very long while, Savannah felt blissfully, incredibly happy.

5

The Far Harbor lighthouse was draped in a soft haze. A cool curtain of fog hung low over the water, and the dense grove of Douglas fir and western hemlock behind the lighthouse loomed dark and mysterious. The dawn sky had been streaked with crimson, predicting that by afternoon thunderstorms would be rumbling their way from the sea over the mountaintops, creating rain that would hit the water like bullets. Winds would stir up whitecaps, and stuttering trees of white lightning would flash across the blackened sky. Living amidst so much nature might not be for the faint of heart, but Dan found it invigorating.

As his running shoes pounded on the wet sand near the water's edge, he thought, not for the first time, how ironic it was that after so many years spent plotting his escape from Coldwater Cove, here he was, back home again, right where he'd started.

He dodged a green tangle of kelp that had ridden onto the pearl gray beach on a surge of tide and decided that Savannah Townsend's recent arrival back in town was additional proof that life tended to have more jigs and jogs than the narrow roads twisting through the jagged Northwest mountains.

The too-early deaths of his sister and brother-in-law had been, hands down, the worst event of his life. But there'd been no time for self-pity as he'd sat vigil beside John's hospital bed, praying for him to regain consciousness—which, thank God, he had.

During his nephew's long recuperation, Dan's attention had been focused on getting John back on his feet. But other events forced him to face the fact that his wife didn't possess the same deep-seated sense of family that he'd been moderately surprised to discover guided his own life.

His first clue had been when Amanda had refused to even visit him in Coldwater Cove, claiming that social obligations and her part-time career as an interior designer to the mega-wealthy made it impossible for her to leave San Francisco for any extended period of time.

By the time the divorce papers had arrived, he'd taken a long hard look at a marriage that should have been declared dead at the altar and vaguely wondered why Amanda had waited so long. As soon as John was back on his feet and had returned to school, Dan had thrown his energies into establishing a new law practice.

The tide ebbed, leaving behind a sparkling

trail of diaphanous sea foam. He pounded up the stone steps leading from the beach and compared the morning solitude with San Francisco's vibrant pulse. Once, in what now seemed like another life, before youthful illusions had been snuffed out by the cold harsh winds of reality, he'd run every morning on this very same beach and daydreamed of bright lights and big cities. The Olympic Peninsula town founded by one of his ancestors had always seemed too provincial, too confining, for someone of Dan O'Halloran's lofty talent and ambition.

The only son of a Coldwater Cove commercial fisherman and homemaker turned charter boat cook, by the time he'd entered junior high school, Dan had a very firm future in mind. The plan, laid out with all the care and precision of the Joint Chiefs preparing for invasion, was to get a prestigious law degree, work for a few years in a high-profile job—prosecution, perhaps—which would set him up for partnership in a respectable big-city law firm.

Rounding out the mental picture was a Tudor-style house like the one belonging to some Wall Street wizard he'd seen profiled in a glossy magazine while waiting for the orthodontist to tighten his braces. The house would boast acres of rolling emerald lawn someone else would mow, a blue tiled swimming pool and a tennis court—red clay, rather than the more pedestrian concrete the public courts at Founders Park were made of, because that's what the mutual fund titan had chosen.

At twelve he wasn't really interested in the family part of his dream, yet from those magazine pages he'd unconsciously absorbed the idea that living in this dream house with him would be a gorgeous, intelligent trophy wife from a good family and their equally attractive, brilliant children.

Dan's laugh was directed inward as he considered how close he'd actually come to achieving his youthful dream. Including the Tudor which had been filled to twelve-foot-high ceilings with pricey Oriental porcelain he'd always been terrified of knocking off those marble pedestals. Befitting his upwardly mobile position and his wife's lofty social status, he dutifully subscribed to the symphony, the ballet, and the opera, and doubted that any of their Pacific Heights friends would ever suspect that he secretly preferred classic Beetles to Beethoven, Willie Nelson to Wagner.

He'd nearly achieved everything he'd ever dreamed of; all that had been missing was the partnership, and if he'd caved in to Amanda's pressure to accept the extremely lucrative offer he'd received from that Montgomery Street law firm the day after his sister's fatal accident, the final piece of the plan would have fallen into place before his thirty-third birthday.

Which just went to show, Dan considered as he yanked off his damp cardinal Stanford sweatshirt and entered his house by the kitchen door, that a guy had better be careful what he wished for.

The house was silent, revealing that John

had already taken off on his summer morning gardening rounds. The aroma of freshly brewed coffee enticed; Dan filled a mug from the Mr. Coffee carafe and took it into the bathroom to drink after his shower.

Ten minutes later he was sitting out on his redwood deck, surveying his domain. The mist had already been burned away by the rising sun.

The moment he'd first seen this house perched on the edge of the cliff, Dan had found it perfect, much preferring the open floor plan and vast expanse of glass that looked out over heart-soaring views to the gloomy San Francisco mansion with its dark silk walls and windows heavily draped in antique brocade that he'd lived in with his former wife. While he still loved the place and figured nothing short of dynamite would ever get him out of it, he'd begun to sense that something was missing. But he hadn't quite gotten a handle on what, exactly, it could be.

When a sporty red BMW convertible pulled up in front of the lighthouse, Dan put the puzzle aside and decided to pay a call on his new neighbor.

Savannah was sanding the dining room chair rail when she realized she was not alone. It was not the first time she'd experienced the feeling. This time, however, when she turned around, she saw Dan standing in the open doorway.

The sunlight streamed over him, gilding the ends of his hair in a way that made her want to run her fingers through it. Heavens, he was good-looking. But having had her fill of good-looking men, Savannah was about to inform him that she was far too busy for neighborly visits when he held up a white bag bearing the ivy-covered-cottage logo of Molly's Muffins and More.

"I figured you might be able to use a little nourishment. Hopefully you haven't turned into one of those California bark eaters during your time in LaLa land."

The enticing, forbidden aromas of deep-fried dough and coffee wafted over the pungent odor of turpentine and paint stripper and nearly made her drool.

"There's something to be said for refined white sugar—in moderation." So much for sending him on his way. Besides, she reasoned, since Dan practically lived next door, she might as well get used to having their paths cross.

Deciding that a few minutes one way or the other really wouldn't make a difference in her overall schedule, she tossed down the sanding block and wiped her hands on the damp cloth she kept dust free in a sealed, oversized plastic bag.

He took two foam cups from a second bag, pulled off the plastic covers, and set them on the thick front door that was currently resting on two sawhorses, awaiting a new paint job and hardware.

She'd arrived at the lighthouse at six o'clock that morning to meet the electrician, who'd made a big deal about squeezing her into his busy schedule. The man's estimate—nearly twice what she'd anticipated and budgeted for—had left her with an aching head. Skipping breakfast, combined with two hours of hard physical labor, had her stomach rumbling.

"Chocolate!" She dove into the bag and pulled out an éclair. When she bit into the gooey cream center, she nearly wept. "Oh, God, I think I love you."

"We aim to please." He selected a bear claw for himself. "I have to admit I was a little worried when Molly didn't have a single edible flower on the menu."

Savannah assured herself that it was an instantaneous sugar high and not Dan's self-satisfied grin and close proximity that jolted her pulse. It took a moment for his words to sink in. When they did, she tilted her head and looked up at him.

"That almost sounds as if you've eaten at Las Casitas."

"I have."

"When?" Deciding that Lilith and Oscar Wilde were right about being able to avoid everything but temptation and convinced that she must have already worked off about a gazillion calories today, Savannah dipped into the bag again, this time choosing a white frosted cinnamon roll studded with fat raisins.

"A couple years ago," he answered. "I attended a prosecutors' conference in Malibu."

"A conference?" The cinnamon roll tasted every bit as sinful as it looked. Savannah feared she'd have to sand woodwork eight hours a day for a solid week to make up for the indulgence. "That implies more than one night."

"Two nights and three excruciatingly boring days spent listening to attorneys, all of whom, like most lawyers, love the sound of their own voices."

"Three days," she repeated. "Did you know I was working there?"

"That fact would have been a little hard to miss, since all the elevators had huge framed pictures of you dipping petunias into melted chocolate while looking incredibly sexy in your white apron and tall chef's hat."

"They were nasturtiums," she corrected absently. "Why didn't you let me know you were staying at the resort? I would have enjoyed seeing you."

That was mostly true. Over the years since high school, Savannah had thought of Dan on occasion, mostly in the over-romanticized, gilt-edged way she suspected most women remembered their first crush.

"I left a note for you when I checked in."

A note. One that Kevin, who, on constant lookout for celebrities, watched over the front desk with an eagle eye, had obviously kept from her. Strangely, for a man whom she'd belatedly discovered hadn't known the meaning of fidelity, her husband had always been unreasonably possessive. When they'd first been married, she'd been somewhat flattered by his jealousy. Now she'd come to understand that he'd merely considered her another trophy, like his state-of-the-art sound system or the black Porsche Targa housed in the three-car garage of their Malibu house.

"I never received any note." She began shredding her paper napkin in lieu of wringing her ex-husband's neck.

Dan didn't look all that surprised, which made her wonder what, exactly, Raine had told Jack about her marriage. And what Jack, in turn, had told his cousin.

"The place was a madhouse, with two conventions there at the same time," he said easily. "It undoubtedly got put in someone else's box."

"That must have been what happened," she agreed.

Savannah had the feeling that neither one of them really believed that explanation.

They sipped their coffee in companionable silence broken by the sound of shingles and layers of tar paper being ripped off the roof overhead. Finally Dan tossed his empty cup into a large brown cardboard box that had originally held a case of Rainier beer that she was using for a trash can, rocked back on his heels, and glanced around.

"I think it's looking better."

Savannah imagined she heard the sound of laughter, but since the voice was too light and high to belong to any of the roofers, decided that it must be the wind whistling through the now open rafters.

"Liar." There were paint cans everywhere, the walls, stripped of paper, revealed patching, and the pine floor was still deeply gouged and in desperate need of sanding and sealing. Reluctantly deciding that her coffee break had lasted long enough, she dropped her foam cup into the box with his and returned to her sanding.

"It's a disaster. But at least it's *my* disaster. Mine and Henry's," she amended.

Dan shrugged out of his leather jacket, tossed it onto the top of a stepladder, picked up an extra putty knife and went to work scraping paint off a nearby windowsill. "Speaking of Henry, I hear you're springing him today."

"This afternoon. After the doctor makes her rounds."

"Better make sure she checks out his heart."

"Why?" Savannah glanced back over her shoulder at him. "Do you know something about his health I don't?" Neither the doctor nor the nurses she'd spoken with had suggested that by moving the elderly man out of Evergreen, she might be risking his life.

He flicked a casual but decidedly masculine look over her. "You really are a fabulous creature, Savannah. Just the sight of you in that getup might set off the old guy's built-in defibrillator."

She was wearing the new T-shirt Ida had given her tucked into the waistband of her oldest jeans. Yet Savannah suddenly felt as if she'd absently run out of the house this morning in her underwear.

"You make it sound as if I'm wearing a leather miniskirt and a sequined spandex tube top," she complained between her teeth as she reattacked the chair rail.

"I've always thought sequined spandex was overkill, but I can't deny that the mental image of you in leather is definitely more than a little appealing." He put down the putty knife and picked up the wire brush she'd been using for detail work.

"I hate to disappoint you, Dan, but I don't even own any leather."

"Don't worry. That can be remedied. I know a guy in town who used to be a member of a biker gang until bad judgment landed him in prison, where, instead of engraving license plates, he learned tailoring.

"After his release six months ago he opened a shop, and business has really taken off. Even Oprah ordered a dress from him, and though I haven't seen him wear it on the air yet, word is that Dan Rather bought a jacket that reads Hard News Guy on the back. Needless to say, everyone in town's been arguing exactly how Rather meant that. . . .

"You know," he warned, "if you're not careful, you're going to sand that wood all the way down to the plaster wall."

Savannah spun back toward him, her planned retort cut off by the friendly warmth in his eyes. "I'm having a hard time picturing Dan Rather buying his clothing from a former felon in Coldwater Cove, Washington."

"My hand to God." He lifted his right hand. "The guy's a client of mine. In fact, he paid his bill with that jacket."

Of course she'd noticed the jacket the moment he'd shown up in her doorway. It was black, looked as soft as butter, and gave him a sexy James Dean rebellious appearance that she

suspected hadn't been encouraged at Stanford
law school.

"That's quite a step, going from prosecuting
criminals to springing Hell's Angels from jail."

"He's not a Hell's Angel, just a wannabe who
learned his lesson the hard way and paid for it
with some hard time. Also, I didn't spring him.
I wrote up his shop's lease agreement after his
release and found him an accountant to handle
bookkeeping and tax stuff."

The leather jacket may be a long way from
Brooks Brothers, but Savannah could more easily imagine Dan arguing a case in a San Francisco federal courtroom than she could picture
him doing routine paperwork for a convict
biker wannabe. Even one who'd sold a jacket to
Dan Rather.

"You don't have to do that," she said as she
realized he appeared inclined to stay. "Surely
you have work to do."

"Not at the moment. I've got to run by a print
shop in Port Townsend later this morning, but
until then I'm free as a bird."

Savannah pursed her lips and nodded.
"Good idea. Having flyers printed up to hand
out at accident scenes." She'd meant the uncharacteristically sarcastic dig as retaliation
for his blatantly sexist defibrillator remark,
but wasn't all that surprised when he remained
unwounded.

"Speaking of accident scenes," he drawled,
"do you know the difference between a lawyer
and a Dalmatian?"

"I have no idea." Her tone dripped with disinterest.

"A Dalmatian knows when to stop chasing the ambulance."

"That's the lamest one yet." She squelched the bubble of answering laughter and felt her neck and shoulder muscles, which had been tied up in knots for weeks, actually relax. "I thought lawyers hated those jokes."

"Actually, there are only two lawyer jokes. The rest are all true." He smiled at her.

"Don't you take anything seriously?" It was not exactly a rhetorical question. Savannah really wanted to know.

"Sure. I'm gravely serious about plague, pestilence, wars, and anyone who hurts defenseless kids or dogs. I'm also a sucker for beautiful women in distress."

When he skimmed another appraising glance over her, Savannah tossed up her chin. That description might admittedly have fit her once, but no longer. Well, at least not as much as it had when she'd first arrived home, she amended, thinking back on how she'd given in to tears this morning after the electrician had packed up his voltage meter and left the lighthouse. But only for five minutes. Then she'd picked herself up, brushed herself off, taken out her sanding block and gone to work.

"Which brings me back to the reason for going to Port Townsend." His deep voice returned her mind to their conversation. "One of my clients is a struggling divorced mother of three who hasn't received a penny of child support in five years. Her ex took off to Montana, but I've got a line on him.

"At least I hope I do. If his pissed-off girlfriend, whose credit cards he maxed out, can be believed, he's moved back to Washington and is currently working as a printer. The shop opens at ten. Meanwhile, I have some time to kill."

"And you couldn't think of anything better to do than scrape paint?"

"Nope. I also couldn't think of anyone I'd rather spend my time with."

His smile was friendly and unthreatening. It also created that now familiar stir. Not knowing how to safely respond to his statement, Savannah returned to her sanding.

6

Savannah watched Henry Hyatt study the bedroom, which, although small, was as tidy as a nun's cell. Framed prints of old sailing ships hung on the wall, and lace curtains dappled the afternoon sunshine, creating dancing dots of light on the antique quilt.

"The girl didn't say anything about me havin' to share the facilities," he grumbled.

"I happen to have a name, Mr. Hyatt," Savannah responded mildly. She'd learned early on in her discussions with Henry that if you gave the man an inch, he'd take it and run for a mile. "It's Savannah."

"Damn fool name if you ask me."

"Nobody asked you," Ida, who'd readied the room for him, snapped. "Not that it's any of your beeswax, but Lilith named Savannah for the town where she was born."

"Good thing Lilith wasn't livin' in Pough-keepsie."

"You get up on the wrong side of the barn door this morning, Henry?" Ida lifted her eyes to the high ceiling. "I knew this was going to be a mistake."

"I didn't ask to come here."

"That's just as well, since I would've probably turned you away. I'm only doing this for Savannah," she told him what Savannah herself already had figured out. "You're damn fortunate my younger granddaughter's such a fool optimist she actually thinks she can turn that wreck of a place you foisted off onto her into something livable."

"The Far Harbor lighthouse has been standing in that same place since before you were born," he reminded her gruffly.

"Which is undoubtedly why it's falling down. Old's old. Whether you're talking people or buildings."

"It's sound enough to have withstood plenty of gales. Including the storm of ought six," he countered gruffly. "Besides, I didn't twist the girl's—"

"Savannah's," she reminded him sharply.

"Hell's bells." He raked arthritic fingers through what was left of his hair. "I'd forgotten what a hardheaded woman you can be."

"Nothing hardheaded about wanting my granddaughter referred to by name—the very same granddaughter who's invited you into her home," she reminded him pointedly.

"Where I have to share the head."

Ida crossed her arms over a scarlet T-shirt

that announced So It's Not Home Sweet
Home . . . Adjust.

"You want a private bathroom? Fine. Since
you're so set on pissin' your life away, I'll drive
you back to Evergreen." Her sneakers squeaked
on the waxed floor as she turned and strode to
the door, pausing to shoot him a dare over her
shoulder. "Well? You coming or not?"

They could have been on the main street of
nineteenth-century Dodge City at high noon.
Both individuals were incredibly strong-willed.
Savannah suspected that until he'd broken his
hip and landed in Evergreen, Henry had been
every bit as accustomed to getting his way as
her grandmother. Ida's edge, Savannah decided,
was that she held the keys to the closest thing
he'd known to a home in a very long while.

"Guess it won't be so bad." He shrugged, as if
he didn't give a damn one way or the other. "So
long as that girl—Savannah," he amended
when Ida hit him with another sharp warning
glare, "doesn't spend all day soaking in the tub
or leave makeup all over the counter."

"Don't worry, Mr. Hyatt," Savannah assured
him. "I'm going to be far too busy for long luxu-
rious bubble baths." Every muscle in her aching
body practically wept with yearning at that idea.

"Thanks to that mess you left her," Ida tacked
on. "You also won't have to worry about makeup, since Savannah's a natural beauty. Never
has needed the stuff."

"Can't argue with you there," he said gruffly.
Savannah sighed. It figured that the first

halfway nice thing he said about her would have to do with her looks. It would be nice, she thought, if just once a man was capable of looking beyond the packaging.

"Sorta reminds me of her mother," Henry continued, unaware of her faint irritation. "But not nearly as flighty."

Since she'd had a long, exhausting day and wasn't up to getting into an argument, Savannah chose not to leap to her mother's defense this time. Besides, it was the truth. Lilith *was* flighty. That had always been part of her appeal.

"I got you something," Ida announced. She marched passed him again, opened the top drawer of a pine dresser and took out a brown paper bag.

"What is it?" Henry's expression suggested he feared the bag could contain anything from rat poison to a lit stick of dynamite.

"Why don't you open it and find out?"

Obviously not quite trusting her, he took the bag and pulled out a T-shirt the deep green of a pine forest. "What's this for?"

Looking nearly as uncomfortable as Henry, Ida shrugged her shoulders, which, while narrow, had carried more than her share of burdens over the years. Savannah would have thought her grandmother was suddenly embarrassed at giving a present to a man who'd done absolutely nothing to deserve it, had it not been for something that looked remarkably like panic in Ida's eyes.

In contrast to the comfortable silence she'd

shared with Dan at the lighthouse this morning, the one settling over the guestroom had the feel of a wet wool blanket.

"I suppose it's a welcoming gift," Savannah said as she studied her grandmother intently.

"I don't need no blamed gift," Henry said.

"Maybe *you* don't need it," Ida countered. "But *I* do." Her eyes cleared. Bright color stained her cheekbones. Proving that age hadn't made her any more patient, she snatched the shirt from his hand and held it up so he could read the message: Please Be Patient. God Isn't Finished with Me Yet.

"If I'm going to be forced to live under the same roof as you, Henry Hyatt, I'm going to need all the help I can get to remind myself that as nasty as you are, you're still a work in progress."

That stated, this time she did leave. She didn't exactly slam the bedroom door behind her, but she came close.

"Damn woman sure has a helluva temper," he grumbled.

"Not that you did anything to provoke her," Savannah suggested mildly.

He cursed, then pressed a palm down onto the single mattress. "This bed is as hard as a piece of old-growth cedar."

Her grandmother wasn't the only one second-guessing the idea to bring Henry into their home. Savannah ground her teeth and tried to remind herself that all this trouble would be worth it once her Far Harbor lighthouse was restored to its gleaming white glory.

"I was informed you preferred a hard mattress for your back."

"It's not as good as the one I used to have when I was living in the lighthouse, but I guess a man could do worse."

"I'm so pleased you approve," Savannah said dryly.

"At least this place doesn't smell of piss."

He was looking out the window at the sweep of emerald lawn, the town, and beyond that, the bay. Savannah watched his scowl soften and saw something that looked like an escaped spark from a fireplace flare hot and high in his faded blue eyes.

Looking as if his bones had given out, he sank down onto the very mattress he'd just complained about, reminding her of the collapsed scarecrow in *The Wizard of Oz*. What appeared to be a staggering emotion moved across his hollowed face in waves.

Savannah had no trouble recognizing the overpowering feeling, having experienced it herself so many times recently.

It was hope.

He was late. Savannah had been pacing the floor, waiting for the past three hours for the delivery of the window treatments. She'd called the store three times in the past forty-five minutes, and each time she'd been assured that the truck was on its way and should be there at any minute.

"Your curtains will be here soon," John assured her. In what had become a daily habit, they were eating lunch together in the garden. Since beginning her dream project, she'd discovered that budgets and deadlines shifted like changing sands in this foreign world of reconstruction. John's unrelenting optimism and amazing patience were proving a balm for frazzled nerves.

"Finally!" A truck was lumbering up the hill; the yellow lettering on the side announced that it was from Linens & Lace, located in Seattle.

The driver didn't offer any excuse for his tardiness. Savannah reminded herself that it didn't really matter. The important thing was that she was finally holding the custom-made curtains she'd pictured so many times in her imagination.

"They're really pretty," John offered as she took the first froths of snowy white lace from the box.

"Didn't they turn out lovely?" She'd had to cut back on her furniture budget to pay for the outrageously expensive lace, but as she draped one of the panels over her hand, admiring what appeared to be bridal veils for windows, Savannah decided the expense had definitely been worth every penny.

Hoping to echo John's remarkable garden, she'd selected a Scottish floral pattern that dated back to the 1860s and had been woven on antique Nottingham looms. The effect worked even better than she'd imagined. The floral lace had brought the garden indoors. But there was one problem.

"I'm afraid the sidelights for the glass panels

on the assistant keeper's cottage door are going to have to go back."

The driver's ruddy face closed up. "You can't send them back." He jabbed a thick finger at the bill of lading attached to his metal clipboard. "It says right here, no returns on monogrammed items."

"But it's the wrong pattern. The rest of the order has fourteen threads per inch. These panels are eight-point, which isn't nearly as delicate."

"They look okay to me."

"They're very attractive." Savannah drew in a calming breath and reminded herself of Ida's old saying about being able to catch more bees with honey than cider. "But they don't match the others. And they're not what I paid for."

"No returns," the man repeated with the stubbornness of an ox. "The salesman should have told you that when you placed your order."

"He did." Savannah ran her fingertips over the lovely *FH* embroidered in the center of the panel. She was not going to let this stubborn, ill-tempered man ruin her lovely mood. Or take away the pleasure from the fact that the rest of the curtains had turned out even more beautiful than she'd dreamed. "I understand the policy, since ripping out a monogram would undoubtedly destroy such delicate lace.

"However," she continued when, appearing to feel he'd won this little skirmish, the driver held out his clipboard again, "the salesman also assured me that all the lace would be fourteen point. The mistake seems to be your company's, not mine."

The man scowled. "I'm not supposed to leave here without a signature. Either you accept the whole shipment or it all goes back."

"I'm not accepting these side panels." A familiar flame flickered beneath her ribs. Her parents had both been emotional, high-strung, dramatic individuals. Their fights had resembled World War III and had, on more than one occasion caused Savannah to become physically ill. They'd also left her hating confrontation of any kind.

Over the years she'd developed the ability to remain firm when it came to her kitchens in the various hotels she'd worked in. Savannah decided that this situation was no different from insisting on the freshest vegetables or the brightest-eyed fish. Still, it was her nature to seek a compromise solution.

"I'm certain, if I call the store manager and explain the situation, you'll be off the hook."

He shrugged his huge shoulders in a way that suggested he didn't really care what she did, so long as she stopped complicating his day. Less than five minutes later he was headed back down the hill, the sidelight panels in his van.

"You did real good," John complimented her.

"I did, didn't I?" Savannah was proud of the way she'd refused to buckle under. "What would you say to going into town and letting me treat you to a hot fudge sundae to celebrate?"

"With double nuts?"

"Absolutely."

"That's a great idea." John helped her pack the lace curtains away in the white tissue paper again. "Can we stop along the way? I have a favor to do for a friend, but it shouldn't take very long."

"Sure." She was already behind schedule. What could a few more minutes hurt? Besides, this was a special day. A day she'd discovered that the world wouldn't tilt off its axis simply if she stood her ground.

John gave her directions to a small, 1930s bungalow–style house near the center of town, across from Founder's Park. It was redbrick with a wide, inviting front porch. An American flag was flying from a bracket attached to one of the porch pillars.

Savannah had driven past the house occasionally since her return to Coldwater Cove and had decided that if there was an award for tacky landscaping, this place would win, hands down. What on earth would possess anyone to plant an entire yard in cheap, dime-store flowers?

Last night's storm had torn the plastic blooms out of ground and scattered many of them into the neighbor's yard. All that remained were a trio of stone ducks, an overturned white plastic birdbath, and a brightly painted wooden whirligig of a pig dressed in a red, white, and blue Uncle Sam suit riding a bicycle.

"Darn." John frowned. "I was afraid the wind would blow all the flowers over."

Savannah parked the car, then waited on the sidewalk while John took out the small box of hand gardening tools he'd placed on the back floor. They were walking side by side toward the bungalow when the front door opened and a man in a wheelchair pushed himself over the threshold.

His age appeared to make him one of Henry Hyatt's contemporaries, but where Henry was thin and wiry, this man possessed a thick chest, huge upper arms that reminded her of tree trunks, and a lined face weathered by years spent outdoors. He was wearing a black-and-red flannel shirt and denim overalls cut above his ankles. Since loggers tended to keep their pants short to prevent them from getting caught in undergrowth and chain saw blades, Savannah guessed that he'd once earned his living felling the huge trees that grew in the peninsula's forests.

"Hello, Mr. Hawthorne," John called out. "I've come to fix your wife's garden."

"You're a good boy, John Martin." A vestige of Maine reverberated in the man's voice. "The wife was fretting about that just this morning. It was all I could do to keep her from coming outside."

"Well, you don't have to worry." John held up a green-handled trowel. "I'll have things back the way they belong real quick." He knelt on the ground and began digging holes in the dark earth still damp from last night's rain. "This is Savannah Townsend. Savannah, this is Mr. Hawthorne."

Savannah nodded. "I'm pleased to meet you,

Mr. Hawthorne." The name rang a bell, but she couldn't place him.

"Same here."

"Savannah bought the Far Harbor lighthouse," John revealed as he began gathering up the scattered blooms.

"Seems I recollect hearin' something about that." The elderly man took a pouch of tobacco from his shirt pocket and began filling a pipe that nearly disappeared in his huge hands. When he pulled an old fashioned strike-anywhere kitchen match from the same pocket and lit it with his thumbnail, Savannah noticed that his index finger ended at the second knuckle.

"Heard you're turnin' the place into some sort of fancy hotel."

"I'm planning a bed-and-breakfast. But it isn't going to be all that fancy." She braced herself for a response she'd heard from local old-timers: that the Far Harbor lighthouse was a dump and she'd bitten off more than any sensible person could chew.

"It's about time somebody did something useful with that place," he surprised her by saying. He lit the pipe and began puffing away, the smoke rising to circle his head in white, cherry-scented rings. "It went to seed when the Coast Guard pulled out. Turned into a real eyesore in the town."

Savannah thought that an ironic comment coming from a man who'd turned his front lawn into a better-living-through-plastics display.

"I'm hoping to bring it back to its former glory."

"Good for you." He puffed some more. "You'd be Ida's youngest granddaughter."

"Yes."

"Good woman, Ida. Hardworking, salt of the earth, and a dandy doctor to boot." He held up the hand that wasn't holding the pipe. "Did a real good job sewing my finger back on when I whacked it off clearing slash over by Forks." More puffs rose from the briar pipe like smoke signals. " 'Course, her meatloaf leaves a bit to be desired, but nobody's perfect."

Savannah smiled. Ida Lindstrom's meatloaf was infamous in Coldwater Cove, but as far as Savannah knew, no one had ever had the heart to tell her that her customary contribution to potluck suppers was as hard as a brick and as dry as sawdust.

"You not plannin' to serve that meatloaf at your hotel, are you?" he asked.

"No, sir, I'm not."

"Then you'll probably do well enough." That settled, he turned his attention to John. "It's startin' to look real good again."

"That's the great advantage of plastic flowers," John said cheerfully.

Knowing how much pride he took in his work, Savannah couldn't quite believe she'd heard John correctly. He tapped some dirt around an orange rose with chartreuse leaves, then rocked back and observed his handiwork as the screen door opened.

"Just in time," Mr. Hawthorne said with a huge huff of obvious relief as an elderly woman came out on the porch. She was wearing a cotton housedress emblazoned with scarlet poppies, a misbuttoned purple cardigan with frayed sleeves, a yellow straw gardening hat adorned with huge pink fabric peonies, and a pair of high green Wellingtons that made her legs look like two pale sticks.

"We've got company, Vada," Mr. Hawthorne said gently. "It's John Martin, come to work in your garden. And Savannah Townsend. You remember, she's Ida's daughter's youngest girl."

He could have been speaking to one of the stone ducks. Vada Hawthorne didn't reveal a single sign that she'd heard him. Seeming in a world of her own making, she made her way down the front steps. Then, muttering beneath her breath, began walking through the rows of replanted flowers.

"Vada's got the Alzheimer's," Mr. Hawthorne explained. "She started getting confused and lost in her mind about five years ago. At first we thought it was just old age, but then things went downhill. It was our son, Jeremy, an ER doc over to Port Angeles, who finally made us realize what was wrong with his mom.

"Even going to the library doesn't seem to spark any memories these days."

It was his mention of the library that made Savannah recognize the name. She remembered, with vivid clarity, that long-ago day she'd walked out of the big brick building with a brand-new library card and a book entitled *Tasty Treats for Young Cooks*. She'd tried out the s'mores that first night.

Over the years Mrs. Hawthorne, who'd been Olympic County librarian for as long as anyone could remember, had continued to supply Savannah with recipes, even using the interlibrary lending program to get more complex cookbooks from Seattle and Tacoma.

Besides feeding a young girl's culinary desires, Vada Hawthorne had taken generations of children on magic-carpet rides to wondrous worlds outside of Coldwater Cove. The librarian's love of books had inspired so many. It wasn't fair that she, of all people, should end her life in such a mental vacuum.

"I'm so sorry."

"Oh, it's not as bad as it was back when she first realized what was happening to her and was scared all the time. This spring she managed to get herself down to Harbor Street and told Daniel O'Halloran that she wanted to divorce me."

"Oh, I'm sure she didn't mean that," Savannah said quickly.

"She sure did mean it," he countered. "Woman got in her mind that if I was shed of her I'd be free to marry again." His voice thickened. He cleared his throat, pulled out a blue-and-white cloth handkerchief and blew his nose with a mighty honk. "We'll be married fifty-five years come Christmas, and there's never been a single day in all those years that I didn't thank the good Lord for giving me my Vada."

"That's so sweet." Savannah had no experience with such long-term commitment; even Ida had left her gambler husband in the fifth year of their marriage after he'd come home from a three-day losing streak and made the mistake of striking his wife. Claiming that if someone hits you, it's a pretty good clue that they don't like you that much—let alone love you—she'd packed her bags and moved from Portland to Coldwater Cove that same day.

"I don't know about sweet." He shrugged his shoulders and appeared self-conscious. "It's just the way things are. These days, about the only thing left from the past that Vada still connects with is her flowers. Course, she can't take care of them anymore, and now that I'm in this contraption, I can't get around the way I used to back when I was younger.

"But then Daniel got the idea for this garden. John planted it and changes it with the seasons, so Vada can believe she's still got plants blooming year-round."

Vada Hawthorne was still talking away at the rainbow plastic flowers when Savannah and John left the house. Savannah no longer found the garden tacky, but as she drove the few blocks to the Sweet Delights ice cream shop, she couldn't decide if the former librarian's garden was the loveliest or saddest thing she'd ever seen.

7

A mental image of Vada Hawthorne stayed with Savannah during her stolen time off with John at the ice cream parlor, as she drove him back to the lighthouse, so he could pick up his bike, then on the long drive to the Christmas tree farm Raine had moved to after marrying Jack. When Savannah had called the law offices earlier, she'd been told Raine was taking a home day.

Her sister answered the door wearing a gray Sheriff's Department T-shirt, jeans, and bare feet.

"You have no idea how good it is to see you," Raine said as she stepped aside and let Savannah into the farmhouse. "I've spent all morning sewing and was about ready to tear my hair out."

"I didn't realize you even knew how to sew."

"I don't, or, more precisely, I didn't. I'm starting to get the hang of it, though it's a lot more dangerous than I would have guessed." She held out her left hand, revealing a Band-aid.

"I've run over my finger three times in the past two hours."

The kitchen looked as if a hurricane had blown through it. Or it had, perhaps, been sacked by a horde of vandals. The table had disappeared beneath pieces of brown, black, and gray fabric. Tissue paper Savannah recognized as pattern pieces were all over the floor. A top-of-the-line sewing machine sat atop the table in the midst of all the chaos; the box on the floor nearby gave proof that it was brand-new.

"May I ask why you're putting yourself through all this?"

"Amy won the part of lead scary tree in her summer day camp's production of *The Wizard of Oz*. I've been sewing damn fabric bark onto a leotard all morning. Thank God it's supposed to be a bare tree. If I had to face leaves, I'd have no choice but to throw myself into the sound."

Despite the concern that had brought her here, Savannah laughed. "Do you have any idea how fortunate you are?"

Raine's scowl instantly turned to a slow, satisfied grin. "Absolutely. Would you like some coffee? It'll just take me a minute to brew it."

"No, thanks. I already inhaled about a pot while I was steaming wallpaper while waiting for the curtain delivery."

"In that outfit?"

Savannah glanced down at her khaki shorts and black, tan, and white striped bateau-neck knit shirt. "What's wrong with it?"

"It's clean. Neat." Raine skimmed a fingernail

down the crease of the shorts. "Starched." She shook her head. "You look as if you just walked off the summer fashion issue of *Vogue*. What the hell do you do, spray yourself with Teflon each morning before you leave the house?"

"I wear an apron."

"An apron," Raine repeated, looking skeptical.

"It's actually more of a smock. To keep the paint and dust off."

"Honey, in order to look half as good as you do right now, the rest of us would have to wear a hazardous waste team incubation suit."

She shook her head in amused disbelief again. "Of course I'm happy to see you, but what's so important that it brought you out to the boonies this afternoon?"

On the long drive to the farm, Savannah had tried to tell herself that she was overreacting. The problem was, she hadn't quite been able to make herself believe that.

"Where's Amy?" She belatedly realized that she hadn't been hit with a ball of blond energy the moment she walked in the front door— which just proved how distracted she was. Normally, she loved any opportunity to see her new niece.

"In Seattle with Lilith. They're having a girls' day on the town. They're shopping at Nordstrom's, having lunch at Pike Place Market, then capping the day off with a trip to the Aquarium."

"Sounds like Mom's really getting into being a grandmother."

"She adores it." Raine took a longer, more probing look at Savannah. "Whatever's bothering you can't be all that bad."

Savannah sat down on one of the kitchen chairs. "John and I took off early today and went out for ice cream and stopped by Vada Hawthorne's house on the way. You remember her, she was town librarian."

"Of course I remember Mrs. Hawthorne." Raine sat across the fabric-strewn table. "She always used to save the new Nancy Drew books for me."

"She introduced me to the *Little House* books. And *Little Women.*" After reading that novel, Savannah had decided that the solidarity she and Raine shared was just like the March sisters'. Needless to say, she'd viewed Raine as the always adventurous Jo, herself as the more settled, domestic Meg. "Did you know she's got Alzheimer's?"

"I heard something about that. How's she doing?"

"Not well." Savannah told Raine about the elderly woman asking Dan for the divorce, then described the garden.

"That was a lovely idea of Dan's."

"John told me later that he'd thought of it after they'd gone to the cemetery to put flowers on Karyn and her husband's grave and they saw all the plastic flowers other people had left on family gravesites.

"I hate thinking of Gram ending up like Mrs. Hawthorne." Savannah took a deep breath. She decided that she'd stalled long enough. "Do you think Gram's got Alzheimer's?"

Instead of immediately denying the suggestion, or laughing it off, Raine folded her hands atop the brown cloth. "I don't know. The thought's occurred to me since I've been back. But I've always managed to convince myself that I'm imagining things—making mush out of a molehill, as our grandmother would say." Raine's attempt at a smile fell flat. "I told you about her outburst in court."

"During Gwen's custody hearing?" Savannah nodded. "Yes. But not the details."

"It wasn't pretty. She ended up telling the entire court the story of how she'd once prescribed birth-control pills for the presiding judge, back when the judge was a college student. At the time I was so busy trying to keep us both from getting tossed into Jack's jail for contempt of court, I put it down to her strong feelings for Gwen and her eccentric personality."

"How do you feel about it now?" Savannah felt a distant pain and realized that she was digging her fingernails into her palms.

"I think she should get a complete physical, but she insists that there's nothing wrong with her."

"You've discussed this with Gram? Without first talking with me?"

"You've been a little distracted," Raine reminded her. "What with your divorce, and trying to restore the lighthouse and beginning a new business. Besides," her tone turned a bit defensive, "I mentioned it to Mother back when you were depressed. We decided that the last thing you needed was one more problem to worry about."

The conversation must have taken place while she'd been hiding beneath her covers. "How nice of you both to decide what's good for me."

"We were only trying to protect you."

"I know." It was consummate Raine, watching out for her little sister. Savannah decided that nothing would be gained by sharing her thoughts that such protection had resulted in her taking too long to acquire a sense of independence. "I also appreciate your concern. But I'm an adult, Raine. From now on, I don't want to be left out of the loop."

There was an awkward moment as the sisters looked at each other. Then, instead of arguing, or behaving as if her feelings were hurt, Raine gave her a slow smile.

"Good for you," she said, her words unknowingly echoing that of Mr. Hawthorne.

"We need a plan," Savannah said.

"A battle plan," Raine agreed. She reached into a cookie jar shaped like Winnie-the-Pooh's honey pot, took out a handful of Oreos, and put them on a plate. "Do you want to confront her directly?"

"We'll undoubtedly have to, eventually." Feeling six years old again, Savannah separated the chocolate halves and scraped the white filling off with her teeth. "But perhaps we should observe her more closely, first, to gather evidence."

"In a controlled setting." Raine took a carton

of milk from the refrigerator and poured them both a tall glass.

"Like a scientific experiment," Savannah said.

"Exactly." Raine crunched a cookie and appeared thoughtful. "You know, we still haven't had a proper celebration for you having bought the lighthouse."

"I thought we'd agreed that we'd wait for the party until all the restoration was done."

"That's your party," Raine reminded her. "There's no reason why I can't throw an earlier one." She nodded again, seeming pleased with this idea. She polished off her milk in long swallows, then took a pen and magnetic pad from the refrigerator door. "We'll invite the entire family, of course. That way we can all watch for signs."

"Do you think that's wise? Gram might notice something's up if everyone's in on it."

"The reason we're doing this is because she isn't all that lucid these days," Raine reminded her. "We'll swear everyone to secrecy and be extra careful not to be too obvious. Besides," she pointed out with the unfailing logic Savannah had always admired, "this way, if one of us slips up, the others can provide backup distraction."

She sounded so confident, Savannah believed her. "What about the menu? I can fix something—"

"You will not. From what Lilith tells me, you're working nearly around the clock now. We'll order out from Oley's," Raine said decisively. "Everyone likes barbecue. And so you won't have to lower yourself to eat red meat,

I'll even split the order between ribs and chicken."

That settled, they picked a time two evenings away. While Raine began calling the other family members to inform them of the dinner, Savannah ate her way through the honey pot cookie jar and hoped with all her heart that their concerns would prove ungrounded.

Pregnant with rain, heavy clouds the color of tarnished silver hung low over Coldwater Cove when Ida awoke. There was something she needed to do. Something important. Something for the family.

"It'll come to you," she assured herself briskly as she tucked in the sheets with tight, hospital corners, straightened the bright handmade quilt, and fluffed the pillows. She had no trouble remembering that Savannah had made the Sunshine and Shadows quilt for her 4-H project the summer she'd turned twelve, so why couldn't she remember the thought that had been teasing at the edge of her mind moments earlier?

"It's not Alzheimer's," she assured herself yet again as she showered. Savannah had installed pretty little soaps that looked like colorful seashells in the bathroom. She'd said that they weren't only for looks, that they had glycerin and some sort of fancy oils in them that would make your skin smooth, but Ida figured at her age, it was a little late to worry about soft skin. "The only thing wrong with me is Old-Timers."

She dressed, pinned her hair up in its usual haphazard bun, and went downstairs to make coffee. By the time she was on her second cup, the caffeine had kicked in.

"Raine's party is tonight," she recalled in a flash of sudden awareness as bright as the lightning that had just lit up the sky outside the kitchen window. "The family will be expecting me to make my meatloaf."

She checked the freezer and wasn't surprised to discover that she didn't have a single pound of ground beef. Savannah had pretty much taken over the cooking since returning home from Los Angeles, and the girl had never been much of a fan of red meat. Ida didn't mind all the meals of fish and chicken since her granddaughter was, after all, a whiz in the kitchen. But she'd put her foot down about the sushi.

"Might as well buy some Glo-eggs down at the Hook, Line, and Sinker," she'd told Savannah at the time. "They're bound to be cheaper."

She rinsed out her mug, then hung it on the cute little hooks Savannah had put up. She made a list of ingredients she'd need, took the keys to her Jeep down from another rack that was new since her granddaughter's return, and picked up her pocketbook, which was right where it belonged on the end of the counter.

Outside, thunder rumbled and lightning flashed. The day was shaping up to be a real frog strangler. As she plucked her rain gear from the hook beside the kitchen door, Ida decided that the fact that she remembered her umbrella proved there was nothing at all wrong with her mind.

"It's going to rain," John announced when he brought the morning paper into the kitchen.

"Sure looks like it." Dan glanced out at the threatening sky. He could vaguely make out the silhouette of the lighthouse in the fog. Farther down the beach, the new Coast Guard light flashed brightly. Dan missed the old red-and-white beacon that had made the Far Harbor lighthouse unique among the others on the strait. He also hoped the guys had finished the roof on Savannah's keeper's house yesterday.

"Do you think the rain will ruin the dinner tonight?" John asked with obvious concern.

"If it's still raining tonight, they'll just move the party indoors. When Jack called yesterday, he said Raine was ordering out from Oley's, so there won't be any outdoor cooking to interfere with."

"That's good. I like Oley's barbecue a lot." John drowned the stack of silver dollar pancakes in blueberry syrup. "Savannah's coming, right?"

"Right." Dan didn't share the details of the sisters' plan to observe their grandmother's mental state in a family setting.

"Good," John said again, with a decisive nod. "I like her a lot, don't you?"

"What's not to like?" Dan chose the maple syrup. "She's gorgeous, friendly—"

"And smells like the garden after it rains," John broke in.

"That is a decided plus."

While the thunder rolled across the fog-blanketed cove, John fell silent. Dan could tell that he was mulling something over. Knowing his nephew would share his thoughts when he was ready, he turned to the sports section to check out last night's box scores.

John was cleaning off the counter ten minutes later when he looked up from putting the pancake batter bowl in the dishwasher. "Do you think you and Savannah might get married?"

"Marriage is a pretty big step," Dan said mildly.

Certainly it was a bigger step than either of them was ready for. Even so, he had been thinking about her a lot lately: during the day when he was wading through legal briefs at the office, in court when he should be keeping his mind on the case he was arguing, and mostly late at night when he was lying alone in bed, watching the lights still on in the lighthouse, and wondering if, just maybe, she was thinking of him, too.

"People usually date for a while before they start thinking about making a commitment like that," he said.

"Then maybe you ought to ask her out on a date," John suggested.

"Maybe I will."

They were in the Tahoe, on the way to Nelson's Green Spot, where John had a weekend day job when his nephew shared another, less optimistic thought.

"You don't think Ida Lindstrom's going to bring her meatloaf to the dinner tonight, do you?"

Dan laughed at the expression of dread on John's face. "I'm afraid that's pretty much a given, Sport."

Ida pushed her cart around the mercantile, gathering up the ingredients for her meatloaf. Eggs, two pounds of ground chuck—because although Savannah insisted the round was less fatty, chuck had more flavor. Then, of course she needed a pound of ground pork, which she had to wait for Glen Harding to grind for her, which wasn't all that much of a hardship since they had a nice chat about the weather and his wife Betty's lumbago, which was doing much better, thanks to the ointment Ida had suggested, Glen revealed.

"I'm pleased as Punch and Judy to hear it," Ida said. It was always rewarding to know that you'd made a difference in someone's life.

She moved on to the vegetable section, where she ran into Winnie Randall pulling back the husks from ears of sweet corn.

"Good morning, Winnie." Ida bagged a fat yellow onion for her meatloaf. "How's your mother doing?" Winnie had recently gotten a nursing home in Gray's Harbor closed down after she'd visited and discovered that her aged mother, Pearl, had acquired bedsores about as dark and deep as Mount St. Helen's craters.

"A lot better." Winnie discarded three more ears of corn. "We've got her at Evergreen, and she seems more alert and coherent. That treatment you had the nurses put on her sores

worked like a charm." Two fat yellow ears made
the cut and ended up in the cart.

"It always does." Ida remembered the case
well. After the horror of finding Pearl in condi-
tions the county would have shut down the dog
pound for, Winnie had checked out Evergreen
six ways to Sunday. Although she trusted the
staff, she'd still asked Ida to drop by and exam-
ine her mother. Ida had driven to the care center that same day and immediately prescribed a
"baker's cure."

The mix of equal parts of granulated sugar and
hydrogen peroxide might be an old remedy and
not nearly as fancy as the medicines being manufactured today, but it still worked, and as far as
Ida was concerned, that was all that mattered.

While she no longer kept office hours, Ida
still considered herself a working physician. A
person didn't retire from the medical profession
the way one might from selling insurance or
working for the telephone company. When you
became a doctor, you signed on for life. Ida
wouldn't have had it any other way.

She exchanged a bit more chitchat, sidestep-
ping questions about Henry's recent move into
her house, Savannah's divorce, and when Raine
was going to make her a great grandmother.
Claiming the need to hurry home to begin
cooking, Ida moved on to aisle six and picked
up the Quaker Oats that was her meatloaf's secret ingredient. She checked her list, satisfied
that she had everything she needed.

As she pushed her cart toward the checkout

counter, where Olivia Brown was waiting behind her newly computerized cash register, a vivid memory of Winnie's mother flashed through Ida's mind. In her years as a doctor, she'd witnessed a lot of tragedies, but the sight of Pearl, who'd once been the prettiest flapper in Coldwater Cove, wasted away to bones and skin and looking like a death camp survivor had been one of the worst.

Deciding that she'd rather drop dead right here in the mercantile than spend the last years of her life in a nursing home, even one as nice as Evergreen admittedly seemed to be, Ida pushed her cart straight past Olivia, who was busy gossiping with Fred, the seventy-year-old bag boy, about Lilith Lindstrom Cooper having had the nerve to show up at the VFW dance.

Old biddy, Ida thought.

"Well, I guess if her war-hero husband can overlook her behavior back in the sixties, the town might as well," Fred was saying as Ida continued out through the automatic doors into the parking lot.

She was putting groceries in the back of the Jeep when a huffing and puffing Olivia—who'd gained fifty pounds since starting work at the market where the Klondike ice cream bars were all too available—finally caught up with her.

8

Savannah was taking a shower in the claw-footed bathtub when the ringing of the phone finally infiltrated through the drumming of the water and the rattle of the hundred-year-old house's copper pipes. She snatched a towel from the rack, shoved aside the curtain, scrambled over the tub's high rim, and, dripping water on the floor, dashed into the bedroom, managing to scoop the receiver from its cradle just as the ringing stopped.

"Damn." Water from her hair streamed off her soap-slick body in rivulets. Wrapping the towel around her, Savannah shoved her wet tangle of hair off her forehead and blinked her eyes against the sting of shampoo.

She stood beside the bed, waiting another long moment for the phone to ring again, hoping that whoever had tried to call would give it another shot. The only sounds were a rumbling warning of thunder and the muffled clang of a buoy from somewhere out in the fog-draped harbor. Even the birds refrained from singing their morning songs, apparently hiding out somewhere in the treetops, anticipating the coming rain.

A louder clap of thunder shook the house, followed by a jolt of lightning that flashed in the bedroom like a strobe light. Old fears sparked at her nerves and made all the hair on her arms and the back of her neck stand up. Reminding herself that she was no longer that fearful child who hid from storms—both natural and emotional—Savannah returned to the bathroom, hoping that the roofers who'd finally finished up yesterday had done as good a job as they'd promised when they'd accepted their hefty check.

"It's about time you got here," Raine complained when Dan arrived at the office.

"I took a little detour to drop John off at the Green Spot, since it was raining too hard for him to ride his bike." With his mind on Savannah, as it had been too often lately, he'd forgotten to turn on his cell phone.

"I figured that might be it. Warren Cunningham's been calling every five minutes for the past half hour. He's in Tokyo, shoring up some sort of Asian Rim finance deal.

"Jack picked his son up about four this morning on a complaint, and since you've taken care of the kid's problems in the past, Warren wants you on the case."

J. C. Cunningham was a sixteen-year-old who spent the school year with his mother in Dallas, and summers and holidays at one of his father's many homes here in Coldwater Cove. Dan suspected a great deal of the trouble he caused was his way of trying to get attention from parents too wrapped up in their own lives to notice that their only son was falling through the cracks.

The boy wasn't really a juvenile delinquent. In fact, he wasn't much more wild than Dan's own cousin Jack, whose teenage stunts had landed him in judicial hot water on more than one occasion during his teen years. Fortunately, Jack had outgrown his infamous reputation and matured into a respectable adult, even following in his father's footsteps as sheriff.

But these were different times and since what once might have been considered normal juvenile transgressions seemed to be leading to more dangerous adult crimes these days, Dan could understand why Jack felt the need to lay down the law.

"What did J.C. do now?"

Raine's lips twitched. "According to Mildred Zumwalt, J.C. and his pals got a little too rambunctious last night and committed a 'drive-by shouting.'"

"That's a new one."

"It's also typically Mildred."

The woman who'd terrified a classroom of eighth graders for nearly half a century appeared to have decided to liven up her golden years by filing lawsuits against everyone in the world. Just last week she'd wanted to sue God for destruction of property when a lightning bolt had struck her tree. No fan of nuisance lawsuits, Dan had been able to talk her out of the suit by patiently reminding the former middle school civics teacher that every defendant had a legal right to answer the charges against him or her in court, and until someone came up with a way to serve a subpoena on God, he doubted there was a judge in the country that would hear the case.

"Mildred is the easy part of this morning's caseload." Raine's expression sobered. "On the flip side, I think Kathi Montgomery might just be ready to file for divorce. Looking at her, I think you're going to want to file for an order of protection as well. I put her in your office."

Dan glanced down the hallway. "It's about time," he murmured.

Jason Montgomery was a former fisherman who'd lost his boat to an Olympia bank and his sense of manhood to the bottle. It was Coldwater Cove's dirty little secret that he'd begun to beat his wife; it was Dan and Jack's dual frustration that short of tossing the guy in jail whenever his behavior got bad enough to result in a 911 call from the neighbors, they'd never been able to talk his wife into testifying against him, or taking the steps necessary to save herself.

She jumped like a startled doe when he opened the office door. The last time he'd tried to talk reason into her, her nose had been slender and delicately sloped. Today it was swollen to twice its size, her top lip had an ugly split, and her flowered print cotton blouse bore rust-colored blood spatters he hoped to hell were from Jason, but suspected were from her broken nose. Bruises new enough to still be blue braceleted both upper arms and darkened the puffy flesh around her left eye. Both eyes were dulled with pain.

A cold rage shot through Dan. For her sake, he controlled it. "Hey, Kathi." They'd dated for a time, in school, when they'd been on the debate team together. It hadn't gone beyond some making out on the bus trips to various competitions around the state. After two months, she'd dumped him for Montgomery, who'd been all-state high school offensive linebacker three years in a row.

"Oh, Dan." Her split lip quivered. Her eyes swam. "I'm so sorry."

"You don't have a damn thing to be sorry for." He crouched down in front of her. When he touched his hand to her hair, she flinched and fear filled her eyes.

"Now there's where you're wrong." She sniffled. "I'm sorry for so many damn things. Especially for having chosen brawn over brain."

The words were the same ones that, suffering from wounded teenage pride, he'd thrown at her when she'd broken up with him. Her soft tone revealed a vestige of the spunk that had drawn him to her in the first place. Back then, before Montgomery had broken her spirit, she'd reminded him a lot of Jamie Lee Curtis in *Halloween*. Unfortunately, Dan thought grimly, Kathi had ended up with her own personal bogeyman.

"I've always believed that there should be a general amnesty for everything we say and do in high school." He took a Kleenex from the box on the table next to the couch and gently dabbed at her swimming eyes. She flinched again when he touched the swelling beneath her black eye.

"I tried to make things right between us. I kept thinking that if only I worked at our marriage harder, if I was more understanding of Jason's feelings, we could make it work."

Dan privately considered that Mother Teresa couldn't have made marriage to that goon work.

"I'd just graduated from school when we got married. I was looking forward to working as a speech therapist, but Jason didn't want me to work outside the home. He said I made it look as if he couldn't support me."

Once again Dan thought the real problem was that Montgomery hadn't wanted Kathi out in the real world where she could meet someone who might truly care about her. Once again he kept his thoughts to himself.

"We moved to Alaska, and we were doing okay. But the fishing wasn't what he'd hoped it would be, so we came back here." She dabbed at her eyes. "Then things got even worse. The more he was out of work, the more he drank. Which made it harder to work. It was a vicious cycle.

"After the boat was repossessed, I went back to work for a private home-care agency. That's when things really started going downhill. . . .

"Then last night he called me a lot of things

I'd just as soon not repeat." She pressed the balled-up tissue against her mouth and struggled for calm.

"You don't have to. That's all in the past, Kathi. What you need to concentrate on is the terrific future that's waiting out there for you."

Dan smiled encouragingly, not because there was anything at all humorous about her situation, but because she needed it.

An hour later, he'd prepared the divorce complaint and had arranged for Kathi to move to a shelter for abused women at least until her husband could be picked up and put behind bars.

Ida had been the impetus behind the shelter back in the late seventies. Bucking initial objection from those who believed that a man's home was his castle where he was entitled to do as he pleased, she'd gone on a statewide speaking tour, pitching her project to the Rotarians, the Elks, the American Legion, PTA, AMA, any group who'd listen and write out a check.

With typical Ida-like candor, she'd told of her own abusive experience, something that wasn't being done in those days when tidy homes in nice neighborhoods had harbored dark secrets that weren't really secrets, and neighbors looked the other way.

Dan would have preferred to cut the wife beater into little pieces of shark bait, but civilization being what it was, he figured he'd have to settle for putting the guy away for a very long time.

That problem taken care of, as well as he could for now, he moved on to J.C., whose situation at least offered a bit of comic relief, he thought as he entered the sheriff's office.

Any prospect of humor instantly died when he viewed Ida sitting in the office, looking like death warmed over. Her complexion was the color of cold ashes, there was a trapped animal look in her eyes, and she was gripping the scarred arms of the wooden chair as if trying to keep herself tethered to earth.

She was also doing something Dan had never seen before. Indeed, he doubted that very few people had ever witnessed the sight of Ida Lindstrom openly weeping.

Henry Hyatt was frying eggs when Savannah entered the kitchen. The aroma of bacon filled the air.

"Ida said I was welcome to help myself," he said defensively, "since I chipped in for the groceries."

"Fine." Savannah looked at the dishes already piled up in the sink and wondered if Henry was expecting her to clean up the mess. "Have you seen my grandmother this morning?"

"Isn't she in her room?"

"No." Ida's bedroom door had been open when Savannah had passed by, the bed neatly made. She wondered if the call had been from Ida and worried that her grandmother had gotten into trouble.

"I don't suppose you could have picked up the phone?"

He shrugged and flipped the eggs. "I was taking the bacon from the pan when it rang. Besides, odds are it wasn't for me."

Savannah had to practically bite her tongue to keep from setting down some house rules. It was, after all, her grandmother's house, which meant that if there was any rule setting to be done, Ida'd be the one to do it.

She went to pour herself a cup of coffee, but the carafe was empty. Deciding to pick up a cup on the way to the lighthouse, she'd taken her raincoat from the rack when she viewed Dan's Tahoe pulling up in front of the house. When she saw her grandmother sitting beside him, she flung open the door and ran out into the rain.

"What happened?" she asked as Dan helped Ida down from the high passenger seat. Her heart clenched when she realized that her grandmother had been crying.

"Nothing that important," Ida insisted. When Dan retrieved two plastic bags of groceries from the back seat, she snatched them out of his hands and marched past Savannah into the house.

"I'll wait out here," Dan offered.

On her grandmother's heels, Savannah didn't take time to respond. "Are you all right?"

"I'm fit as a fiddler." Ida's red-rimmed gaze circled the kitchen.

"Then why did Dan drive you home? Where's the Jeep?"

"At the market, and you don't have to worry, it's not wrecked or anything." She muttered something under her breath, then shot Henry a stern look. "I'm not cleaning this mess up."

"Don't get your britches in a twist, I'm planning to take care of it." Ignoring her sputtered protest, he took the bags, put them on the counter, and began putting the groceries away. "You'd better sit down." His blue eyes swept over her. "You look like hell."

"You're no Paul Newman yourself," she shot back as she grabbed the ground meat from him and yanked open the refrigerator door.

"Grandmother," Savannah repeated with dwindling patience, "what happened?"

"I told you, nothing important." Ida slammed the door shut. The look she shot her granddaughter was even harder than the one she'd used to scant avail on Henry. "Just a little mix-up at the market."

"What kind of mix-up?"

"The mixed-up kind," Ida retorted. "And that's all I'm going to say about it."

Savannah may have toughened up over the last weeks, but she suspected that even Genghis Khan would have had difficulty facing down Ida at her most resolute. Dragging her hands through her hair, she decided to get answers from another source.

Dan was waiting for her on the front porch. He was leaning back in the porch swing, his booted feet propped on the railing. The driving rain had lightened to mist.

"What happened?" she repeated. "Why was my grandmother crying?"

The expression of sympathy she viewed on his face when he looked up at her made her dread his answer. "I suppose crying is a standard reaction when you get arrested for shoplifting."

"Arrested?" His words buzzed like a swarm of wasps. Savannah latched onto the loudest one. "Jack arrested my grandmother?"

"He didn't exactly arrest her." Dan sighed, dropped his boots to the porch floor and leaned forward, his fingers linked between his knees. "He just took her down to the station for her own protection. . . . It's a little complicated."

Name one thing about her life that wasn't these days. She was living proof that trouble, like nature, seemed to abhor a vacuum.

"My grandmother wouldn't steal anything." About this Savannah was very sure.

"I know that. So does Jack. Hell, Olivia Brown knows it, too. The trouble is, the new owners of the mercantile are from the city, and they established a no-tolerance policy for shoplifters.

"Olivia was afraid she would lose her job if she didn't call the sheriff, especially since Fred Potter was there to witness Ida breezing past the checkout with a cartload of groceries."

The wicker creaked as Savannah sank onto the porch swing beside him. "Oh, God. . . . She forgot to pay for them."

"That'd be my guess. Needless to say, she was pretty shook up when Jack arrived a couple minutes after Olivia stopped her from leaving. He didn't want to let her drive home by herself."

"I can understand that. But how did you end up getting recruited?"

"I happened to walk in the door of the sheriff's office right after Jack struck out trying to get hold of you or Raine. I knew Raine was on her way to Tacoma to take a deposition and figured you were already at the lighthouse. So I volunteered to chauffeur Ida home.

"Jack's going to come by with a deputy later on today to drop off the Jeep, but you might want to hide the keys for a while, at least until your grandmother gets a clean bill of health."

She wasn't surprised he knew about Ida's problems. Undoubtedly Raine had told her husband, who'd told his cousin, about tonight's dinner plans.

"The trick, of course, is getting her to agree to a comprehensive physical in the first place— short of tying her up and dragging her into the city." Savannah's voice was as flat as her spirits.

"We'll think of something."

"It's not your problem."

"You're family, Savannah. When Jack married Raine, that made you part of the clan. And we O'Hallorans stick together."

Clan. It was a strange, old-fashioned word for a concept as foreign to Savannah as Amazonia. For years her immediate family had consisted of Ida and Raine. Lately Lilith, too, had returned home to be part of that nuclear unit, which had expanded to include Raine's husband Jack and his daughter Amy, as well as Cooper Ryan and Gwen.

Her father had sent her an invitation to his wedding in London last year, but it had taken place on Christmas, the busiest time of the year at Las Casitas, not that Savannah was all that sure she would have gone even if it had occurred during the off-season. Still, even if she counted Reggie's new wife, whom she'd never met, the number didn't begin to come close to that of the O'Hallorans, who'd first settled on the peninsula over a hundred years ago and had seemed to take to heart the biblical admonition to be fruitful and multiply.

They were sitting very close together, close enough for her to see the change in his eyes. Distracted and unwillingly fascinated by the blue flame, she wasn't prepared for him to touch his mouth to hers. For a brief moment, her already unstable world tilted.

Because it would have been so easy—too easy—to sink into the tender kiss, because she could still feel the hum of it vibrating on her lips, Savannah pulled back, seeking solid ground.

"What was that for?" Her voice sounded too defensive even to her own ears.

"Luck." The familiar grin flashed. His hand lifted, as if to touch her face, then merely tugged on a curl that had fallen across her cheek instead. "See you tonight."

Because she didn't want to let him know that he had, in that fleeting instant, made her feel things she'd forgotten she could feel, things she had no business feeling, Savannah resisted the schoolgirlish urge to stay on the porch until he'd driven out of sight.

Instead, she went back into the house, searching for Ida, who'd sequestered herself in the den and tartly informed Savannah through the closed door that she was busy with household accounts and did not want to be disturbed.

There were no lingering tears in her grandmother's voice. No tremor, no confusion. She sounded as resolute as she'd been in the days when she'd served as a stabilizing rock for two little girls, who, without her, could have drifted so far astray.

Myriad memories, both good and bad, assaulted Savannah, ricocheting in her mind like gunfire as she drove to the library to research Alzheimer's before tonight's dinner. She felt the moisture on her face, realized she was crying, and swiped at the tears with the back of her hand.

Surrendering a day's work on the lighthouse wouldn't begin to make up for the personal sacrifices Ida Lindstrom had made for her granddaughters, but it was a start.

9

"Some of the symptoms are right on the mark," Savannah said to Raine when the sisters had slipped away to the back porch of the farmhouse before dinner. Afraid she might be overheard by either Henry or Ida if she called from the house, Savannah had waited until she'd arrived at the farm to tell her sister about today's research trip. "But others don't fit at all."

"I imagine each case is different," Raine mused as she skimmed through the pages Savannah had copied.

"That's what all the books say." Savannah took a sip of the red wine that had been Dan's contribution to the family dinner. "They also say the warning signs may apply to dementias other than Alzheimer's."

"Terrific." Raine sighed and looked out over the acres of conical blue-green spruce and firs.

"All the more reason to get Gram to the doctor as soon as possible."

As they silently sipped their wine and considered the difficulties involved in that challenge, it was Savannah's turn to sigh.

Displaying an ability to compartmentalize that Savannah had always admired, Raine switched conversational gears. "With all that's been happening, we haven't had a chance to talk about you. How are you doing?"

"Better than last week. The shingles are finally all replaced, so I can finally start finishing up the inside. I ran by to check on things before I drove here, and wonders of wonders, the roofs weren't leaking."

"That is good news. But I wasn't asking about the lighthouse. How are you doing now that you've put some time and distance between yourself and the weasel?"

"I've turned the corner on that, too. At least I haven't had the nightmare for two weeks." Savannah didn't mention that concerns about Ida had precluded a great deal of sleep.

"What nightmare?" Raine was looking at her in that same deep way that Dan had on more than one occasion. Savannah decided it must be a lawyer thing.

"Didn't I tell you about it?"

"No."

Savannah wished she hadn't brought the subject up. She also knew that since Raine had definitely inherited their grandmother's stubbornness, it wouldn't do any good trying to dodge the issue now. "I dream I'm getting married at the lighthouse."

"That's not such a bad start."

"For you, perhaps." Savannah was pleased her sister seemed to be basking in marital bliss, but she had no intention of ever walking down the aisle again. Better, she'd decided, to stick to things she did well. "It's a garden wedding. In the summer, I think, because the sky is wide and blue and I'm surrounded by John Martin's flowers."

"It sounds gorgeous. So what's the problem? Is this one of those naked dreams?"

"No, I'm wearing a gorgeous, traditional white satin gown, with lace and seed pearls and about a mile-long train."

"If you tell me the groom is Kevin, I'll understand why you consider it a nightmare."

"It's him. And I'm feeling as stupidly blissful as I did in Monaco—until after we exchange vows, when, instead of lifting my veil, he pulls a hedge clipper out of his tuxedo and clips off my wings."

Raine lifted a brow. "Your wings?"

"Wings," Savannah repeated. "They're even prettier than my gown, all gossamer silver and gold, as delicate as a spider's web. I begin to cry, and ask him what he's doing, and he answers that now that I'm married, I won't need them anymore."

"And what do you say?"

"I try telling him that I need to fly. That I've flown since I was a child, and that's when it happens."

"What?"

"All the guests stand up, and they're wearing white-and-black masks, like the comedy ones that are the flip side of drama?"

"Right."

"And they all say 'Silly girl, you've been fooling yourself. You never learned how to fly.' When they start to laugh, I try to run away, but they're all standing on my train, so I grab the hedge clippers from Kevin and hack it off. Then I run away, off the edge of the cliff."

"And?"

"I don't know. I remember thinking that if I look down, I'll fall, like that Roadrunner cartoon. But then I wake up."

"Well." Raine looked out over the fields of Christmas trees again. "It doesn't exactly take a shrink to figure out that you're facing big freedom issues, which is certainly expected, given your situation."

"It's true, though," Savannah insisted earnestly. "I have never really flown. You and Mother were always the ones with the wings in this family."

"Me?" Raine looked honestly surprised by that idea.

"You left here, went to Harvard, then on to New York, forged a life for yourself—"

"A life, you'll note, that I was more than happy to give up."

"Still, you were brave enough to try. And succeed. All on your own."

"Going off to cooking school in Paris took a lot of nerve," Raine pointed out.

"I was homesick for months."

"So was I when I was at Harvard. And it was even worse when I first arrived in Manhattan."

"Really? But you always used to talk about how you couldn't wait to get away from here. And how much more exciting life was in the big city."

Savannah thought that Raine was definitely proof that the world kept turning and changing. Oh, Raine still practiced law, and had kept ties to her former firm with her Asian Rim business, but she had put far behind her the eighty-hour weeks that had defined her life as a high-powered New York litigator.

Savannah was still amazed that Raine had settled down on a Christmas tree farm in this small, remote town, become a stepmother to one child, and claimed to want more of her own. Still, she thought now, she'd never seen her sister looking more radiant.

"You know what they say about not appreciating something until you don't have it anymore." Raine shrugged. "Besides, mostly I was missing you and Ida."

"But you got over that."

"Let's just say I learned to adapt."

"I don't think I ever really did, which was one of the reasons I eloped with Kevin. At the time, getting married seemed a better choice than returning home a failure."

Just as Lilith had done so many times. Raine didn't say it, but Savannah knew they were both thinking about their mother.

"No one could ever consider you a failure," Raine argued with the unwavering loyalty Savannah had always been able to count on. "Especially these days. What you're doing with the lighthouse is nothing short of a miracle. To tell you the truth, sis, I wasn't honestly sure you'd be able to pull it off."

"Neither was I," Savannah admitted. "But if luck holds, I'll be open for Christmas."

Despite having gotten behind schedule in the beginning, she still had four months to pull off her miracle. The mental picture of the restored buildings lit up with bright white lights for the holidays warmed the heart she'd feared had been shattered. She could practically hear the crackle of the logs and smell the cedar in the fireplace, welcoming guests to her lighthouse.

"Do you realize," Raine said, as if the thought had just occurred to her, "that this will be the first holiday season in years that we're all back home together?"

"With Amy beginning a new generation."

"To us." The late afternoon sun made the wine gleam like rubies as Raine raised her glass. "And all four generations of strong, soaring Lindstrom women."

Savannah lifted her own wineglass to her sister's toast, her attention momentarily drawn to her fingernails. They were chipped and torn from scraping moldy, water-stained layers of paper off walls.

Not so long ago, her French manicure had been kept flawless by weekly visits to a Beverly Hills salon. Her nails may have been perfect, but her life had been a mess. As difficult as things were now, she couldn't imagine returning to that former existence she'd managed to convince herself was everything she'd ever wanted.

She might not be soaring up there with the eagles yet, but having tested her wings, she was finally learning to fly. And despite having hit a few air pockets, it was wonderful.

"I'm glad you're fixing up the lighthouse," Amy O'Halloran said after the family had gathered around the dining room table. "I like it a lot, especially the flowers John planted, though it's sad that bad boys broke the windows."

With her long, golden curls and bright blue eyes, the six-year-old girl was the most beautiful child Savannah had ever seen. She was also precocious, unrelentingly curious about everything around her, and despite having lost her mother to cancer, amazingly well-adjusted. Savannah thought that said a lot about Raine's husband.

"Well, they've all been replaced now."

"I saw that when we were driving home from town yesterday. Mommy said you're going to make it as pretty as it used to be, before I was born."

Savannah watched the pleasure move across Raine's face when Jack's daughter called her Mommy. "That's my plan."

"Speaking of plans," Lilith trilled, "thanks to Mother's army of volunteers, this year's Sawdust Festival is going to be the best one yet. We're even having a palm reader."

"Damn foolish notion, if you ask me," Ida muttered.

"I thought you liked Raven."

"She's okay—for one of those New Age types," Ida allowed. Tonight's sweatshirt was bright purple and proclaimed Age and Treachery Will Always Overcome Youth and Skill.

"Mebbe this year you can liven things up by bein' arrested again," Henry suggested with a sly grin. When she'd discovered that Ida had invited her boarder to the family dinner, Savannah had worried he'd make an already delicate situation worse.

"That was nearly half a century ago. And every one of those years, you have to bring it up, Henry Hyatt. A gentleman would just let sleeping dogs out of the bag."

"Never been much of a gentleman," Henry said, proving himself a master of understatement. "And it's damn hard to forget the sight of a woman setting up a mobile castration clinic in the parking lot."

"If I've told you once, I've told you a thousand times, it wasn't a castration clinic!" Ida huffed. She'd yet to reveal any lack of memory this evening, which once again had Savannah hoping that she and Raine were overreacting to what were merely the normal signs of aging.

"Daddy, what's a castration clinic?" Amy asked.

Jack exchanged a resigned look with Raine. "It's sort of a medical office, honey."

"That's precisely what it was, Amy, dear," Ida concurred. She turned toward Dan. "Times were tough in the logging business that year, and people were having trouble feeding the children they already had. Seemed like a good idea to offer two-for-one pricing to help the situation."

"Vasectomies," Savannah murmured in explanation, for Dan's ears alone.

He arched a brow and looked across the table at Ida, who'd folded her arms and was daring him with a look to criticize her behavior. "Makes sense to me," he said easily.

"We Lindstrom women have a knack for stirring things up," Lilith said with a radiant smile, "which is why we're so fortunate that Coldwater Cove's sheriff is part of the family."

When Jack had the good sense not to suggest that he couldn't let his marriage keep him from doing his duty, Lilith deftly turned the conversation back to this year's festivities.

"No one's supposed to know it yet, but Becky Brennan's going to be this year's Sawdust Queen," she announced.

"Oh, goodie!" Amy jumped up and down in her chair and clapped her hands. "Becky's my baby-sitter. I like her a lot. She plays Barbie with me and reads *Lilly's Purple Plastic Purse* over and over again, just the way Gramma Lilith does."

"That's one of my favorite stories," Lilith said with her trademark dazzling smile that had once lit up the silver screen. "I'm not surprised Becky likes it, too."

Raine and Savannah exchanged a look. Savannah had no doubt they were thinking the same thing: that for a woman who'd found motherhood so difficult, Lilith seemed to be reveling in her new role as Gramma Lilith.

"Oh, Savannah, darling." Lilith turned toward her daughter. "Don't forget, the rehearsal for the queen's pageant is tomorrow afternoon."

"Pageant?"

"Didn't I tell you?"

"No."

"Oh, dear. I've been so busy lately, it must have slipped my mind." Savannah didn't trust her mother's innocent tone. Despite her B-movie acting career, Lilith had never been a convincing liar. "We've added something new this year. All the former queens are going to be on hand for Becky's coronation. Roxie Denton, at All That Jazz Dance Academy, has worked out the cutest choreography number."

"I was planning to sand floors this weekend."

"Oh, you can't do that!" Lilith pressed her hand—which had never known a chipped nail—against the front of her scarlet silk blouse. "You can work anytime. But how often do you get to dance across the stage to an orchestra playing Joe Cocker's 'You Are So Beautiful'?"

"I wasn't aware Coldwater Cove had an orchestra." Sensing that Dan was doing his best to smother his laughter, Savannah refused to look at him.

"Well, actually, it's not exactly an orchestra," Lilith admitted.

"It's the Davis twins playing trumpets, Archie McCoy on guitar, his sister Aretha on keyboard and Joe Bob Preston singing the song," Cooper

Ryan, who was sitting beside his wife, revealed. "They're not half bad."

"Heard a lot worse," Henry supplied gruffly.

"So they're not the Grateful Dead or the Eagles. It'll still be fun," Lilith continued to coax.

There had been a time, in the not so distant past, when Savannah would have caved in to her mother's coaxing. But that was in another lifetime—before she'd gotten her wings.

"It sounds like quite a show, but you'll have to do it without me. As much as I'd like to help you out, Mother, I've too much work to do."

"But, darling—"

"No." Resisting Lilith was not for the faint-hearted. Savannah managed, with an effort, to firm up her mild tone. "I'll try to drop by the park for an hour or so. But I'm not playing rural Rockettes."

"Well." Lilith's expressive eyes narrowed. An expectant silence fell over the dining room. As she submitted to her mother's long, silent look, Savannah sensed she wasn't the only one at the table holding her breath. Her nerves tangled like a ball of barbed wire in her stomach.

Finally, Lilith's lips curled in a slow, pleased, almost feline smile. "Brava, dear."

She was an adult, an adult who'd suffered, survived, and had gotten on with her life. She was no longer the child who slept with her nightlight on, who cowered in closets or had tea parties with an imaginary mother who wore cozy aprons and didn't look or smell like a movie star. Her mother's obvious approval shouldn't mean so much.

It shouldn't, but, damn it, it did.

Savannah thought back on all the missed dance recitals, birthdays, and holidays, and realized she'd been waiting to hear those words all her life.

The mood in the room lightened. There was laughter. The conversation continued, as if the little battle of feminine wills had never taken place.

Dan reached beneath the table and took hold of Savannah's hand, his fingers squeezing hers in a friendly, encouraging way. Feeling immensely pleased with herself, she glanced up at him, intending to return his gesture with a smile.

But then she found herself getting lost in his quiet, confident blue eyes, just as she'd done when they'd been sitting together on the porch earlier today. The other voices faded into the distance; it was as if the rest of the family had suddenly vanished.

"I can't wait to ride the merry-go-round," Amy was announcing. "The big white horse with the gold saddle and the pretty flowers in its mane is my favorite. I like the happy music. Do you like to ride merry-go-rounds, Aunt Savannah?"

She forced her attention back to her niece, who, she belatedly realized, was looking across the table at her expectantly. Dan released her hand. The moment, which she guessed had lasted no longer than a few seconds but had seemed like an eternity, ended.

As she assured Amy that she did, indeed, love to ride merry-go-rounds, Savannah felt a growing unease building somewhere in the region of her heart.

10

"Well, Gram certainly seemed quite lucid tonight," Savannah said as she slid pieces of apple cobbler onto plates.

"Didn't she?" Raine's face lit up with a hopeful optimism that made Savannah think how odd it was that in this case, she was turning out to be the more cautious sister.

A born lawyer, before her marriage to Jack, Raine had always been more logical, more likely to study all sides of a problem before making a decision. Savannah, on the other hand, had always followed her heart. *And look how that turned out.*

"That's what's been so troubling about this." She went to the freezer and took out a half gallon of ice cream. "The memory lapses and confusion seem to come and go. Sometimes, like tonight, she's as sharp as ever." The scent of vanilla bean mingled with the rich aroma of baked apples, brown sugar, and cinnamon, reminding Savannah of when she'd been nine years old and had seen an old-fashioned ice cream churn in the window of Granny's Attic. She'd brought it home, and she and Raine and Ida had spent that evening on the porch, taking turns cranking. The handle had broken the second time they'd used it, but she'd never regretted having spent a week's allowance. Savannah had never tasted anything as sweet as that homemade ice cream they'd made together on that perfect summer day.

"But there are other times, like the incident at the market and when I bought the lighthouse, when she just seems to glitch out."

Raine glanced over at Savannah with surprise. "You didn't tell me anything about a problem when you bought the lighthouse."

"It didn't really register at the time. I was tired and excited, and I guess I wanted to overlook the fact that I don't think she knew what I was talking about when I first came home. After all my reading today, it sort of clicked into place."

She began scooping ice cream atop the cobbler. "I had a thought during dinner. What if we do an intervention, like families do when someone they love is an alcoholic or drug addicted?"

"It wouldn't be easy, but it'd be for her own good." Raine nodded, looking more like her Xena the Warrior-Princess self. Her jaw was set, her eyes clear and focused on her goal. "And that's all that matters. Do you want to do it tonight?"

Balancing protecting Ida's pride with possibly protecting her life was proving more than a little difficult. They were, Savannah thought sadly, caught between Ida and a hard place.

"Now that we've come up with a plan of action, we might as well get it over with while we're all here together."

"Then it's settled. I'll put Amy to bed after dessert." While Savannah returned the carton to the freezer, Raine picked up two of the plates.

Having decided on a plan of action, they returned to the dining room. As she picked at her cobbler, Savannah listened to Ida regale the family with a lively tale of another Sawdust Festival when she'd delivered Polly Lawson's twins in the pie judging tent.

"Fool girl spent all day in labor, but didn't tell anyone because she was waiting around to make sure she won the blue ribbon for her lemon meringue pie."

"Did she?" Amy asked, wide-eyed.

"No. Gladys Quincy won it, like she always did in those days, for her blueberry buckle. But Polly won the red. She also took home the grand prize—two of the cutest red-haired babies you ever saw."

Her grandmother's memory appeared as clear as the special-occasion Waterford crystal adorning the table, her vivid detail and colorful description making the story come alive.

It was going to be all right, Savannah assured herself firmly. Her grandmother Ida would be all right. She could not—would not—allow herself to think otherwise.

* * *

After dinner they moved to the cozy living room. Savannah was, at first, relieved when Ida didn't interrupt Raine, who, being the attorney in the family, had chosen to make the opening argument. Their grandmother didn't so much as flinch as Raine listed all the incidents of memory loss and of apparent disorientation that the family had documented.

Savannah hoped Ida was listening. The way her grandmother was staring out the front window made it difficult to tell for certain.

Finally, having lost momentum when she didn't get any feedback, Raine ran down. Savannah watched as Jack put a comforting arm around his wife and, despite her recent vow to become totally independent, envied Raine, just a little, for having someone who obviously loved and cared for her so very much in her life.

"Is that all you have to say?" Ida asked. Her small, wiry frame was practically swallowed up by the wing chair.

"For now," Raine answered.

She continued to sit there for another long minute, still as stone. Then she turned to Savannah. "I suppose you agree with your sister?"

"You haven't exactly been yourself the past few months," Savannah said carefully.

"It's called aging. I don't like to admit it, but I'm not exactly a spring chicken anymore." Her voice was as brittle as dried autumn leaves. "Besides, everyone suffers from memory lapses from time to time. You forgot to return the plumber's call yesterday."

"Savannah has a lot on her mind right now, Mother," Lilith tried to help out.

"And I don't?" Ida folded her arms across the front of her purple sweatshirt. "I never thought I'd live to see the day that my own family turned against me."

"We're not turning against you, Gram," Savannah argued. "We're trying to take care of you."

"I'm not a child, Savannah. And I can damn well take care of myself, thank you very much."

"You may not be a child," Henry entered the family conversation uninvited. "But you're a damn fool."

"Just because you sit in front of the television and watch *Jeopardy!* every day doesn't make you Alex Trebek," Ida returned grumpily. "You don't know everything, Henry Hyatt."

"Got that right enough. But I spent enough time in Evergreen to know when someone's not right in the head." He met her glare with a hard, level look of his own. "And you're not."

Ida's curse was one Savannah had never heard come out of her grandmother's mouth. "I don't have Alzheimer's."

"Then why don't you put your money where your big mouth is and prove it? Or aren't you a betting woman?"

Crimson flags of color waved high on Ida's cheeks. Her mouth pulled into a tight line, and her eyes snapped with barely restrained temper.

Savannah felt torn. Part of her thought she shouldn't let Henry talk to her grandmother that way. After all, he was only a boarder in Ida's house; he had no business even being at this dinner tonight, let alone barging into family matters.

But another, stronger part realized that just perhaps he could reach Ida on a level none of the rest of them could. They were contemporaries who'd already learned that Bette Davis wasn't kidding when she proclaimed that old age wasn't for sissies.

"My husband was a gambler," Ida said. "Being married to him taught me to bet only on myself."

"Then do it," Henry prodded. He reached into a pocket, pulled out a small wad of bills, and peeled a rumpled one from beneath the rubber band. "Here's twenty bucks that says you're too chicken to give up control long enough to let some other doc do the tests." He slapped the money onto the coffee table.

The color in her grandmother's face flared hotter and brighter. "You're on." Ida dug into her purse, retrieved a crisp bill of her own, tossed it next to his, then added another. "And ten more says I don't have Alzheimer's." She speared a look toward Savannah. "You satisfied now?"

"It's a start." Savannah refused to let her grandmother's practiced glare cower her. "I'll be more satisfied once you actually make the appointment for the tests, and happier still after you've completed them."

"Ha!" Ida dug into the black pocketbook she'd had for as long as Savannah could remember and pulled out a piece of paper that she placed with great ceremony next to the money. "I'm proud of the way you girls turned out. You're both bright and courageous, and except for screwing up your marriage, which unfortunately is pretty much run-of-the-mill for us Lindstrom women, you've made yourselves a real good life. . . .

"But you're going to have to get up a lot earlier in the morning to stay ahead of your grandmother."

Savannah leaned forward and picked up the piece of yellow paper. She skimmed the lines, then handed the paper to Raine, who arched a brow as she read it, then passed it on to Lilith.

"Mother!" Lilith shook her head, her expression filled with fondness touched with exasperation. "Why didn't you tell us you'd arranged for tests next week?"

"A woman's entitled to some secrets," Ida huffed. "Besides, ever since you girls set up this dinner, I've been looking forward to seeing how you were planning to handle the intervention."

"You knew all along," Raine guessed resignedly.

"I'm not a fool, Raine. Nor do I tolerate fools. You're both bright girls. I knew it was only a matter of time before you decided to try to lay down the law. After that little mistake in the mercantile, you really didn't have much choice.

"The way I see it, if my family's worried enough to resort to subterfuge, the least I can do is ease your minds. But not until after the Sawdust Festival," she said firmly. "This is the first year I'm in charge, and my reputation's at stake. If I'm not there to keep everyone on their toes, the whole weekend could just go to hell on a Harley."

Savannah wouldn't be able completely to put her concerns behind her until Ida's doctors presented them with test results that revealed that they'd exaggerated their fears. However, the comforting familiarity of her grandmother's malapropism and characteristically brisk, matter-of-fact attitude gave birth to a faint ray of light that brightened, ever so slightly, her dark and looming fear.

After they'd driven home, Ida went directly to bed, declaring herself exhausted from all the family intrigue. Henry looked inclined to make it a night, as well, when Savannah stopped him at the bottom of the stairs.

"Thank you."

He looked down at her hand, resting atop his on the newel post, as if wondering how it had gotten there. "For what?"

"For helping us with Grandmother. That was a very nice thing to do."

"Hasn't it sunk in yet, girl?" he asked gruffly. "I'm never nice."

"Liar." She leaned forward and brushed her lips against his cheek.

Henry flamed lobster red. "What the hell was that for?" he asked, unknowingly nearly echoing her words of this morning when Dan had kissed her.

"Because you're a fraud, Henry Hyatt." She'd seen through the gruffness to the man beneath, the man who'd lived the solitary life of a lighthouse keeper not so much because he didn't want to have any interaction with neighbors, but because he loved the Far Harbor lighthouse and cared about others' safety enough to make personal sacrifices.

She smiled. "Good night."

He muttered something that could have been "good night" in return, then made his way upstairs. Watching him, Savannah thought she detected a bit of a spring in his step.

Savannah was back at the lighthouse, energetically sanding the floor of the keeper's cottage, when Dan showed up with an electric sander of his own, rented from the same hardware store where she'd gotten hers. He was wearing a sleeveless sweatshirt, ragged shorts that looked as if he'd whacked away at a pair of jeans with a pocket knife, and work boots. His body looked as hard and dark as teak. She decided that it should be against the law for any man to look so seductively male—at least this early in the morning.

"Don't you have to work?"

"It's Saturday." He didn't mention that he'd dropped by the women's shelter to take Kathi Montgomery some peanut butter fudge from Coldwater Cove Confectionery before coming here. It had always been her favorite. He'd been glad to discover it still was.

Kathi's bruises were starting to turn an ugly purplish green, but as they'd sat out on the deck of the middle-class house, watching a pair of hummingbirds spin and whirl in a noisy battle over claim to a bright red glass feeder, she'd seemed a bit more relaxed. Neither Jack nor the state police had been able to locate her husband yet, but just knowing that she was no longer having to handle her domestic problems all alone had given her strength and taken some of the fear from her eyes. When he'd left, she was talking about returning to work. Dan had taken that as a very positive sign.

"I figured you could use some help."

She looked around the enormous expanse of flooring left to sand. "I can't deny an extra hand would be nice, but you don't have to—"

"I know. But I want to, Savannah. Besides, the hardware store was having a special on sander rentals, and hey, I've never been one to overlook a good deal."

Though it was a lousy joke, she laughed, which made him feel as if he'd just scaled Mount Olympus.

The work was hard, hot, and dusty. Savannah didn't even try to tell herself that she was grateful for Dan's presence because he was cutting the work and the time it took to do it in half. The truth was that they worked well together, passing each other with an easy rhythm, each choosing rooms without discussion. Even when they were working in different locations, there was an easy camaraderie that she'd only felt when working in a kitchen where the entire staff had slipped into a mind sync and performed as if in a ballet.

She smiled behind her dust mask at the idea

that there was anything at all ballet-like about this particular work. Obviously, she was becoming too fanciful. If she wasn't careful, the next thing she knew she'd start seeing Lucy's ghost.

Dan was upstairs when she moved into the closet of the downstairs bedroom. One of the planks beneath her sneakers creaked, then tilted when she stepped on it. Curious, she turned off her sander, knelt, and, using the putty knife she kept in the new leather tool belt she wore on her hips, she pried up the board.

"Treasure," she murmured, looking down into a small space that contained what appeared to be personal items. She reached in and pulled out a Bull Durham tobacco bag filled, she discovered, with marbles.

She tugged down her mask. "Dan, come look," she called out over the roar of the sander's motor overhead.

He cut it off. She heard his footsteps coming down the stairs.

"Did Henry and Ruth Hyatt ever have children?" he asked as he observed her find.

"Not that I know of."

"Then they're probably Henry's." Delving deeper into the space, he retrieved a few more items: a top wound with white string, a small model of a clipper ship, complete with yellowed newspaper sails, a stuffed one-eyed brown teddy bear, and a tarnished silver–framed photo of an obviously pregnant woman and small boy.

"Oh, that must be Henry and his mother."

"That'd be my guess. He was a cute kid."

"I think he'd hate to hear you say that. But he had been cute," Savannah agreed. His nearly white blond hair had been cut like the Dutch Boy paint boy, and he was wearing a miniature sailor suit with short pants accessorized by a pair of incongruous cowboy boots and jingly spurs. A wide Huck Finn grin wreathed his freckled face. "From the state of Lucy's pregnancy, this photo must have been taken shortly before her death."

Lucy Hyatt's smile was warmed with intimacy and lit up her eyes in a way that revealed an unmistakable love for whoever was holding the camera. Standing in front of the mother and son was a small fox terrier.

"She looks so happy," she murmured. "Not at all like a woman who's planning to run away with her lover."

"Perhaps her lover is the one holding the camera."

Upstairs a door slammed, the sudden sound echoing in the empty rooms. The temperature in the house seemed to drop at least ten degrees.

"Must be another storm coming," Dan said, glancing up toward the ceiling.

"That must be it," Savannah agreed with a bit more assurance than she was feeling. This was not the first time she'd experienced a strange sense of . . . something . . . while working on the lighthouse buildings. Something that defied her facile explanations.

Putting that fanciful thought away, she studied the photograph in more detail. The Far Harbor lighthouse was in the background. "Since I doubt if she would have risked inviting a lover here to the lighthouse, it had to have been her husband who took the picture."

"I'd guess you're right. Especially since Henry's in the picture with her. But if that's the case, from the way she's looking at him, you have to wonder why Lucy even took a lover."

"I guess we'll never know." Savannah sighed. She was about to put the board back in place— saving the personal items for Henry—when she realized that there was still one more thing in the space.

The small journal had a cover that was the same dark gray as the shadows in the room, which was what had prevented her from seeing it right away. The yellowed, fragile pages were edged in gilt, and the front page revealed, in a slanted, feminine script, that the book was *Lucy Randall Hyatt's Far Harbor Adventure. Book One.*

She looked up at Dan and saw her own excitement reflected in his eyes. "Treasure," they said together.

They took the book out to the garden bench overlooking the water. There were no workmen scheduled for today, and with John working at the nursery, they were all alone save for the seagulls.

The first entry was headed "Farmersburg, Iowa." " 'Dear Diary,' " Savannah read. " 'It's nearly time to leave for the train station. I still cannot quite believe that I've chosen to leave my family and travel halfway across the country to a place I've never been to marry a man I've never met.

" 'But Harlan Hyatt's letters make me think that he must be a nice and considerate man, and I must admit that his obvious love of his surroundings is contagious. I've always wanted to see the sea. Now, in a mere few days, I'll be living in a lighthouse.' "

Savannah glanced up from the pages. "She must have been a mail-order bride."

"Sounds like it." Dan eased back on the bench and put his arm comfortably around her shoulder in a gesture so quick and smooth she almost didn't see it coming. She went still for a moment but didn't pull away.

" 'Needless to say, Hannah's still against what she refers to as "Lucy's latest act of impulsiveness," but how could she possibly understand how badly I want to leave Farmersburg? For I know that I would surely suffocate if I were forced to spend the rest of my days living under my sister and brother-in-law's roof, teaching reading and writing to a classroom of students who'd rather be running free outdoors and playing Aunt Lucy to Hannah's children into my dotage.

" 'My older sister keeps pointing out that there's no earthly need for me to travel so far to find a husband. Indeed, I've received numerous proposals, most recently from John Hoffman. With her usual eagle eye toward security, Hannah insists a woman could do far worse than marry such a successful hog farmer, but the thought of spending my days and nights living with the smell of pig manure quite honestly makes me gag.'

"Well," Savannah said, "I can certainly identify with that."

"Hey, you have to be grateful to pig farmers. After all, a life without smothered pork chops would undoubtedly be a life not worth living."

"I like a man who knows his priorities," Savannah said dryly.

He grinned and tugged on the gilded tips of her hair. "Don't worry. You're far above pork products on my personal priority list."

"That's certainly one of my higher achievements—being ranked above pork products."

She returned to the journal. " 'As for my other prospects, I've grown up with all the men around here. I've worked in the fields with them, talked with them on market day, and even danced with many of them at the grange, but there's not a single one I'd want to put his boots next to my bed. Or his mouth and hands on my body.' "

"Sounds as if Lucy certainly had her priorities right," Dan murmured.

The warmth of his body so near hers and the crisp tang of male sweat emanating from his skin was causing her mind to create erotic pictures that were awakening needs that Savannah told herself were nothing more than hormonal aberrations. Hoping Lucy would move on to the travelogue part of the story, Savannah ignored the provocative comment and kept on reading.

" 'Of course I haven't told Hannah this last part for fear of scandalizing her. While she and Jacob may indeed have a full and love-filled marriage, outwardly they've always appeared so distant from each other, it's hard to imagine how my sister managed to conceive three children.

" 'In each of his letters, Harlan warns me that lighthouse life, with its days and sometimes months cut off from civilization, can get lonely and monotonous. Yet his rousing stories of storms and shipwrecks lead me to suppose that he doesn't begin to know the meaning of monotony. And surely the loneliness I feel surrounded by my family is far worse than any isolation due to geography.' "

"I know that feeling," Dan surprised her by saying.

Savannah looked up at him. "Me, too," she admitted. She wondered if he was talking about his marriage, then reminded herself that she wasn't interested in his relationship with other women, most of all with his ex-wife.

Liar.

" 'Besides,' " she continued, " 'the way Harlan always ends with a witty anecdote suggests he'll be an amusing companion, and if the photograph accompanying his first letter even remotely resembles his actual countenance, he's a robust, handsome man. I blush as I write these words and pray that this journal never falls into anyone else's hands, but such strong, confident features suggest that he will prove a good lover. I only hope that he will find me adequate in that respect, as well.' "

"Hey, you can't stop there," Dan complained when she closed the journal. "We were just getting to the good part."

"That's all there is."

"Of course there's more. They didn't get Henry by mail order. And she must have liked sex enough to do it at least twice because she was pregnant when she died."

"It's the end of the book. Which is just as well, since I was starting to feel like a voyeur." A hot, shockingly needy voyeur who had begun to tingle in places she hadn't even realized *could* tingle.

"If Lucy hadn't wanted us to find her journal, she wouldn't have kept it."

"She didn't exactly leave it out on the bookshelf in plain sight."

"True. But she didn't burn it, either, which would have been the more logical thing to do. Especially if she was about to abandon her husband and son."

"Leaving Henry has always been the part of the story that's bothered me," Savannah said. "I can't imagine any mother abandoning her child."

"Not every woman has your nurturing instincts."

"No." When Lilith came immediately to mind, Savannah breathed a soft sigh.

"Your mother loved you, Savannah." He drew her a little closer, so their thighs and hips were touching. A flare of heat threatened to melt her jeans to her skin. "In her own flawed way."

"We weren't talking about Lilith." She'd gotten over any resentment against her mother for not having lived up to some idealized Mother Knows Best image that had probably never existed in the real world and now was seen only on Nick at Nite. So why were there those out-of-the-blue times that it still hurt? Like now.

"But you were thinking about her."

"Now you can read my mind?" Savannah welcomed the quick flare of irritation. It took her mind off her growing desire—a desire every bit as unwise as it was unruly.

"No. But I'm getting pretty good at reading your face. A piece of advice, sweetheart." He framed the face in question between his palms. "If you decide to change careers again, I wouldn't recommend following in your maternal grandfather's gambling shoes, because you'd make a lousy poker player. That lovely face would give you away every time."

His voice was rough and deep and rumbled through her like distant thunder. Without taking his eyes from Savannah's, giving her ample time to read his intention, he slowly lowered his head.

11

Having expected power, Savannah was surprised when he skimmed his lips up her cheek with a touch that, while feathery, still caused the breath she'd been holding to shudder out. She felt his smile against her too-warm skin. Then, appearing to have all the time and patience in the world, he caught her lower lip between his teeth. His eyes, which had returned to hers, darkened as he nibbled lightly, seductively.

Oh, the man is good, Savannah thought as renewed arousal began to flow through her veins like a thick, golden river. He knew how to coax a woman, to make her want. To make her ache.

"Dan." It was a whisper, blown away by a gust of wind swirling around the lighthouse. "Kiss me."

"I am." His teeth closed tighter, not hard enough to cause pain, but enough to make her breath tangle in her throat.

"No." Lucy Hyatt's journal fell to the ground unnoticed as Savannah pressed her hands against his chest. Her fingers tangled in the material of his shirt as she strained closer, so close that a whisper of breeze from the strait couldn't have come between them. "I mean, *really* kiss me."

He smiled again. With his mouth and with his eyes. "I am." He soothed the pink mark his teeth had made with the tip of his tongue. "I will."

And he did.

But still he took his time, drawing out the pleasure, his kiss slow but exquisitely scintillating. How could such a strong, firm mouth be so blissfully tender? Savannah wondered as his lips brushed against hers with the delicacy of butterfly wings. Once, twice, then a third time, lingering in a way that caused her eyelids to drift shut and her bones to melt.

Gulls cried as they whirled and dive-bombed for fish, a buoy clanged, a ferry whistled as it pulled out of the harbor. Savannah didn't notice. Her entire world narrowed down to the feel of Dan's mouth, his dark, mysterious male taste, the strength of his hands as they slipped beneath her T-shirt, the caressing, velvety touch of his fingertips skimming up her spine, rough and soft at the same time.

Her head spun. She felt so light she could have floated right up to the sky; so warm she might have swallowed the sun.

A lone gull flew past, his shriek rending the salt-tinged air, then fading away on the wind as he flew out toward the horizon.

Dan lifted his head and drew her away just enough to allow him to look down into her face again.

"That was even better than I remembered." He brushed the pad of his thumb against her tingling lips.

"I'm surprised you remember anything," Savannah said. "After all, we only had one date." *And you never called the next day. Like you promised.* A feminine teenage pique she was surprised to discover lurking inside her uncurled like a serpent.

He didn't appear at all embarrassed. A bit chagrined, perhaps, she thought. But that didn't stop his eyes from lighting up with that easy humor she was starting to expect from him.

"After which I never called you again."

"Really? I don't recall that." She tossed her head, pretending indifference.

"Unfortunately, I do. I also remember feeling lower than a snake in a rut for a long time after that," he said against her mouth. "I was wrong. An idiot." He was punctuating his words with kisses. "Feel free to stop me any time."

"When you say something that isn't true, I will." With all the problems she'd had to face lately, it was nice to be able to find humor in something.

"My only excuse for my behavior back then is that I was too scared to think straight."

"I refuse to believe you were actually afraid of me."

"Not of you." Taking her hand, he lifted it to his lips in a gesture so natural she couldn't think of a single reason to complain. "Well, maybe just a little. You were, after all, the closest thing to a living, breathing goddess Coldwater Cove had ever seen. That's pretty intimidating for a kid who tended to stumble all over his feet whenever you got within sniffing distance."

He made her giggle by snuffling at her neck. Savannah couldn't remember the last time she'd giggled. He was also making it more and more difficult for her to remember exactly why this was a mistake.

"Speaking of which," he said against the sensitive skin behind her ear, "have I mentioned that you still smell damn good? Light and fresh and pretty. Like a garden after a summer shower."

"That sounds remarkably like a line."

Dan groaned inwardly as he heard himself say the words and figured a guy was getting pretty rusty when he had to steal seduction lines from his thirteen-year-old nephew.

"You're right. It is. And not a very original one. But that doesn't make it any less true." He touched his mouth to her chin. Her cheek. Her temple. "It's a scent all your own, Savannah. The kind that gets beneath a man's skin. It stays in his mind and has him imagining making love to you in a sun-dappled meadow of wildflowers."

She drew back. Hitched in a breath. "Dan . . . I'm not ready for this."

Because he wasn't certain that he was ready for it, either, Dan reminded himself that just because a woman smelled great and looked even better shouldn't be reason enough to drag her off to bed.

There were other, more important things . . .

like admiring her mind. Her resiliency. Her warm heart, generous nature, and deep-seated sense of family. Oh, hell.

Better watch it, O'Halloran, an inner voice of reason counseled. *You're getting dangerously close to the edge of a very steep cliff.*

"I have a feeling I'm going to regret asking, but you've piqued my curiosity," she said.

"About what?" Having been sidetracked by the thought of how easy it would be to fall headfirst off that cliff, it took Dan a moment to realize that she was talking to him.

"What it was about a teenage girl you found so frightening you had to resort to the age-old ploy of pulling a disappearing act?"

"Oh, that." He shrugged, pretending a casualness that was at odds with the way he was feeling. "I'm admittedly a little vague on all the details of that night, but I do recall a moment, somewhere between when I brought you up here to watch the submarine races and when I kissed you good night on Ida's front porch, when I actually found myself thinking of ever-afters."

"That's another line."

"Actually, that one is the truth. It was also one helluva terrifying idea for a hormone-driven kid who was about to head off to college to be contemplating."

"Oh. Well." He could tell, of all the excuses he might have offered, Savannah definitely hadn't expected that one.

A trio of fat-billed pelicans flew by as she considered his answer. A ship steamed past, carrying cargo from the Port of Seattle to far-off places.

"That was a long time ago," she decided, telling him nothing that he hadn't already been telling himself. "We're both different people now."

"If there's one thing the law has taught me, it's that people don't change, Savannah. Circumstances do. Times do. But deep down inside, where it really counts, we remain pretty much the same."

"I refuse to believe that." Her hair fanned out like a gilt banner as she firmly shook her head. Her chin rose along with a flash of pride. "I've changed."

Savannah bent down and picked up the journal. "We'd better get back to work."

"That's one idea. Or we could just stay out here and neck."

Her lips twitched, giving him the impression that she was fighting a smile. The way her eyes darkened to a deep jade suggested that Savannah was also struggling against the same unbidden desire that kept digging its unruly claws into him.

"Work," she repeated with that firmness he'd watched her develop since she'd returned to Coldwater Cove. "I have a man arriving from Gray's Harbor first thing Monday morning with a truckload of stain, and before he agreed to come all this way, I had to promise him that the floors would be ready."

Wondering how many males with blood still flowing in their veins could deny this woman anything, Dan pushed himself off the bench and followed her back down the garden path. As he watched the feminine sway of her hips in khaki shorts that amazingly still held a knife-edge crease, he decided that this place really did have the best view on the peninsula.

"Hey, Captain Bligh," he called out.

She glanced back over her shoulder, impatience replacing the earlier touch of reluctant desire on her face. "What now?"

"You're right. You have gotten tougher. And you know what?"

"What?"

"It looks damn good on you."

Savannah didn't respond, but she didn't need to. Dan read both pride and pleasure in her remarkable eyes and decided that it was enough. For now.

The Sawdust Festival was, hands down, the most important annual event to occur in Coldwater Cove, surpassing even the Fourth of July as the highpoint of the year. It was part carnival, part county fair, part logging competition, along with a lot of music and even more food—an all-around good time.

The rain that had been falling off and on all week stopped a few hours before the festival began. As a full moon rose in a clear deep purple sky over Founder's Park, not a single person challenged Lilith's assertion that ancient pagan gods had pulled off a weather miracle.

Japanese lanterns had been strung around the town square, illuminating the George Strait wannabe crooning somebody-done-somebody-wrong songs in the lacy Victorian bandstand. Smoke from Oley's portable barbecue drifted on air enlivened by the sound of guitars, the plink of horseshoes hitting iron stakes, and the wasp-like drone coming from the far end of the park, where men and women wielding souped-up chainsaws were turning huge logs into sawdust.

"Oh, look," Raine said. "There's Lilith's friend." She pointed in the direction of a fifty-something woman seated in a booth painted with gold stars and silver crescent moons. Wooden beads had been woven into jet black hair that fell straight as rain to her waist. She was wearing a flowing purple caftan embroidered with yet more moons. "Let's get our fortunes told."

Savannah looked at her sister with surprise. "I can't believe that you, of all people, are suggesting we spend ten dollars to hear someone wearing more turquoise than is probably found in the entire state of New Mexico tell us that we're going to meet tall, dark, handsome strangers who'll take us on a sea cruise."

"Lilith says she's not a fake."

"Our mother also burns bonfires to ancient goddesses and draws down the moon."

"Well, there is that," Raine agreed, glancing across the green to where Lilith and Amy were riding the carousel. Amy was astride her favorite flower-bedecked white horse; Lilith had, unsurprisingly, chosen a dragon with shiny green scales. "But it'll still be a kick. When was the last time you had any real fun?"

Because she'd almost managed to convince herself that it hadn't really meant anything, that they'd only been responding to sensual ideas stimulated by Lucy's journal, Savannah decided not to mention her little interlude with Dan on the garden bench.

"No wonder you win all your cases," she muttered as she allowed Raine to pull her by the hand toward the fortune-teller's booth. They could have been children again, with her big sister leading the way. "It's useless trying to argue with you."

"Try telling Amy that," Raine complained lightly. "She's begun questioning everything Jack or I tell her. Jack assures me that it's just a new phase, but sometimes, when I find myself arguing with a six-year-old, it's hard to remember that I once tried cases in a New York federal court."

"It could be a phase," Savannah said. "Or it could be that you're going to have another lawyer in the family."

Raine laughed at that. "Heaven help us."

They handed over their money, and after Raven had correctly pegged Raine's recent marriage and career change, she also predicted more children.

"How many more?" Raine asked.

"Two," the fortune-teller said with conviction. "A boy who will resemble his father and a little girl who'll look like the best of both of you."

The amazing thing about the prediction, Savannah thought, was that Raine actually seemed to believe it. Or perhaps, she corrected as she watched her sister's face light up, perhaps she wanted to believe it.

It was Savannah's turn next. "You've recently been badly hurt." Raven Moonsilver's fingernails were short, lacquered in a blinding amethyst metallic shade and adorned with airbrushed silver stars that matched her caftan. She trailed a purple tip across Savannah's palm. "By a man."

"Name me one woman over the age of ten who hasn't," Savannah suggested mildly.

"Ah, but it was not your heart that was so cruelly wounded, but your confidence. Along with your pride."

Savannah assured herself that again, she certainly wasn't alone in that regard. The same thing was undoubtedly happening to women all over the world at this very minute.

"You are an old soul. You have lived other lives that have touched many." Savannah rolled her eyes and waited to hear she'd been Marie Antoinette.

"I know you are skeptical." The silver replica of a Northwest tribal totem the fortune-teller was wearing in one earlobe glinted in the light of the Japanese lanterns as the woman nodded with apparent approval. "This is good. When you finally break through the wall of disbelief, you will no longer have a single doubt."

She studied Savannah's palm in greater detail. "I see someone."

"Here it comes," Savannah couldn't resist telling Raine. "My tall, dark stranger."

"I know you're joking. But this is a woman." Raven Moonsilver's eyes narrowed. Her fingers, gleaming with silver rings, tightened around Savannah's. "A woman caught between the realms."

"Surely you're not talking about a ghost?" Raine asked with interest, earning a sharp, warning look from Savannah. There was no point in encouraging the woman.

"A spirit," the fortune-teller corrected. She was crushing Savannah's hand now. "A lost soul who needs your help to free herself from the bonds that are holding her to this mortal coil."

Savannah tugged her hand free. "How am I supposed to do that?"

"It's not for me to tell you. Open your heart and the answer will come to you."

"Open your heart," Savannah was still muttering five minutes later as they followed the high-pitched, wasp-like drone toward the timed chain-saw art competition where Raine had arranged to meet Jack. "The answer will come to you.

"Gee, talk about wasting money. Even if Mother hadn't told her, which Lilith undoubtedly did, everyone in the county knows I bought the Far Harbor lighthouse. It's also no secret that the lighthouse is supposed to be haunted. The woman is obviously a fraud."

"It's not impossible that she could be in touch with Lucy."

"Then she should be the one to help her. I have enough to do trying to fix up Lucy's house."

"Are you sure you haven't sensed anything? Nothing out of the ordinary has happened there?"

Savannah decided that Dan's kiss momentarily tilting her world wasn't what Raine was re-

ferring to. "Nothing worth mentioning. Perhaps
there have been a few occasions . . ."

Her voice drifted off as she thought of the
slamming door, the times she'd been working
alone late at night and heard soft, breathy
sounds that resembled sighs but were undoubtedly only the wind in the tops of the trees.

"What kind of occasions?"

"Nothing. Just shutters banging in the wind,
rafters creaking, glass rattling. You know how
spooky old houses can be late at night."

She thought of the journal but decided that
didn't count, either. People were constantly
finding all sorts of things hidden in old houses.
Whatever her reasons for hiding her journal,
Savannah refused to believe that Lucy was attempting to send her some sort of secret message from beyond the grave.

They'd reached the sawdust ring where the
competition was to take place. Savannah stood
with Raine and Jack, watching as a man turned
a log into a wooden statue of a bear holding up
a fish, in a record time of six minutes. Deciding
that chainsaw art really wasn't her thing, Savannah wandered on, pausing to observe the
women's ax-throwing contest.

"Now there's a frightening sight," said a familiar deep voice behind her as one ax landed right
in the middle of the red bull's-eye with a loud
thud. "A female with a double-headed axe."

She turned and didn't even try to hide her
smile. "Hi."

"Hi, yourself." Dan skimmed a look over her.

"You're still the most gorgeous Sawdust Queen ever."

She glanced across the lawn to the fir-draped royal arbor where fifteen-year-old Becky Brennan stood laughing with friends and flirting with a group of star-struck teenage males. The boys were wearing jeans so new they looked as if they'd stand up by themselves, Garth Brooks–style shirts, boots, and Stetsons. The numbers pinned to the back of those colorful western-cut shirts revealed they were contestants in the battle of the country band competition.

"Becky's lovely." The memory of being impossibly young and carefree, feeling for at least one night that she'd been the most special girl on earth, was bittersweet.

"Adorable," he agreed. "But she can't hold a candle to you. You take a man's breath away."

She shrugged. "Luck of the genes."

"Perhaps that has something to do with it." He reached behind his back and pulled out a bouquet wrapped in green tissue. "But as my mom always used to remind Karyn, beauty is as beauty does. And you, sweetheart, do real well."

"Oh, they're lovely." Savannah murmured as she lifted the bouquet to her nose and breathed in its delicate scent.

A man who excelled at outward romantic gestures, Kevin had gifted her with a dozen long-stemmed roses at every holiday during their marriage. She'd finally realized that it hadn't taken any effort to have his secretary place a call to the florist.

Other men, most particularly wealthy resort guests who, arrogantly overlooking the fact that she was married, seemed to believe that she could be seduced by a gift of long-stemmed red roses. They had, of course, been wrong.

No man had ever given her wildflowers.

"They're growing all around my house," Dan said. "Whenever I look at them, I think of you. Of course, that's not unusual, since thinking about you seems to be what I've been doing most of the time lately."

When his remark reminded her of his comment about wanting to make love to her in a field of wildflowers, her mutinous hormones spiked.

"How do you feel about roller coasters?" Dan asked suddenly.

"I used to love them—until my life became one."

"The Ferris wheel, then. What would you say to coming for a ride in the sky with me, Savannah?"

Torn between prudence and pleasure, Savannah looked up at the revolving double wheel that was lit up like a gigantic Christmas tree.

"If that suggestion doesn't tickle your fancy, we've got just enough time to make the greased pole climb."

"It's a tough choice." She laughed and made her decision. "But the Ferris wheel it is."

"Terrific." Dan linked his fingers with hers as they strolled hand-in-hand beneath the fairy lights twinkling like stars amid the leaves of the huge red-leaf oaks.

*　*　*

The festival was turning out to be a grand success. As she made her way toward the pie-judging tent, Ida decided that this year's event would go down as the best on record.

"Whoever takes over next year will have a helluvan act to follow," Henry said. He munched on a hot dog loaded with the works as he and Ida watched the teams of loggers trying to climb the towering greased pole.

"I was thinking pretty much the same thing. But I didn't say it because I didn't want to sound like I was bragging on myself."

His salty curse was learned during a decade spent in the merchant marines before he'd returned home to take over the lighthouse duties from his father. "It isn't bragging if it's the truth."

Ida glanced over at him in surprise. "You keep handing out compliments like that and I'm going to think that you've been taken over by one of those pod people or something."

He shrugged. Then his eyes narrowed as he watched her dig into her pocketbook and pull out a plastic bottle of aspirin. "You okay?"

"I'm fine." She swallowed two white tablets with a sip of her iced tea. "It's just a little noisy, what with all the chainsaws whining away and those drums. Whose idea was it to have a battle of the bands, anyway?"

"Lilith said it was yours."

"Oh. Well, like I said, it's a great idea. Brought more young people in."

Strangely, the pounding behind her eyes seemed to have synchronized itself with the throbbing sound of the drums coming from the Victorian bandstand. She glanced around at the crowds of teenagers with satisfaction. There must be a third more in the park than Florence Heron had managed to pull in last year.

Of course, to give Florence her due, it had probably been thirty years since the woman had spoken with any teenager other than the boy who delivered her morning *Coldwater Cove Chronicle*. And then she was likely to scold him for tossing the paper in the rhododendron bush.

What had begun as an act of altruism—bringing foster kids into her home—had turned out to benefit her, as well. Ida had quickly discovered that being around the younger generation helped her stay young. They'd admittedly been a challenge, but she'd always thrived on challenges.

She was thinking that they were also good company when the park, and everyone in it, suddenly went all fuzzy, as if she were looking through a camera lens that had suddenly gone out of focus. Ida blinked.

"Henry." She reached out to steady herself, her fingers digging into his arm.

His brows drew together as he looked down at her. "What's wrong?"

"I don't know." She was struggling to focus when she heard someone call her name. Ida was vastly relieved when her vision cleared, allowing her to view the teenager standing at the other side of the sawdust horseshoe pit.

"Why, it's Gwen." The momentary blurriness was immediately forgotten.

Henry followed her surprised gaze. "You talking about that little girl who looks like she stuck a wet finger in a light socket?"

"That's her." The bright red Little Orphan Annie curls were longer than they'd been when Gwen had left Coldwater Cove two months ago, and even more unruly. "She wasn't due home from science camp for another three days. I guess she came early so she could attend the festival."

The problem was, Ida thought, the serious expression on the teenager's face as she approached didn't give the impression that she'd come here tonight to have a good time. Ida cast a glance upward toward the heavens and said a quick, silent prayer. *Please don't let her be in trouble with the law again.*

Never having known a stable home until she'd landed in Coldwater Cove, in the past Gwen's chosen response to unpleasant experiences—of which she'd had more than her share—had been to shoplift. Ida dearly hoped she'd put such self-destructive behavior behind her.

"Hello, darling." Tamping down her concerns, Ida hugged the foster child she'd grown so fond of.

"Hi, Mama Ida." Gwen hugged her back. Her youthful body had lost all its pregnancy weight. The jeans clinging to her hips were so baggy, Ida figured there was room for a second teenage girl inside them.

"You're home early."

"I know." She'd matured, Ida realized, looking up into the sober face that was more woman than child. Of course that wasn't very surprising. Carrying a baby for nine long months, only to give it up the day after it was born, was bound to make any girl grow up a bit faster than most.

"There's something I need to talk with you about," Gwen said. "Something I've been thinking a lot about while I was in Texas. Something that wouldn't wait three more days."

Ida felt a sharp, tension-caused twinge behind her eye. She ignored it.

"This might not be the best time or place to be talking about this," Henry warned. Ida sensed he was trying to forestall the conversation out of concern for her.

"Nonsense, Henry," she argued. "If Gwen skipped science camp graduation, it must be important." The weekly reports from the counselors had been unanimously glowing.

"What is it, dear?" Ida asked with feigned calm, even as she feared she knew exactly what Gwen was about to say.

The teenager drew in a deep breath, then slowly let it out. "It's about my baby."

Her words echoed in Ida's ears as if she were speaking from the bottom of the cove. Slender teenage hands raked through bright curls, but Ida didn't notice their tremor. Every atom of her attention was riveted on Gwen's lips, which now seemed to be moving in slow motion. Her voice had the odd, drawn-out sound of an old 45 record played at 33 1/3 speed. "I think I want her back."

12

They were riding up backwards, higher and higher, until the people on the ground resembled toy action figures.

"Oh, look," Savannah pointed out. "There's John." She was surprised to see the teenager holding hands with a tall blond girl who was wearing a plastic lei over her sweater and carrying a stuffed animal nearly as big as she was. "I didn't realize he had a girlfriend."

"They sort of tumbled into puppy love this past spring when they met at the Special Olympics," Dan said. "Cindy fell into Coldwater Cove when she was two. By the time they pulled her out, she'd already been brain-damaged."

The Ferris wheel jerked to a halt. Down below, people were getting off, others getting on. "If the scuttlebutt is to be believed, her father never quite forgave her mother for what he considered her carelessness. Plus, the burdens of taking care of a toddler are tough enough without tossing a mental handicap into the mix."

The wheel began to move again, picking up speed.

"The guy left Mrs. Kellstrom with the chore of teaching their daughter how to walk and talk and do all that other basic stuff again from scratch."

"That must have been horribly difficult."

"I suppose it may help that she's a nurse. Even so, it would have to be a helluva test of strength. But she obviously did a great job, because Cindy Kellstrom's one of the nicest, most hardworking kids I've ever met."

She sounds a lot like John, Savannah thought. "They look sweet together," she said as the wheel stopped again, leaving them at the very top, with a bird's-eye view of John buying his girlfriend a cone of fluffy pink cotton candy.

"They are kind of cute," he agreed. "Of course I'm not looking forward to dealing with his wounded heart when they break up, which they're bound to do at their age, but I suppose we all have to learn from experience."

"I suppose so." Savannah heard the laughter and shrieks from the Tilt-a-Wheel and watched as it dipped and spun, the riders pressed hard against the side by centrifugal force.

"That's exactly how I felt when my marriage broke up," she murmured, surprised when she realized she'd said the words out loud.

He followed her gaze. "Dizzy and sick to your stomach?"

"No." She watched the floor drop away. The wheel spun faster. The people shrieked louder. Savannah's hands tightened on the metal bar in front of them as the wheel began its rapid descent.

"Well, the sick-to-the-stomach description pretty much fits." Or at least it had the morning after she'd left Kevin when she'd awakened at the Beverly Wilshire with a killer hangover. "But mostly I felt as if the bottom had dropped out of my life."

"Perhaps that's not so bad." He pried her hands off the bar and held them between his as they swooshed past the ticket taker and headed back up again. "Maybe the bottom should drop out of all our lives every so often, if for no other reason than to let some fresh air in."

"That's a nice philosophy. But the next time I feel my life getting a little stuffy, I believe I'll just open a window."

She'd lost track of John and Cindy. But looking out over the park, Savannah could make out her grandmother and Henry. Miracle of miracles, they seemed to be actually getting along as they ate hot dogs and watched men trying to scale towering greased poles. Not far away, Lilith and Amy had moved on to the spinning teacup ride.

"Want to talk about it?" he asked mildly.

"Not particularly."

"He hurt you." It was not a question.

"Yes." So much for fun, Savannah thought.

"Did he hit you?"

"Of course not." She glanced at Dan in surprise. She was even more surprised to see something new in his eyes. Something dar and dangerous. "It's not that big a deal." She shrugged. "Divorce hurts. However it happens."

"Mine didn't."

"Really?"

"I suspected I was making a mistake the day I got married. I think Amanda did, too."

"Then why did you go through with it?"

"Beats me. Because five hundred of her father's closest friends were coming to dinner?"

"Don't joke. Since you brought it up, I'd really like to know." Surely he couldn't take what was supposed to be a lifetime commitment so casually?

"Okay." His expression turned pensive. Unreadable. "I suppose the simplest way to put it is that Amanda and I were unlucky enough to meet at a time when we were both asking ourselves that old song lyric, 'Is that all there is?' There was a brief chemical flash, but we were adults who'd admittedly been around the block a few times. Neither of us would have gotten married just for lust."

Savannah worried when the idea of Dan lusting after some society blond named Amanda caused a stir of something that felt uncomfortably like jealousy.

"The bottom line was that she thought I had something she wanted. And I thought she had something I wanted. By the time we finally called it quits, the only thing either of us wanted from the other was freedom."

"That's sad."

"I'm certainly not a proponent of divorce.

But in some cases, like ours, where both parties are financially independent, with no kids, and seemingly unable to do anything but make each other miserable, it might be the best solution all around."

"I suppose I can understand that." But she couldn't really identify. "I was never miserable."

They'd reached the bottom again. When the ticket taker leaned forward to open the bar, Dan shoved a bill into his hand.

"We'll be staying a bit longer." The man looked inclined to argue. He glanced over at the ticket booth, then back toward Dan again. Massive shoulders that appeared to have been carved from oak shrugged. He jammed the money into the pocket of his black T-shirt. "Suit yourself."

"Now then." Dan put his arm around Savannah and drew her closer as they slowly climbed back up to the top of the double wheel. "You were saying? About not being miserable?"

"I wasn't. Really," she insisted, meeting his openly skeptical look. "In fact, for a long time, I thought I was blissfully happy."

"Women who are blissful in their marriages don't usually get divorced."

"True." She sighed and wondered how she could possibly explain her behavior to Dan since she was just beginning to understand it herself. "You'd have to know Kevin to understand."

Dan decided that it would probably be best if he never met the weasel.

Neither of them said anything for an entire revolution. Dan was a patient man. Years of in-

terrogating individuals on the witness stand
had taught him to use silence well.

"I met him right after I'd graduated from
culinary school. I'd gotten a job as an assistant
to the assistant pastry chef at the Whitfield
Palace hotel in Paris."

Dan whistled softly. "When deluxe will no
longer do," he murmured the slogan of the
worldwide luxury hotel. "I'm impressed." He
didn't mention that he and Amanda had stayed
at that same hotel on their honeymoon. *Had Savannah been working there then?* he wondered.

"Kevin had just been hired as assistant manager of customer services. Before that he'd been
night manager at the Hôtel de Paris in Monaco.
The day he arrived, I ran into him at the end of
my shift. He was sitting at a corner table, all
alone in the deserted dining room, poring over
a tourist guide of popular Paris sights, trying to
figure out the way to the Eiffel Tower."

"Which you promptly offered to show him."

She looked surprised. "Yes. How did you
know that?"

"Lucky guess," he said dryly.

"Well, anyway," she forged on, "it was Paris
in the spring, I was horribly homesick and lonely, and he was just enough years older to seem
so much more worldly than most of the boys I
knew. He was also suave and sophisticated and
looked incredibly handsome in his Italian
suits."

"If you don't mind, I'd just as soon skip the
roll call of attributes."

"But that's just my point," Savannah said earnestly. "He seemed like every young girl's romantic fantasy. Like Prince Charming. He even shared my dream of someday owning a little inn together, and he made it seem so wonderfully romantic. . . .

"Even after we eloped, whenever I thought I sensed cracks in the facade of what I wanted to believe was our perfect marriage, he convinced me that I was only imagining things. The hotel business gets a lot of women—about-to-be-divorced women, lonely women, career women on business trips who want a fling away from home. He told me that some of those women may occasionally come on to him, but I didn't need to worry because I was the special one. I was the only woman he could ever want."

She managed a sad smile. "Unfortunately, I discovered that I wasn't the only woman he was telling all those pretty words to.

"My ex-husband was manipulative, seductive, and unfortunately without any moral core. After I came home, Ida described his charm as being the oily kind that washes off in the shower."

"That's probably one of the few things your grandmother has ever said that I understand." Dan skimmed his fingers over her shoulder to toy with the ends of her hair. "I'm sorry."

He honestly *was* sorry she'd been hurt. But Dan couldn't really regret her marriage breaking up, because if the husband had been the paragon she'd mistaken him for, Savannah would still be happily whipping up soufflés in Malibu instead of sitting here at the top of Coldwater Cove with him.

"So was I. I was sorry, hurt, and angry, and I've recently realized exactly how much of my self-confidence and self-respect he stole while I wasn't looking." She fell silent and looked out over the midnight-dark waters of the cove.

The carousel's cheery calliope drifted up from the midway. The twangy sounds of a country guitar and fiddle band rode on air scented with popcorn, peanuts, fir, and sawdust. Once again Dan waited.

"You know about Lilith," she said, turning back toward him. "About her life before Cooper. Her marriages."

"I've heard a few stories."

"I love my mother. . . . Really," she insisted when he didn't immediately respond.

"I believe you."

"I've always loved her. And I was never as angry about her behavior as Raine seemed to be."

"Perhaps you were too busy bottling your anger up."

That suggestion hit a little too close for comfort. "All right. I have to admit to wondering recently, now that we're all home again, if in my need to avoid confrontation, I'd managed to convince myself that Lilith's behavior didn't disturb me as much as it did Raine.

"Maybe one of these days I'll work that out. But what I have realized, since I discovered Kevin making love—"

"Not love."

"What?" His quiet comment sidetracked her.

"I've never met the guy, but from the little you've said, and what I've inferred from Jack and Raine, I'm guessing the weasel doesn't know the first thing about love."

She wondered if becoming an attorney had made him so perceptive, or if he'd chosen the law because of what appeared to be a natural talent for reading people.

"It's difficult to love someone else when you're so enamored with yourself," she responded dryly. "When I discovered he'd been having an affair with the head of the resort's legal department, I think what really hurt, more than his infidelity, was that deep down inside, I'd known it all along.

"It was as if we had this secret, unspoken contract. Kevin screwed around, and I knew it, and he knew that I knew it. So by overlooking his lapses in monogamy, on some level, so long as he remained discreet and we could both continue to lie about his behavior, I believed that I was keeping my marriage intact."

"Then he breached the contract by bringing the affair out into the open," Dan suggested.

"I think I was the last person at Las Casitas to know." She shook her head. "No, that's not exactly right. I was the last person to *acknowledge* it."

Except for a few general comments to her family, and telling Raine whatever details her sister needed to handle the legal aspects of her divorce, Savannah really hadn't talked about the breakup of her marriage.

She'd been too embarrassed. Too ashamed. Now she realized that Kevin was the one who should be ashamed.

"The entire time I was growing up, I swore that I wouldn't make the same mistakes regarding men that Lilith did. I promised myself that when I got married it would be for keeps."

"Given Lilith's marital history, I suppose it makes a certain cockeyed sense that you'd stick out a bad relationship longer than you should have. But I still can't understand why you married a jerk like that in the first place."

"Neither can I, now. I suppose I read too many fairy tales growing up. I was waiting to get swept off my feet, so when Kevin proposed eloping to Monte Carlo a week after we met, I thought it was what love was supposed to feel like."

She was looking out over the park again in a way that had Dan suspecting that she was seeing that long-ago day she'd exchanged vows with a guy that was so very wrong for her. Even though he could see how she'd gotten herself in such an impossible situation, he was still surprised that a girl who'd always seemed like the princess of Coldwater Cove could have ended up playing the role of Cinderella.

"Sometimes it's mutual. Guys can get swept off their feet, too. My folks only knew each other a week when they got married."

"Really?"

"Really. Dad had just graduated from college, and since the Air Force had paid for his education, he was about to ship out to Vietnam, which, I suppose, admittedly helped move the timetable up a little.

"Mom was the nurse who gave him his inoculations, and he insists that he fell head over heels. Literally. He fainted right after she stuck the needle in."

A silvery laugh bubbled from between Savannah's lips. Luscious lips Dan could still taste. Lips he wanted to taste again. "That's a wonderful story."

"I've always thought so. Dad hates Mom to tell it because he says it makes him sound like a wuss. They'll celebrate their thirty-seventh anniversary next spring.

"My grandparents didn't even take that long to get married. Gramps was in the navy. He met Gram when she was handing out doughnuts at a USO during World War II, and they eloped that same night, had eight kids, and are still crazy about each other. In fact, the way they slow dance at family reunions is downright embarrassing."

She smiled. "It sounds as if war has been very good for your family."

"They would have all gotten together, anyway," he said with a shrug. "As Gramps always says, you can't fight destiny."

Savannah looked skeptical, but she didn't argue.

They fell silent. Enjoying the night. Enjoying each other. Music from far below played on. The Ferris wheel continued its revolutions. When they stopped at the top again, Dan cupped her cheek in the hand that had been playing with her hair and turned her face toward him.

"Advance warning, Savannah. I'm going to kiss you. If you don't want me to, you'd better say so now."

She didn't say a word. She didn't need to. Her eyes, two limpid pools of need, gave Dan the answer he needed.

All it took was the taste of her to make him hard. Dan wasn't gentle this time. Unable to get enough of her, his mouth turned hot and hungry. Needing more, he used his thumb to coax her lips open.

The kiss grew more and more ravenous as he swallowed her soft moans and throaty whimpers.

Dan wanted to touch her. To taste her. Everywhere. He imagined his mouth on her flesh, following the lush curves while his hands played hot licks on her body—that incredible body that he was literally aching to be inside.

"If we're not careful, we're going to end up falling into the cove." He wondered if that would cool them off and decided they'd just set the water to boiling instead.

She drew her head back and blinked slowly. Sometime during the heated kiss, her hand had landed in his lap. Dan ground his teeth as she absently stroked him. "It just might be worth it."

Because he was on the verge of exploding, he took hold of her hand to keep them both out of trouble. "You keep touching me that way, sweetheart, and you may just end up getting us both arrested for disorderly conduct when I rip off your clothes and ravish you atop a amusement ride in a public park."

"Ravishing sounds pretty good," she admitted as the wheel jolted again.

"Maybe later." With his gaze still on hers, he kissed her again, lightly this time, and watched a mingling of pleasure and need rise in her eyes. "When we both have our feet on the ground again."

Before she could respond, they'd reached the end of Dan's money. "Time's up," the ticket taker said firmly.

Wanting to be alone with Savannah, this time Dan didn't argue. They'd no sooner started back across the park when John came running up to them.

"I've been looking all over for you, Savannah," he said. He was obviously agitated and out of breath.

Her fingers tightened on Dan's. He felt her hand turn cold. "Did something happen to my grandmother?"

"No. Dr. Lindstrom's fine. But she sent me to get you. She said it's an urgent family problem and you all need to go back to the house right away. She and Henry and Gwen are waiting for you at the car. With Raine and Jack."

"Gwen's here?"

John nodded earnestly. "I think she's what the problem is about."

Savannah's gaze cut from John to Dan.

"Perhaps it's not as bad as it sounds," he said encouragingly.

"We can always hope." She did not sound encouraged.

As they headed toward the parking lot, Dan reminded himself that Savannah had made a substantial financial and emotional commitment here in Coldwater Cove. She wouldn't be going anywhere.

There would be plenty of time to pick up where they'd left off. Hopefully sooner rather than later.

13

"I didn't say for certain that I wanted her back," Gwen insisted after they'd gathered in the front parlor of Ida's home.

To keep Amy out of the discussion, Henry, Jack, and John had taken her upstairs to watch a National Geographic video about whales on Ida's bedroom television. Since he was the attorney who'd written up the initial adoption agreement, Dan had stayed downstairs with the Lindstrom women and Gwen.

"I said I was *thinking* about it." The teenager's bottom lip thrust out as she turned to Raine. "When I signed the adoption contract, you told me I could change my mind."

"There's a window of opportunity," Raine agreed. "But just like adoption, it's not a decision to be made lightly, Gwen."

"Which is why you need to be very, very sure about this, darling," Lilith added.

"I know. That's why I need to go see her," Gwen insisted, her eyes glistening. "So I can make up my mind."

Savannah exchanged a worried glance with her sister, then with her mother, then finally directed her gaze toward Ida, whose complexion appeared oddly putty colored.

"Are you all right?" she asked her grandmother.

"I wish everyone would stop asking me that," Ida snapped. "Besides, how can anyone be all right? This is a mess."

"I-I-I'm s-s-sorry." The tears began to fall. Gwen's hands were clasped together so tightly her knuckles were white. "I've really tried not to think about her. But I do. And I know you'll all think I'm behaving irresponsibly, but I have this h-h-huge empty feeling in me that won't go away."

She scrubbed at the free-falling moisture, appearing so like a child herself that Savannah felt like crying too. Gwen closed her eyes. Her lashes looked like thin threads of copper silk against her splotchy, freckled cheeks.

"I can't stop wondering what she looks like now. If she's got h-h-hair. If she's h-h-happy."

Savannah didn't think she'd ever seen anyone look so wretched. Gwen hadn't even been this distraught the day at the hospital when she'd handed her infant daughter over to Terri and Bill Stevenson. She knelt beside the chair the teen was slumped in and took her in her arms.

"It'll be all right," she said reassuringly. Somehow, whatever Gwen's decision, the family would find a way to work the problem out, as they had so many others over the years.

"I just need to see her, Savannah," Gwen repeated through her tears. Her voice was shaky, but determined. "To m-m-make sure."

After a great deal of discussion, and a decidedly uncomfortable telephone call to the Stevensons, it was decided that Savannah would drive Gwen to Sequim first thing in the morning.

Both Dan and Raine objected when the parties involved opted against bringing attorneys into the meeting at this point, but after a great deal of argument—which became heated for a few moments—they were overruled.

"I'll keep my cell phone on," Dan promised as Savannah walked with him out to the Tahoe. His voice was resigned, but she could tell he still wasn't happy with the arrangement for the private meeting she'd worked out with the Stevensons.

"If you or Gwen need any legal advice, or if you just need a friend to talk to, all you have to do is call. I can be there in thirty minutes."

And he'd come, Savannah thought. Without hesitation, without question. Because he cared. She tried to think how long it had been since she'd been able to count on anyone but her grandmother or sister.

Too long, she realized. Perhaps even forever. It was nice knowing that she could count on Dan O'Halloran. Nicer still knowing that she could count on herself.

Savannah was beginning to view her divorce not as something she'd suffered through and survived—like mumps or a tax audit—but as a born-again experience. She'd been gifted with a new beginning, a chance to reinvent Savannah Townsend. And so far, she thought with a burst of pride, she was doing a pretty damn good job of it.

"We'll be fine."

"Oh, you're a lot better than fine, sweet-heart." They'd reached the truck. Ignoring the interested side glances from the others, he drew her into his arms. Ignoring the looks from her family, Savannah went.

He didn't kiss her. Just held her, offering comfort and strength. Allowing herself to accept both, just for a minute, Savannah circled her arms around his waist and rested her head against his shoulder.

She watched him leave and felt a sudden, cowardly urge to go with him. Despite how far she'd come in a few short months, as she got ready for bed, Savannah couldn't help dreading tomorrow. She washed her face in the old pedestal sink in the bathroom she shared with Henry and thought how, if given the choice, she would rather have discovered Kevin sleeping with the entire LA Lakers cheerleader squad in their custom-made king-sized bed that looked out over the sea than watch Gwen suffering such emotional pain.

While she brushed her teeth, she decided that it would be easier to go through a dozen divorces than risk shattering the fragile new family bonds of her longtime friends, whose idea to adopt this particular baby had been hers in the first place.

Even with all those unpleasant prospects tumbling around in her mind, as she crawled between the sheets that smelled of the Mrs. Stewart's bluing Ida used in the wash, Savannah thought back to the kiss she'd shared with Dan. Had it been only a few hours ago? It seemed much, much longer.

But even the distance of time hadn't stopped the moment from being permanently etched in her mind. She knew that years from now, when she was Ida's age, looking back on the fortunes and follies of her life, she'd recall in vivid detail sitting atop the world with Daniel O'Halloran and feeling as if she could have reached out and grabbed a handful of the glittering stars that had been stitched against the night sky like brilliants on velvet.

Unfortunately, Gwen's return home had sent her crashing back to earth.

A rose bush climbed a white lattice trellis outside the window, its fragrance perfuming the room. The late summer roses were overblown, as if to put on one last spectacular display before autumn frost would curl their serrated green leaves and turn the blossoms from wine red velvet to a sad dead brown that would crush between your fingers, then blow away like dust. Like her old life.

The house was dark and mostly quiet. If she was very still, she could hear the faint nighttime rustling of bird wings in the monkey puzzle tree on the front lawn, the distant bark of a dog, Henry's muffled snores from beyond the violet papered wall. She could not hear anything from Gwen's room. But Savannah sensed the teen's silent weeping and knew that she wasn't the only person in the house finding sleep difficult tonight.

The lady or the tiger? Savannah worried as she spent the long night staring up at the shadows moving across the swirled plaster ceiling. Each door held potential heartbreak.

The day dawned pastel pink and silver. A veil of soft, hazy mist lay low over the cove. The mood in the kitchen was strained, cautious, as if a wrong word could set off a deadly chain reaction. Ida remained uncharacteristically silent, as though determined not to influence what Savannah knew could be the most important decision Gwen would ever make. Henry had chosen to stay upstairs, displaying either surprising sensitivity or, more likely, a desire to avoid any more emotional storms.

The morning sun flashed buttery yellow bars on the asphalt as Savannah drove along the narrow, twisting road that ran along the coastline to Sequim. Gwen didn't say a word. But the brittle metallic tension surrounding her was so palatable, Savannah imagined she could taste it.

Bill and Terri Stevenson were refugees from California who'd bought a house built in the late 1800s as a summer estate for a wealthy Seattle lumber baron. A former wine master at a world-renowned Napa Valley vineyard who'd grown weary of fighting the accountants who seemed to be running the larger wineries lately, Bill had opted out of the rat race. These days he was focusing on the work he loved, turning his carefully tended grapes into award-winning wines while his wife Terri, a graphic artist, designed labels featuring the century-old stone castle-like building that harkened back to the original owner's German roots. Terri also handled the equally successful advertising and marketing end of the business.

It was a modern-day cottage industry, one that allowed the couple to work at home and lavish attention on their newly adopted daughter.

Since the day was bright blue, they all sat outside, as they had that first day, on a little patio overlooking the duck pond and the sweep of vineyards set in dark soil that stretched nearly to the strait. Only a few months ago, the vines had been bright and spring green with promise; now they were dark, their limbs bending with ripening, deep purple grapes approaching harvest.

Baby Lily, dressed in a frilly dress the color of lilacs and pink ruffled socks, was strapped into an infant swing beneath a blue and white fringed awning. The day the infant had been born, Savannah thought her face had resembled a sweet, round pink pumpkin. She'd changed considerably since then. Her satiny skin was the peachy cream of a true redhead, like her birth mother, and a fuzz had sprouted on her formerly bald head like coppery thistle-down. The sweet scent of Johnson's baby pow-

der suggested she'd been bathed shortly before
Gwen and Savannah's arrival.

Oblivious to her surroundings or the tension
in the air, she was cooing happily to herself,
sounding a bit like the doves that gathered beneath Savannah's bedroom window each morning. It would have been obvious to anyone that
this was a contented child, a baby who was well
and truly loved.

For the first time in her life, as they exchanged
small talk, Savannah understood the old saying
about the elephant in the living room. It hovered
there, huge and menacing as they discussed the
prospect of a good harvest despite the need for
more rain in what was known as the Olympic
Sunbelt, Gwen's summer at science camp, and
Savannah's ongoing restoration of the lighthouse. It was as if all the participants at the possibly life-altering meeting were avoiding the
subject they'd all come together to discuss.

Finally Bill, after sharing his hopes for this
year's merlot, broke the conversational ice.

"We've been worried about you," he told Gwen.

She tossed up her chin. Insecurity radiated
from her slender body that had lost all its baby
weight. "Worried that I'd change my mind?"

The girl who, not so long ago, had dared Jack,
Raine, and an Olympic County judge to throw
her back into the revolving door of the state's
foster care system, had returned. Which only revealed, Savannah thought, how frightened she
really was beneath that truculent exterior.

"No," he said in the quiet, thoughtful way

that was such a contrast to his wife's more ebullient personality. "We've been worried about how you've been dealing with your decision. For your sake."

"You've had a great deal to overcome already in your young life, Gwen," Terri said gently. "We hated thinking that giving up your baby may have caused you any more pain."

"Not that we regret adopting Lily." Bill's tone was calm; the emotion swirling in his normally calm brown eyes was not.

"She's the best thing that could ever happen to us." Terri's voice choked up. Her eyes swam. "The answer to all our prayers." She reached blindly for her husband, who linked his fingers with hers.

His hands were rough and dark, his knuckles scraped, and Savannah either saw, or imagined she saw, dirt around his ragged cuticles. They were not the hands of some San Francisco yuppie who one spring day awakened with a whim to make a nice little wine to serve at small gatherings of the kind of attractive, articulate friends so often depicted in wine advertising.

They were the hands of a working man, a man more comfortable laboring in soil than pushing a pen behind a desk.

But she'd also seen how gentle those very same hands could be when he'd placed his daughter into her swing.

"We told you that we're proponents of open adoption," he reminded Gwen. "We haven't changed our minds. We adore Lily, which is why we can understand how much you must love her, too. The way we see it, a child can't have too much love."

Savannah could tell from Gwen's expression that his response was not what she'd expected. She'd come here today to fight; by offering to share their lives, they may have managed to disarm her.

When the tears the teenager had so stubbornly held back on the drive from Coldwater Cove began to trail silently down her face, Savannah realized that they were right back where they'd been three months ago. Once again her grandmother was right. It was a mess.

"You realize that if you keep it up, you're going to wear a damn hole in the rug," Henry told Ida.

Her nerves about as jumpy as a frog in a French restaurant, Ida spun back toward him, her hands on her narrow hips. "It's my house."

"It's also your blood pressure." He pointed the remote at the TV he'd been watching and hit the mute. "Speaking of which, when was the last time you had it checked?"

"I'm a doctor. I can check it myself."

"So?"

"So what?" Just when she was beginning to think that having this man living under her roof might be tolerable, he'd begun to irritate her all over again.

"So when did you check it? At your age, you can't be too careful."

"I'm younger than you."

"Mebbe. By a few years. But like you said, old's old."

If there was one thing Ida hated worse than having someone try to tell her what to do, it was having her own words tossed back in her face. Especially when she couldn't quite remember them. Though it sounded like something she might have said, she allowed.

They stared at each other.

She might not be as young as she once was, but her will was still strong as cold forged steel. Unfortunately, it was beginning to look as if she'd met her match in Henry Hyatt.

He finally shrugged. "Stubborn as a Missouri mule."

He turned the sound back on, the noise of the Seahawks game grating on her nerves.

Ida left the parlor and began pacing the wide planks of the front porch. What was keeping them? She'd never been patient. A change-of-life surprise baby, she'd come barreling into her parents' life just at the time they'd begun looking forward to slowing down and perhaps bouncing a grandchild or two on their knees. Looking back on it now, her mind on babies anyway because of Gwen's pickle, Ida realized that trying to keep up with a child who didn't know the meaning of the word *slow* would have been a challenge.

Her weary mother had, on more than one occasion, accused Ida of possessing the attention span of a hummingbird. Which, now that she thought about it, was much the same thing she'd always said about her own daughter. It was the first time in fifty years that it had ever occurred to her that she and Lilith might have anything in common. It was a thought that merited some consideration.

Once she'd quit worrying about Gwen.

She stared toward the direction of Sequim, as if she could will Savannah's little red car to appear. But the only car on the road was Melvin Baxter's old clunker of a Buick he insisted on calling a classic, when what it really was was a wreck. The sky between the mountains and the cove was a clear robin's egg blue, marred only by the puffy white contrail of a jet flying high overhead, the plane's body glinting like quicksilver.

Quicksilver. That had been the word her mother had used to describe her mind, which had admittedly hopped from subject to subject, never seeming to find a topic worthy of interest. Her grades had been mediocre at best, which, since she was a girl and not expected to have a career, wouldn't have worried her parents overmuch had it not been for their concern that her unfortunate habit of speaking her mind would greatly diminish her marriage potential.

Then, on a Christmas Eve she'd never forget, two weeks before her fifteenth birthday, Ida's life had drastically and inexorably changed. As she'd been doing since she was old enough to ride along on the wooden sled, she'd gone out into the New Hampshire woods with her father to cut down their Christmas tree. A typical taciturn New Englander, John Lindstrom had not mentioned the pain that had been lurking beneath his ribcage when he'd awakened that morning.

Indeed, there'd been scant time for conversation as Ida had been downstairs impatiently waiting for him, already bundled up in woolens and boots.

Her mother had always been a perfectionist when it came to the family's annual tree, and it had taken a great deal of trekking through knee-deep snow to find a spruce Ingrid Lindstom wouldn't be able to find fault with.

They'd been returning down the mountain with their lush blue-green prize when her father's knees had suddenly buckled and he'd come crashing to the snowy ground in the same way the tree had fallen to the ax.

The next few hours of terror passed in a mind-numbing blur, but, frightened as she'd been, the instant Ida rushed into the emergency room behind her father's stretcher, she felt suddenly whisked from her boring, black-and-white world into a Technicolor wonderland. She could have been Dorothy, landing in Oz.

The bustling, foreign world of medicine that caused her mother to fret so was the most fascinating thing Ida had ever seen. She was fascinated by the nurses, whose starched white uniforms rustled like dry leaves and whose crepe-soled shoes made not a sound as they moved through the halls in a brisk, efficient manner. Even today, Ida could recall in vivid detail the little boy who had fallen through the ice while skating and had miraculously escaped anything worse than a probable head cold.

Another man had been sitting on a gurney, his long legs dangling over the side. He was pressing his hand against a blood-soaked white towel as he'd awaited stitches for a nasty cut on his forehead. Ida overheard his wife telling the nurse that he'd received the wound when he'd leaned too far forward to put the star on the top of the tree and had fallen off the ladder.

There were more people crowded into the emergency room, more than she would have expected for such a small population, all of them dependent on the larger-than-life white-jacketed individuals who moved among them like gods who'd strolled down from Mount Olympus to play with the mortals.

It was only years later, when she was in medical school, that it would dawn on Ida that the doctors had all been men. Not that it would have mattered if she *had* realized that the only women in the emergency room had been wives, mothers, or nurses. She'd discovered her true calling on that memorable Christmas Eve, the one thing in all the world that could capture and hold her attention.

The god attending her father informed the family that John Lindstrom would live. He would, however, have to remain in the hospital for the next six weeks. "To allow his heart to rest," the doctor had explained to his relieved wife and spellbound daughter.

Ida visited her father every day. She drank in

the always changing sights and sounds and scents like a girl who'd spent years crawling across parched desert sands and had finally stumbled across a sparkling oasis. And she was never, ever bored.

Nor had she ever suffered a moment's boredom during all the years she'd served as Coldwater Cove's general practitioner, caring for entire families in a way that made her an intricate part of the community.

She'd kept up with the times, attending seminars and spending her nights reading medical journals to learn new techniques, new methods of healing.

But the one thing Ida had never been able to learn was patience.

14

"Can I hold her?" Gwen asked.

"Of course," Terri and Bill said together.

They exchanged a quick look, then Terri rose, lifted Lily from the swing, and carefully placed her, one mother to the other, into Gwen's arms. It escaped no one's attention that this was a reversal of the gesture of that morning in the hospital when Gwen had surrendered her child to the Stevensons' for safekeeping.

Lily stopped cooing. Her brow furrowed beneath the pink elastic headband. Eyes as wide and blue as a china plate observed this newcomer with sober intensity. On some deeper level, Savannah realized that all three adults on the patio were holding their breaths. Watching the turbulent emotions move across Gwen's face, she feared the teenage mother had forgotten how to breathe. Gwen's yearning was painful to watch.

It was as if they'd all been turned to stone—

or wood, like the life-size tableau of the crèche
and the wise men Ida put out on the front yard
every Christmas.

Then it happened.

"She smiled at me!" Gwen exclaimed.

Terri beamed through unshed tears. "She's
been doing that more and more lately. It's like
looking into the sun, isn't it?"

"Yes." Gwen's voice was filled with an awe
that, Savannah belatedly realized, she hadn't
been allowed to experience the day she'd given
birth to Lily.

Concerned for Gwen's feelings, attempting to
help smooth over the wrenching pain of loss,
the family had inadvertently stolen any sense of
maternity from her. Only Terri, who'd insisted
that the baby be photographed with her birth
mother, had begun to understand the complex
emotions the teenager might be experiencing
on that unforgettable day.

"She's grown so much," Gwen said softly.

"Like a weed," Bill said.

"A beautiful, one-of-a-kind weed," Terri said.
"She looks like you, Gwen."

"Do you think so?" Hope and an unmistakable maternal pride warred on the freckled face.

"Absolutely," Terri and Bill said in unison.

Gwen ran her finger down her daughter's
cheek. "I decided to give her up for adoption in
the first place because she needed a better mother,
a better family than I could be right now."

None of them challenged that truthful ap-
praisal.

"Until that day I was panhandling on the ferry and Mama Ida took me home with her, I never felt as if I belonged anywhere. It's hard to fit in when you're being dragged from home to home, always changing schools."

She smoothed the frilly organdy skirt. Lily cooed and kicked her plump, stocking-clad feet. "I want Lily to know where she belongs. To know who her family is."

Gwen bit her bottom lip as she dragged her gaze from her daughter, out across the rolling vineyard, then back to the Stevensons.

"You're her family. I love her with my whole heart. I always will." She sighed, a sad little shimmer of sound. "But she belongs with you."

Bill and Terri exchanged another look. If the subject hadn't been so serious, if so much hadn't been at stake, Savannah might have envied their silent marital conversation. She couldn't remember ever sharing such obvious telepathy with Kevin.

"We want you to be very, very sure about this, Gwen," Bill said. Again, his voice was gentle, but firmer than Savannah had ever heard it. "We're willing to make accommodations for your feelings and whatever need you have to be included in Lily's life. Within reason," he tacked on.

"But you can't go changing your mind every few months. It'd be too hard on all of us—you, Terri, and me, and most of all it would be too hard on Lily."

"I know." Gwen hugged her daughter closer. Her expression was hidden by her cap of red hair as she brushed her lips against the top of the baby's head.

"I didn't really want to take her away from you. On the way home from science camp, I was thinking that maybe we could share her. Not just on special days, like her birthdays, or Christmas. But all the time."

She turned to Terri. "It must be hard being a working mother."

"It takes some juggling," Terri allowed. "But she's a remarkably easy child, and at this age, I can keep her with me while I'm working."

Gwen considered that. "My mother always said I ruined her life."

Savannah couldn't let that hurtful statement go unchallenged. "I never knew your mother, Gwen." But she'd heard the stories from Raine and Ida, horrific stories of drugs and prostitution and child abuse. "But since we're all ultimately responsible for our own behavior, I have to point out that your mother ruined her own life."

"Yeah. That's what the counselor said."

The only thing that had worried Savannah about Gwen going to off to science camp was that her court-appointed weekly therapy would be interrupted. She was moderately relieved at this indication that at least some of the self-esteem Gwen had developed while living with Ida had stuck during her time away from home.

"It'd be confusing for Lily to have two mothers." Gwen sighed again with obvious sadness and resignation. "But I want her to grow up knowing that *she* never ruined my life. That I

loved her." She hitched in a shaky breath.
"More than anything."

"Absolutely," Terri said.

"I'm going to register with one of those bureaus that let adopted kids find their natural parents when they're adults. That way, if she ever wants to m-m-meet me"—she struggled against renewed tears—"she can."

Terri nodded. "I believe that's a very wise, very mature decision. And you can trust us to support Lily if—and when—she wants to discover what a brave, special woman her birth mother is."

In contrast to the first time they'd all sat together out here on the patio, sheltered from a spring rain, as Gwen gave Lily back to Terri and good-byes were said and hugs exchanged, there were no tears. Savannah suspected the teenager was cried out.

"I understand how hard it is to lose a child." Savannah said as they drove back home.

Gwen glanced over at her with surprise. "Did you have to give away a baby?"

"No. I had a miscarriage early in my pregnancy. It was the same day I brought home a new crib."

It had been painted in a gleaming white enamel that shone like sunshine on new snow and had been topped with a ridiculously feminine, peony-hued ruffled canopy made for a princess.

The crib had still been in the nursery, a vivid pink and white reminder of her loss, when Savannah had returned from the hospital. Despite her doctor's instructions to rest, she'd spent the entire afternoon with screwdrivers and wrenches, taking it apart and putting it away. She'd hoped that if she didn't have to look at the symbol of so much hope and happiness, she'd feel better. Of course she hadn't.

"That must have been awful."

"I thought my heart would break."

"But it didn't break," Gwen said, with obvious hope.

"It was pretty much shattered," Savannah contradicted, deciding that she owed Gwen the absolute truth.

Savannah had never told anyone but Raine about her miscarriage. Not even her grandmother, partly because she hadn't wanted Ida to worry, partly because she hadn't wanted to think about it herself. She decided the fact that she could talk about it with Gwen now, without that horrid, wrenching pain, was yet more proof of personal growth.

"It's gotten better. But I can't imagine that I'll ever put it entirely out of my mind."

"I'll never forget Lily," Gwen said with a sad little sigh.

"No. You won't."

"When I was a little kid, the only thing I ever wanted was a mom who loved me and who'd take care of me."

"I felt the same way a lot of times."

"Yeah. I guess Lilith wasn't a very good mom."

"I think she was just too young to take care of two children." But not once had she ever ac-

cused her daughters of causing the turmoil her
life had been for so many years, as Gwen's
mother had done.

"Yeah," Gwen repeated. "She was probably
too young to be a mother. Like me."

A thoughtful little silence filled the car. Wanting
to leave Gwen to her thoughts, Savannah didn't
speak until they were nearing the lighthouse.

"How are you with a paintbrush? I'm finishing up the trim on the inside of the lantern
room today and could really use some help."

"You're just trying to get my mind off Lily."

"Partly," Savannah agreed. "But mostly, I honestly could use another hand. John also said
something about planting mums today." She
knew that Gwen loved to garden; indeed, the garden she'd created in Ida's back yard had proven a
beautiful place for Lilith's and Raine's weddings.

"Okay. If you and John Martin really need
help, I guess I could pitch in." She hitched in an
audible breath. "Thank you. For coming with me
today. For letting me make my own decision."

"It was your decision to make," Savannah
said mildly.

"I know." Gwen stared out the passenger
window, pretending grave interest in the trees
flashing by, then turned back toward Savannah.
"Thank you for being my family."

Savannah smiled. "That's the easy part."

That crisis dealt with, Savannah found herself embroiled in yet another problem when it
came time for her grandmother's visit to the

doctor. Independent to the bone, Ida, whose shirt informed them all that I May Have Many Faults, But Being Wrong Isn't One of Them, was not at all pleased when she came downstairs and found her daughter and both her granddaughters waiting. Even though Gwen had professed a desire to go with them, she had reluctantly headed off to the high school to get her books and confirm her schedule for her upcoming senior year.

"It's just a routine physical," Ida grumbled. "I don't need an entourage."

Raine folded her arms and met her grandmother's stubborn glare straight on. "Tough."

The grandfather clock in the front hall announced the half hour with a peal of Westminster chimes. Ida checked the time on her own watch—the one she'd worn for as long as Savannah could remember, with a wide leather band, round white face, and red sweep hand that ticked off the seconds.

Then she shot a look at Henry, who was sitting at the table, drinking coffee and pretending to read the morning paper. Savannah had known he was pretending when ten minutes had gone by without his turning the page.

"I left you a cold meatloaf sandwich for lunch," Ida told him. "It's wrapped in waxed paper in the fridge."

"Sounds real good." Savannah gave him points for lying with a straight face. "Thanks."

"You're a guest," Ida reminded him briskly. She turned toward the others. "Well, since I seem to be stuck with you three, we might as well get going."

It was, Savannah thought as she followed her grandmother out the kitchen door, one of the few times she'd ever seen Ida Lindstrom surrender without a prolonged fight.

The day seemed a month long. While Ida may have always found medicine fascinating, Savannah, forced to wait with her mother and sister while her grandmother—clad in a white cotton hospital gown that hung past her knees—was moved from room to room, cubicle to cubicle, found it bewildering and frightening.

Armed with informational brochures found in the waiting room, she, Raine, and Lilith learned more detail about tests they'd mostly only seen on *ER* or *Chicago Hope*. There were tests to determine how long it took for Ida's blood to clot, tests to measure her glucose level, and the amount of fat and cholesterol in her blood. There were chest x-rays, a CAT scan, and an EKG, which a friendly, chatty technician had explained was necessary to check heart function, since clots could often be thrown off from the heart and enter the arteries of the brain.

Exhausted herself when the battery of tests were finally concluded, Savannah couldn't imagine how Ida was feeling.

When the neurologist, Dr. Burke, finally brought the family into his office, Ida was already there. Despite the grueling day, she looked a great deal more chipper than Savannah felt, and if appearances were anything to go by, Raine and Lilith were also wrung out.

Lilith looked especially drawn. Her normally smooth forehead had been furrowed for hours, her midnight blue eyes lacked their usual sparkle, and concern carved deep brackets along both sides of her mouth, drawing her lips down. For the first time in memory, Savannah's mother looked not just her age, but older.

"I've already heard the verdict." Ida stood up when they entered, pocketbook clutched in her hands. "Since I can't see any point in sitting here while you all rehash it, I'll wait down in the cafeteria. Those fool tests cost me breakfast and lunch and I'm starving."

Savannah decided that the fact that the doctor was letting Ida walk out of his office instead of admitting her immediately was a good thing. Then again, she considered, from her reading, she knew that Alzheimer's patients could live with the disease for years before hospitalization became necessary.

She was vastly relieved when the doctor skipped the getting-to-know you small talk and went straight to the point.

"Dr. Lindstrom tells me that you've been concerned about recent memory lapses she's been experiencing."

"We've been worried she may have Alzheimer's," Raine, equally to the point, answered.

"Alzheimer's is admittedly something we all worry about, especially on those days we can't find our car keys." When he folded his hands on his desk, Savannah found herself studying them, as she had Bill's yesterday. They were capable hands, she decided, in their own way as reassuring as the plethora of framed diplomas covering the walls.

"But I don't believe that's Dr. Lindstrom's problem."

"Is that good news? Or bad news?" Savannah asked.

"Obviously, in the case of dementia, all diagnoses are relative."

"Excuse me if I don't find any diagnosis of dementia very comforting," Lilith interjected.

"I understand." The look he gave her suggested he just might. "It's one of those words that doesn't come with any positive connotations. Still, if we were talking about my grandmother—"

"Which we're not," Raine broke in.

"Actually, we could be," he countered mildly. "My maternal grandmother was diagnosed with multi-infarct dementia five years ago. MID is the second leading cause of progressive mental deterioration, or, in layman's terms, tissue death in the brain."

Savannah heard her sister let out a breath. "What causes it?"

"MID is caused by damage or death to brain cells due to a deprivation of oxygen and nutrients."

"That sounds like a stroke." Savannah felt the blood leave her face.

She'd secretly worried about this, but had

been afraid to let herself even consider the possibility. A friend—a pastry chef at the resort she'd worked at in Atlantic City—had suffered a stroke that had left the thirty-seven-year-old woman unable to speak and completely paralyzed on one side. When she had finally gotten her voice back months later, she'd sounded like a slow-minded toddler, and when Savannah had left, she'd only been able to get around with a walker.

"Surely we would have noticed if Mother had suffered a stroke," Lilith insisted.

"Not necessarily. Transient ischemic attacks, or TIA—which are essentially ministrokes—aren't that easy to spot, especially in the elderly, since the symptoms—dizziness, clumsiness, fainting, numbness, forgetfulness—are brief, usually lasting less than five minutes, and they tend to get dismissed as a normal process of aging."

"She fell off a kitchen stool this past spring," Raine said flatly. "She was hospitalized, but no one ever diagnosed a stroke."

"I've only been on staff for three weeks, so I don't have any personal knowledge of the incident. But looking at her chart, I can understand why the admitting physician wasn't overly concerned, especially since she didn't reveal any other symptoms at the time."

"I don't know anything about strokes," Lilith murmured.

"That's not surprising. In this information age, you can't turn on your television without hearing about the dramatic new techniques in preventing or treating cardiovascular problems or cancer. But while approximately half a million people a year have strokes, they don't garner the same press. I suppose part of the reason is that strokes are harder to pin down. Most people, when they have a heart attack, suffer much the same damage.

"But strokes are different. Unique. Our brains consume the largest percentage of our body's energy—about twenty-five percent," he said, slipping into a pedantic mode that made him sound like a medical school professor, which, Savannah noted from one of the diplomas, he'd once been. "There are twenty billion neurons in the brain and each of those makes, on average, ten thousand connections. Our brains are the miracle of our human frames, the supercomputers of the universe, so to speak. They're also our greatest human mystery.

"In fact, it was only about three hundred years ago that physicians first started noticing that some people without any signs of head injuries would suddenly complain of head pain and collapse. Since the condition seemed to appear from out of the blue, a stroke of bad luck, so to speak, they started calling it a stroke. And the name stuck."

"That's an interesting bit of medical history," Raine said dryly. She was clearly impatient, as was Savannah. But of the two of them, Raine had always had the greater need for controlling her environment and everyone in it. "But what's my grandmother's prognosis?"

"These things are very individual." Savannah

suspected the doctor's vague answer only irritated Raine further. "But TIAs *are* the most predictive risk factor for a more serious cerebral-thrombosis stroke."

Lilith, sitting between Raine and Savannah, moaned softly. Raine took hold of her left hand, Savannah her right.

"Thrombosis is caused by narrowing of the arteries to the brain, right?" That was what Savannah's friend had suffered.

"Exactly." Dr. Burke nodded in a way that reminded her of the gold stars her third-grade teacher used to put on her spelling tests. "In fact, it's the same type of atherosclerosis that results in heart attacks.

"Unfortunately, not only do TIAs multiply the risk for cerebral thrombosis tenfold, approximately a third of patients who experience them suffer a stroke within five years. Half within a year."

"Well, I asked for a prognosis," Raine muttered grimly.

"It's not as bad as it sounds," the doctor said. "In many cases, MID is not only preventable, it's treatable. Daily low-dose aspirin can help prevent the internal blood clots that cause TIAs. It also appears to stabilize mental decline. Some test study subjects also show improved cognition."

"I don't believe this." Lilith's face was also now a study in frustration. "That sounds remarkably like a neurologist's version of 'take two aspirin and call me in the morning.'"

"I realize it sounds simplistic," Dr. Burke

countered. "But aspirin has been proven to be an extremely effective preventative. Of course, in the case of a cerebral hemorrhage, it can increase bleeding, but that's definitely not what we're dealing with in Dr. Lindstrom's case.

"In her favor is the fact that she doesn't have additional risk factors. She's not overweight, her cholesterol is within the acceptable range, she's never smoked, only drinks occasionally and exercises regularly, and she has a positive, forward-thinking attitude that helps her deal with stress. Those are all very encouraging factors."

Savannah desperately wished she could be encouraged.

They continued to question him for another half hour, during which he impressed Savannah by neither retreating behind a wall of medical jargon nor appearing offended when Raine fell back into her cross-examination mode, grilling him as if he were a hostile witness she had on the stand.

Afterwards, they found Ida sitting at a cafeteria table with a trio of women in scrubs. Savannah smiled when she heard her grandmother advising one of the women on the best way to treat colic.

But as they left the hospital, Savannah heard the doctor's words replaying inside her head and suddenly felt the same way she had when she'd let go of Ida's hand during a shopping trip she'd taken with her grandmother—just the two of them, which had made the day extra special—to buy birthday presents for Raine at Nordstrom's in Seattle.

She couldn't recall how old she'd been, but she must have been very young because she remembered, with absolute clarity, feeling like Hansel and Gretel in the forest, right before they'd found the wicked witch's house. Right before they were put in the cage to be fattened up for eating.

As she remembered the rush of relief she'd felt when she'd been lifted out of that teeming sea of adult legs, Savannah desperately wished that there was something she could do to save her grandmother, the same way Ida had rescued her.

15

It was late afternoon, almost evening. Raine had returned to the farm, Ida was up in her room, napping, Savannah hoped. After hearing the less than encouraging diagnosis from the others, Gwen had also gone upstairs, ostensibly to get a start on this year's reading list for her honor's English class. Savannah suspected she was doing what the rest of them were doing—worrying.

Henry was nowhere to be found, but a note on the refrigerator said that he'd be back in time for dinner, which he'd pick up from Papa Joe's on the way home. Savannah found that little act of charity the sole positive note in a miserable day.

Feeling too cooped up and edgy to stay in the house, she went out on the porch and was surprised to find Lilith still there.

"I thought you'd gone home."

"I'm not in any hurry, since it's Cooper's monthly poker night and my den will be full of cops."

"I'll bet you never thought you'd be married to a policeman." Savannah sat down on the steps.

"I never thought I'd be married again, period." Lilith opened her purse, then seeming to remember she'd quit smoking on her wedding day, closed it again. "But then again, Cooper's special."

"He is that."

"And you know what they say about second marriages being a prime example of the triumph of hope over experience. Of course in my case, my third marriage was proof of love triumphing over experience."

"I think I've had enough experience for one lifetime."

"That's what you say now," Lilith said. "But you'll get over it."

"That's just the point. I don't *want* to get over it. I can't think of a single reason to get married. Except to have children," she said in afterthought, thinking of how Amy seemed to have made such a difference in Raine's life.

"I'm glad I had you and Raine. But it undoubtedly would have been easier on all of us if I'd married Cooper the first time."

As much as she honestly loved her father, Savannah couldn't argue with that.

They fell into a companionable silence, watching as dusk draped long purple shadows over the town. The old-fashioned gaslights on Harbor Street flickered on; the pink and blue neon bordering the Orca Theater's marquee, which had seemed terribly old-fashioned when Savannah had been a teenager, had come back into vogue.

"Do you think she's going to be okay?" Lilith asked.

"She has to be." Savannah would not allow herself to think otherwise.

Lilith nodded. "I honestly can't imagine life without Mother. She's always seemed as strong as the trees surrounding the town. It was always so good to know that whatever trouble I got into, she would be here, whenever I needed her."

"When any of us needed her."

They sighed.

"I wonder how old you have to be before you stop being your mother's daughter," Lilith murmured.

Savannah had been wondering that same thing herself lately. "I don't think you ever do." She paused, then decided that since burying her feelings deep inside her to keep the peace had definitely proven harmful, she'd be straight with her mother now.

"When I first came home, I think there was a part of me, a part I was afraid to admit even to myself, who blamed you for everything that had gone wrong in my life."

"Well, of course you did."

"You knew?"

"You don't have to look so surprised. My own life may have been a disaster for years, but that doesn't mean that I couldn't recognize when my daughters were making mistakes. It was obvious that in your own individual ways, both you and Raine were struggling to be the opposite of me."

Her faint smile seemed to be directed inward. "Raine, of course, is the most like me. I was five when your grandmother divorced my father. That hurt me more than I think Ida realized at the time, but I've recently come to the conclusion that I wasted a great many years desperate for men to find me attractive, to make up for the loss of my father."

"You *are* attractive," Savannah pointed out. "And Raine has never depended on her looks."

But she could have. The funny thing was, her sister had never realized how lovely she was. Determined to be admired for her mind, Raine had set her feet firmly on her legal career path and hadn't allowed herself so much as a sideways glance until she'd come home to Coldwater Cove and fallen in love with Jack.

"Owen Cantrell was the most brilliant, egocentric, ruthless man I've ever met," Lilith revealed. "I've no doubt that his being an attorney is one of the reasons Raine chose law as a profession. As she grew older, it was obvious that she was trying to win her absent father's approval—and love—by being equally ruthless."

As much as she loved her sister, Savannah decided that that unflattering observation made some sense. "But Reggie isn't anything like Owen Cantrell. I've never doubted that my father loves me. In his own way."

The same way a two-year-old loves a shiny new toy. When it came to penning lyrics that the rebels and wannabe rebels of the world could identify with, Savannah suspected that Reggie Townsend was as brilliant as Raine's famous defense attorney father. But Reggie's attention span was incredibly short, and he'd never demonstrated an ability for long-term commitment.

She had not a single doubt that if there ever came a moment when performing in front of adoring crowds no longer gave him a rush, a moment when music wasn't fun anymore, her father would hang up his electric guitar without a backward glance.

"Reggie's my favorite ex-husband, but he's certainly been no model of stability for you, darling. Why, he's been married more times than I have. It's only understandable that you were trying so hard not to repeat your parents' serial marriages, you willingly blinded yourself to your own husband's lack of decency."

It was the same conclusion Savannah had come to. The same one she'd shared with Dan atop the Ferris wheel. But accustomed to her beautiful, willful mother's life-long disregard for the consequences of her actions, she was surprised by Lilith's uncharacteristic insight.

"When did you get so smart?"

Lilith laughed the trademark crystal laugh that had been as popular with movie-going fans as her screams. "What a polite, Savannah-like way of asking when I started to grow up." She lifted a fond hand and smoothed Savannah's hair back over her shoulder. "I've discovered that wisdom—the little I've acquired at any rate—is one of the few advantages of turning fifty."

How strange, Savannah thought, that such a light maternal touch could cause an easing of the tension that had practically twisted her into knots during the long stressful day at the hospital.

"I love you," she said on a burst of heartfelt emotion.

"I love you, too, darling." Lilith's voice turned husky. "And I do so want for you to be happy. As happy as I am. As your sister is."

They were sharing a mother-daughter hug when Dan's Tahoe pulled up in front of the house. He and Henry emerged, the older man carrying two red-and-white pizza boxes.

"How did things go?" Dan asked.

Once again, as she had with Gwen, Savannah shared the condensed version of the doctor's diagnosis.

"Could have been worse," Henry volunteered. "I know lots of folks who've had TIAs and never had a major stroke."

Savannah wanted to find comfort in his words, yet couldn't help thinking that a great many of those people could well be patients at Evergreen.

"It's tough." Dan sat down beside her, untangled her hands, which she was unconsciously twisting together in her lap, and linked his fingers with hers. "But Ida's a tough old bird. My money's on her."

"Mine, too." Lilith, who had been watching them with open maternal interest, stood up. "I've been meaning to talk with Gwen about a new school wardrobe. Obviously she can't wear last year's maternity clothes."

Gracing both Savannah and Dan with a satisfied, almost feline smile, she deftly shepherded Henry into the house.

"My mother," Savannah said wryly, as she retrieved her hand, "has never been known for her subtlety."

"I can't imagine her any other way. She's one of a kind. Like her daughter." He leaned over and sniffed at her neck. "Thank you."

She pulled back just far enough to look up at him. "For what?"

"For smelling so damn good." He combed his fingers through the long waves Lilith had smoothed earlier. "Do you know, it's gotten so I wake up imagining your perfume on my pillow?"

So he'd been dreaming of her, too. "It's undoubtedly pollen," she said mildly. "Perhaps you should start closing your window at night."

Dan reluctantly decided against suggesting that perhaps she ought to just start spending the night in his bed so he could wake up with the real thing instead of some lingering remnants of the dreams that had him starting each morning with a cold shower.

"Now there's an idea."

Because it had been too long since he'd kissed her, because he'd been thinking of little else all day, he touched his mouth to hers, encouraged when her arms lifted and wrapped around his neck.

Her lips heated. Clung. Then parted to allow him to deepen the kiss. Which he did.

A nagging voice in the back of his mind was trying to send a warning to his body that the house behind them was full of people who could, at any minute, decide to come out on the porch.

As a woman of the world who could undoubtedly recognize sexual undercurrents, Lilith wouldn't. But Gwen was a teenager, so impulsiveness was a given, and while Henry had actually been behaving like a human being lately, it was not unthinkable that he'd come outside just for the sheer pleasure of screwing up the moment.

As for Ida, she'd managed to put the fear of God into the entire male population of Coldwater Cove High. Every boy in school had known that getting caught going beyond first base with either Raine or Savannah was a sure-fire way to make your life a misery.

Obviously she wouldn't expect her divorced granddaughter to still be a virgin, but Dan suspected the contrary female wouldn't hesitate to make her displeasure known if she thought for a moment that he might be taking advantage of the recent upheavals in Savannah's life.

Which he wasn't. But damn, how he wanted her. Dan knew he was in deep, deep trouble when even the prospect of Ida Lindstrom's ire didn't do a thing to lesson the hunger that had him in a vice grip.

Reluctantly relinquishing her lips, he settled for skimming his mouth along the fragrant skin just beneath her slender jaw. "Lord, you taste good." Down the line of her throat. "Even better than you smell."

Dan might be a little uncertain about all his feelings where this woman was concerned, but he knew damn well that he was too old to be making out on Savannah Townsend's front porch.

"Come home with me, Savannah." She hitched in a breath as he touched his mouth to the hollow of her throat and felt her pulse leap. "I want you."

"I know." She briefly closed her eyes. When she opened them again, they gleamed with arousal in the gloaming. "I want you, too." Dan watched as that arousal was slowly replaced by regret and knew that she wasn't ready. Not yet.

"But?"

"It's too soon. While I admittedly haven't gone out with a man for years, I have the feeling that I'm not the kind of woman who goes to bed on the first date."

She smiled, a slight, tentative smile that still had enough warmth to knock him back on his heels if he hadn't already been sitting down. "Which we haven't even had yet."

"Objection sustained." He ran his hand over her shoulder, which today was clad in a black silk that brought out the fire in her hair. As soft as the silk was, Dan suspected that her skin would be a great deal softer.

"I've been remiss."

His hand continued down her bare arm. The night was getting cool. If she wasn't going to allow him to take her somewhere private and warm her all over, he was going to have to let her go into the house.

"How about coming sailing with me tomorrow evening?" he asked. "It'll give me something to look forward to while I'm in court all day battling for my client's custody of a batch of frozen bull sperm."

"You are kidding."

"Hey, it's not exactly on a par with fighting for truth, justice and the American Way. But the sperm in question just happens to belong to a champion rodeo bull owned by a syndicate that went bust when the members decided to branch out and invest in Thoroughbreds. A couple test tubes of that stuff would probably have paid for your new roof."

"What an appealing thought," she murmured. "But I'll be wallpapering the kitchen of the assistant keeper's house tomorrow evening."

Still drawn by her scent, he leaned closer again and nibbled on her earlobe. "No, you won't."

She stiffened in his arms. Then drew back. "Excuse me?"

The fire had turned to ice. Dan had already discovered enough of what pleasured Savannah to know he could melt it. "You're not wallpapering the kitchen because it's already done."

She folded her arms and gave him an accusing look that wasn't quite the display of gratitude he'd been hoping for. "Are you telling me that you hung my wallpaper?"

Hell. She definitely was not pleased.

"I knew your schedule was tight enough that losing today would cost you, so I thought I'd give you a hand."

"Didn't you have any law work to do?"

"The nice thing about being your own boss is you can give yourself an afternoon off from time to time. Besides, I had help, so it didn't take that long."

He watched the awareness dawn. "That's where Henry was?"

"The guy's got a real talent with a paste brush, which was fortunate since, left to my own devices, I would undoubtedly still be there, turning the air blue with my curses.

"Hanging wallpaper," he said dryly, "is not quite the snap they make it out to be on that video at Olson's hardware store."

"I appreciate the help," she allowed. A bit reluctantly, Dan thought. "But I don't need it."

"There's such a thing as being too independent, sweetheart." He took hold of her hand. When she'd first returned home, her palms had been smooth. The row of calluses were mute evidence of how hard she'd been working all these weeks. Yet as much as he admired her determination to toughen up and handle everything by herself, there were limits. "All of us can use a little help from time to time."

She seemed to be processing that suggestion as she looked out over the town. Warm yellow lights curved around the cove, reminding Dan of the train layout he'd earned a Boy Scout merit badge for building back in the sixth grade. The breeze from the water was rustling the leaves in the trees.

"Besides," he reminded her quietly, "Henry's part owner of the lighthouse. He jumped at the chance to work on his old home."

"Oh. Of course he would want to be involved. I should have thought of that."

"You've had a lot on your mind lately."

Her soft sigh confirmed that statement.

"I apologize if I overstepped my bounds, Savannah." He brushed a kiss against her knuckles. "If I promise to never lift a hand to help you again, will you come sailing with me?"

She laughed lightly, as he'd meant her to, then turned back to him, her eyes meeting his. "I may have overreacted, just a bit. . . . Thank you."

"It was my pleasure. So, is that a yes?"

This time her sigh was one of surrender. But the warmth that had returned to her eyes revealed that it wasn't a reluctant one. "Yes."

Having been born in Coldwater Cove, Dan had grown up on the water. But he couldn't remember ever enjoying an afternoon more than this one. Just the sight of Savannah—her face lifted to the sun, her hair blowing in the breeze like a gold and bronze flag—was enough to take his breath away.

But it was more than the fact that she reminded him of some mythical mermaid. It was the ease with which she laughed and talked with him. They'd stopped at the house so she could check on her grandmother, who'd complained about the way everyone was fussing over her lately. During the brief stop, Savannah had run upstairs to admire the new clothes Lilith and Gwen had brought home from the Dancing Deer Dress Shoppe, leaving him to dodge some pointed questions about his intentions that had Dan thinking that Ida would have made one helluva prosecutor.

He was in his thirties, successful, and, he liked to think, a pretty good catch for the right woman. Yet Savannah's grandmother had managed to send the clock reeling backwards in a way that had him feeling like a hormone-driven, sweaty-palmed seventeen-year-old promising to bring Savannah straight home after their date. And no speeding.

Now, as he maneuvered the skiff over the water, enjoying the sound of her laughter, the way the wind and sun brought color into her high cheekbones, Dan decided that the brief discomfort spent undergoing Ida's cross-examination had been worth it.

He was also considering sailing away with Savannah to some faraway island where they could spend their days basking in the sunshine on spun-sugar beaches and their nights making mad, passionate love.

Jack and Raine had gone to Bora Bora for their honeymoon, and both had waxed so enthusiastic about the South Seas island, he was tempted to try it out for himself.

"Something funny?" she asked, making him realize that he'd laughed out loud at the fanciful idea of the two of them sailing off into the sunset.

"I was just wondering how far it is to Tahiti."

"I have no idea. But I suspect it's a bit far for a first date."

"Next time, then."

Rather than point out that the idea was ridiculously impractical, Savannah smiled. "Perhaps."

It was, Dan told himself, enough for now.

16

As the air became crisper and the leaves began to turn colors, Savannah's days fell into a predictable, yet enjoyable routine.

She'd get up early every morning so she could cook breakfast for the family. Cold cereal might be fine for summer vacation, but she was determined to send Gwen off to school properly fortified. She also took the time to observe Ida closely, watching for any additional signs of TIAs, but other than her usual malapropisms, her grandmother seemed as mentally sharp as ever. What she insisted on referring to as her "spells" when she would discuss them, which was hardly ever, seemed to have passed.

Days were spent at the lighthouse, which, thanks to part-time help from Dan, Henry, and John—who'd constructed a greenhouse on the grounds to supply her with fresh flowers—was coming closer to being completed with each passing day. Optimistic enough to believe that she would actually make her scheduled holiday opening, she'd placed ads in a few magazines and had brochures printed up which she'd sent out to travel agencies.

Things were definitely looking up.

Savannah was determined to never again define herself by a relationship, but she couldn't deny that she'd be hard pressed to find a better relationship than the one she had with Dan.

He was smart, funny, sexy, and, best of all, he thought she was all those things, too. He didn't expect her to be some starry-eyed young girl afraid to speak her mind. He didn't even seem to expect her to look like a model all the time, which was a good thing since her nails were a disaster, her hair was in dire need of a trim, and there had been more than one occasion when, pressed for time, she'd actually taken jeans straight from the dryer and put them on without bothering to first starch and iron them.

Just last week Raine, who'd dropped by the lighthouse to see the progress, had marveled that even after a day spent cleaning sticky labels off acres of new window glass, her little sister was still fashion magazine material. Savannah, of course, knew otherwise. In what she'd come to realize was her own version of her sister's attempt to be the perfect New York attorney, she'd spent a great many years *looking* perfect. It had always been an important part of her image. Her identity. It had also been exhausting.

She may be all too aware of her loosening

standards, but amazingly, Dan seemed to believe she was beautiful however she looked. Even that day she'd forgotten to wear a cap while painting the ceiling and ended up with Glacier White paint spatters in her hair.

Not only did he spend every weekend working on the lighthouse with her, as her project progressed Savannah discovered she could talk with him about anything. And everything.

He didn't think she was whining when she complained that the new flashing those outrageously expensive roofers had installed around one of the chimneys had ripped off during an early autumn storm, causing rain damage inside the house. She'd ended up having to restain a section of floor, which wasn't as bad as it might have been, since they did it together on a Saturday.

He assured her that she wasn't being overly critical when the faucets for the assistant keeper's bathroom arrived in chrome, rather than the antique brass she'd ordered. And when the plumber did not show up as promised to install the Jacuzzi tub in the bathroom she'd built beneath the stairs leading to the lantern room— which she'd turned into a bedroom with a stunning 360-degree view—he'd written a terse legal letter that had encouraged the man to quickly finish the job.

They continued to spend nearly every evening together, at easy outings for which she didn't even have to dress up: barbecue at Oley's, sails on the sound, eating ice cream cones while they watched the ferry dock and the tourists—

not as many now that Labor Day had come and gone—disembark.

While not a professional chef, he had, on more than one occasion, fixed dinner. She'd never had a man cook for her before, but that first night, as she'd sipped a crisp Blue Mountain chardonnay while he whipped up a platter of Dungeness crab cakes, grilled corn, and crisp green salad, Savannah decided that the experience came pretty close to heaven.

Since the chemistry between them was as strong as ever, stronger since they'd been practicing such strict self-denial, their relationship wasn't totally platonic. Savannah loved to kiss him, adored the flex of his back muscles beneath her fingertips and reveled in the way he touched her in return.

She knew he wanted her. He told her that again and again with his lips, his hands, the rigid power of his erection that would press against her stomach as they made out like two frustrated teenagers on his wide suede couch. With each day that passed, she wanted Dan more, too.

But she had discovered that there was a difference between attraction and commitment. Having grown up watching marriage promises get ripped to pieces, Savannah had vowed that when she got married, it would be forever. Of course it hadn't been, or she wouldn't even be thinking about making love with Dan O'Halloran—which was something she thought about too much lately.

Since her divorce she'd made a new vow:

there would be no more broken promises. To get naked with Dan could risk new cracks in a heart that had only recently mended.

Not that she believed he'd hurt her deliberately. He was the most natural, genuinely caring man she'd ever met. Dan O'Halloran was probably as close as she'd ever find to the perfect man. The kind of man a woman could imagine spending the rest of her life with.

If she were looking for a man to spend the rest of her life with. Which, of course, she wasn't.

"I've made a decision," Ida said.

Savannah was working on her menu plan. Thanksgiving was three weeks away, and she was sitting at the kitchen table, planning the menu. Raine had offered to have the family dinner at the farm, but since her sister's culinary talents generally involved nuking meals in the microwave or heating up takeout, despite her desire to move into the lighthouse before the holiday weekend, Savannah had insisted on preparing the meal here at the house.

She did, after all, have a great deal to be thankful for this year.

"What decision is that, Gram?" she asked absently, trying to decide between chestnut and oyster dressing.

On the other hand, perhaps Amy would prefer sausage or cornbread. Maybe she could make all four, baking them in separate pans. The problem with that idea was that Ida's old oven was definitely not as spacious as the state-of-the-art commercial one she'd installed in the lighthouse.

"I want to adopt Gwen."

That got Savannah's attention. She put her pen down and looked up at her grandmother. "What?"

"I said, I want to adopt Gwen."

"Why?"

"To make her part of the family, of course."

"She's already part of the family."

"Not legally." Ignoring Dr. Burke's warning about caffeine intake, Ida poured herself her third cup of coffee of the day and sat down at the table. "She's still underage. There's not a single thing to keep Old Fussbudget from showing up at the house and taking her away from us."

Old Fussbudget, Savannah knew, was Gwen's probation officer.

"Gwen's behavior has been exemplary. She's back at the top of her class, and unless something drastic happens, she looks to be a shoo-in for valedictorian."

"The girl's always gotten good grades, which is amazing when you consider what she's been through."

"Perhaps school was a refuge."

"That's the way I always saw it," Ida agreed. "But you know how screwed up Social Services can be. They don't seem to care about grades, or the fact that she's always made honor roll, even the semester she had the baby. They've still put her in more foster homes than Carters has Pilgrims."

Her eyes were flint, her jaw jutted out in a

way Savannah recognized all too well. When her grandmother set her mind to something, you had three choices: give in, get out of the way, or get run over.

"Have you discussed this with Raine?"

"Not yet. But Raine's family. I figured it'd look better if we had some other lawyer take care of it for us."

Savannah knew exactly what other lawyer she was referring to. "Have you mentioned this adoption plan to Gwen?"

"Of course not. I didn't want to get the girl's hopes up. I figured I'd let Dan get all the initial paperwork done, then I'll surprise her with the news on Thanksgiving Day."

Savannah had no doubt that the teenager would be thrilled. There was, however, one possible major stumbling block to the plan. "I hate to bring this up, but what about your age?"

"What about it?"

She could have been trying to cross a minefield. "Well, you're a bit older than most adoptive parents," she said carefully.

"You surprise me, Savannah. Of all my family, I never thought you'd be one to throw cold water on my parade."

"I wasn't—"

"Fine." Ida stood up. "Then you'll ask Dan to get started with the necessary paperwork."

"Why can't you do that?"

"Because he'll probably have a whole laundry list of reasons why it's impractical and why Social Services is going to balk at the idea and why I might want to consider slowing down instead of taking on the responsibility of a teenager in my early seventies."

Make that her *late* seventies. "There's nothing wrong with slowing down a bit." Savannah would dearly love to do exactly that. For just one day.

"Some old ladies might be content spending all their time knitting or playing bingo. But I'm like a salamander. If I don't keep going forward, I die.

"So," Ida finished up, "since I have no intention of wasting time arguing with a man whose butt I spanked when I brought him into this world, I figure you can be the one to ask him. Seems he'll do just about anything for you these days."

That stated, Ida left the room on a step that was, Savannah had to admit, pretty lively for a woman pushing eighty.

"Ida's age might not be a problem to her," Dan said two days later. They were at his house, where he was cooking dinner again. "But unfortunately, from what I could determine from my conversation with Old Fussbudget today, it is to Social Services. If Gwen were only older—"

"If she were older, she'd legally be an adult and wouldn't need to be adopted to protect her interests in the first place," Savannah pointed out.

"If the law were logical, the world wouldn't need lawyers." He poured two glasses of wine and handed one to her.

"I know. But there must be something we can do."

"I checked over the guardianship papers. They're pretty tightly written. There would have to be an extremely compelling reason for Old Fussbudget and her minions to pull Gwen from Ida's home, especially since she's only got a few months to go until she turns eighteen."

"Six," Savannah said. "A lot can happen in six months." Wasn't she living proof of that?

"An alternative idea occurred to me while I was shaving this morning. We could get her declared an emancipated minor."

"Can you do that?"

He grinned. "Piece of cake. As long as she keeps out of trouble," he qualified.

"If she dares shoplift again, I'll personally kill her for upsetting Gram."

"Well, that would certainly take care of the custody issue. Though I have to admit, sweetheart, the idea of trying to kiss you through a set of prison bars isn't all that appealing."

She laughed, then moved over to the glass wall and looked out at the rising harvest moon that was splashing a coppery sheen over the wine-dark water.

"Every time I come here, I feel as if I've just stepped onto the bridge of the starship *Enterprise*," she murmured. As magnificent as Dan's house was from outside, the inside was even more stunning. The ceiling soared at least fifteen feet overhead, and a two-story stone fireplace took up nearly an entire wall. "Or the *Millennium Falcon*. Just before it went into warp speed."

He came up behind her. "Believe me, sweetheart, when I finally talk you into my bed, I'm going to do my best to keep the pace a bit slower than that."

"Promises, promises," she laughed lightly as she leaned back against him.

"So, what's my surprise?" He nuzzled her neck.

"Surprise?" The touch of his mouth on her skin was enough to wipe her mind as clear as the glass window.

"When I came by the lighthouse to pick you up this evening, you told me you had a surprise for me."

"Oh. I do." The brief discussion about Ida had made her forget. He murmured a protest when she slipped out of his light embrace and retrieved her purse.

" 'Lucy Hyatt's Far Harbor Adventure, Volume Two,' " he read aloud from the cover of the small notebook. "Where did you find this?"

"In the attic of the keeper's house. I was putting some storage boxes up there when I noticed that the chimney looked strange. I pulled out a couple loose bricks, and there it was."

"The lady certainly did work hard at hiding her journals," he mused. "So, are there any juicy parts in it?"

"I don't know. I wanted to save it to read with you."

His wineglass paused on the way to his mouth. Something flickered in his eyes. "I think I'll take that as a compliment."

"It was meant as one," she said as they settled down on the couch.

" 'The journey to Washington was even more thrilling than I could possibly have imagined,' " Savannah began to read, trying to keep her mind off the fact that they were in the very same spot where they'd driven each other to distraction only last night.

" 'The snow-capped Rocky Mountains were spectacular. When the train reached the top of its climb before going down the other side, the clouds cleared, revealing meadows ablaze with wildflowers as far as the eye could see, and crystal streams flowing from ancient glaciers. I felt as though I'd been granted a glimpse of Paradise. Indeed, had not I not been so eager to meet my husband-to-be, I would have been more than happy to spend eternity in that heavenly place.' "

"The Rockies have their appeal. But I'll still take the Olympics any day," Dan decided.

"Me, too." It crossed Savannah's mind that of all the places she'd lived over the world, this was the only one that had ever felt like home.

" 'Coldwater Cove, while not as breathtaking as the Rockies, proved every bit as charming as Harlan had described it,' " she continued. " 'While his letters had suggested that he was not a man prone to embellishment or untruths, as Hannah had reminded me on a daily basis, it's not unusual for a man to prevaricate.' "

"I wonder if Hannah's speaking from personal experience."

"She's a woman. My guess would be yes."

Dan didn't comment, but instead picked up reading the story.

" 'During the trip westward, the train passed through a number of small towns—some barely more than rough outposts—and in truth, there were times I feared that my destination may turn out to be equally rustic. But when I viewed the town, I was momentarily confused and wondered if the train had changed direction during the night and somehow ended up in New England.

" 'The buildings on the main street—Harbor Street, I was later to learn—are of substantial red brick that gives the impression that this town will not soon blow away, like the eerie, sad ghost towns I'd seen throughout Colorado and eastern Oregon and Washington. If buildings could make a statement, these are saying that Coldwater Cove is here to stay.' "

"She was right," Savannah said, thinking of her lighthouse.

"Absolutely. 'Wooden sidewalks line Harbor Street, which, despite being dirt, is remarkably unrutted. Huge houses, suggesting prosperity, line the top of the cliff which overlooks the Cove.' She's talking about your grandmother's house."

"I think so." Savannah had never thought of her grandmother's Victorian as a symbol of prosperity. To her it had always represented a haven.

" 'A grassy green square is the centerpiece of the town, the new bright red brick tower rising like a beacon; the clock face on each of the compass points can be seen for miles.

" 'Standing guard over all is the Far Harbor Lighthouse. *Harlan's lighthouse,* I thought to myself as I viewed the glorious white structure gleaming like marble in the midday sun. *My lighthouse.*' "

Dan smiled down at Savannah. "Your lighthouse now."

She smiled back. Their eyes met. And held.

"Savannah . . ."

He pulled her close and fastened his mouth on hers, the kiss so mindblinding that Savannah nearly dropped her glass.

"If you keep that up," she said after they'd come up for air, "you're going to have wine all over your clothes."

"I was hoping, if I keep it up a bit longer, we'll both end up naked and it won't matter." He skimmed a finger along her shoulder.

"Think about it, Savannah." The treacherous touch continued downward, causing a giddy pleasure to bloom beneath her hand-painted sweatshirt depicting a row of Coldwater Cove's famous Victorians. "You spill your wine on me." Needs she'd been fighting for weeks coiled inside her as his fingertip swirled around her nipple.

"Then I'll spill mine on you." His stroking hand moved to her other breast, treating it to a torture every bit as sublime. Her head reeled. "Then I'll lick it off." Her body throbbed. "Every last drop."

"I knew I should have taken time for lunch." Her complaint was wrenched on a husky, ragged moan she could barely recognize as her own voice. "One glass of wine and my head's spinning."

"That's a start."

His bold grin promised wicked delights. He put his glass on the pine coffee table with deliberate slowness, giving her time to back away, as she had on past nights. When she didn't move, he took her glass from her nerveless fingers and placed it beside his.

"Let's see if we can make the rest of you spin."

Since he was already doing a pretty good job of that, Savannah didn't, couldn't, respond. But her eyes gave him her answer.

Dan exhaled a deep breath. Then stood up, scooped her off the couch, and carried her across the room and up the stairs to the loft.

17

Dan put her down beside the bed, then paused to light the fire he'd set in the stone fireplace before leaving for work.

And then he was back, standing in front of her.

"I want to do this right." He brushed her hair back from her face, his touch as hot as his eyes. "Tell me what you want me to do to you. . . . With you."

"Anything." Her breath was ragged. Savannah didn't even attempt to control it. "Everything."

It was as if her words had opened a dam, releasing a torrent of passion too long denied. He dragged her down onto the bed. Savannah went willingly. Eagerly.

Her sweatshirt was ripped over her head and sent flying across the room. Her jeans were dragged down her legs. Her own hands were no less urgent. She tore at his shirt; buttons scattered across the wood floor as she yanked it off

him, exposing a rock-hard chest that gleamed
like polished teak in the flickering light.

He turned her in his arms, braceleted her
wrists in one hand and held them over her head.
Having invited this, having dreamed of it, hot
erotic dreams that had her waking up unfulfilled
amid tangled sheets, Savannah closed her eyes,
hung on tightly and followed him into the flames.

His mouth was everywhere, relentlessly nip-
ping and licking and sucking. Savaging her.
Thrilling her. His teeth scraped against first one
taut nipple, then the other, creating tremors of
delicious excitement to ripple beneath her hot
skin. His tongue stroked a trail of sparks up the
moist flesh of her inner thigh, drawing a primal
sound from deep in her throat.

Springs creaked. The fire hissed and crack-
led. The air grew as thick and steamy as the
Olympic rain forest in summer.

His fingers tangled in the downy curls between her thighs. When his warm breath ruffled them, Savannah went hot and cold at the
same time, like a woman in the grip of a fever.
He parted the swollen pink flesh.

More physically needy that she'd ever been in
her life, Savannah drew in a deep, shuddering
breath and bent her leg.

He lifted his head. "Open your eyes, Savannah."

She forced open lids that had turned unreasonably heavy and found herself looking up
into eyes that gleamed like molten cobalt in
the flickering glow. There was a warrior's
fierceness to his face that might have fright-

ened her had she not already experienced his tenderness.

He smiled and the warrior turned to rogue. "Beautiful."

Then he was kissing her hard and deep, the same way he'd kissed her mouth, but then he'd merely stolen her breath. Now he was stealing her sanity.

Coherent thought disintegrated as his greedy tongue invaded the giving folds of her body, seeking intimate secrets while his teeth toyed with the ultrasensitive nub, creating a need so sharp Savannah feared she'd surely shatter.

Her stomach grew taut, her thighs tensed, a flush spread over her breasts. A final flick of his tongue caused her body to explode in a violent, dizzying release.

But still he wouldn't stop.

"I can't," she gasped as he began to drive her up again.

"You can." His clever, wicked touch was making her mad. "*We* can."

And they did. Again and again, until her body hummed from a thousand erratic pulses and his lips were wet with her orgasms.

And still it wasn't enough. Needing to touch him as he'd touched her, wanting to make him feel that same need that had escalated to a pleasure just this side of pain, Savannah pulled her hands free.

They fretted over him. Her ragged fingernails dug into his skin. It was hot and slick and moist.

"I want you." She returned her mouth to his. "All of you." She tasted herself on his lips. Desire flared. Hotter, higher. "Inside of me."

"Thank God." His voice was rough and tortured. He cursed beneath his breath as he drew away long enough to yank open the drawer of the bedside table and retrieve a condom. "Remind me to plan this better next time."

Then he was kneeling between her thighs. With his gaze on hers, he lifted her hips and slid smoothly, gloriously into her.

Breathing a shimmering sigh of pleasure, Savannah wrapped her legs tighter around his hips and began to move with him, instinctively knowing his rhythm as if they'd made love a hundred, a thousand times before.

She would not have thought it possible, but soon, amazingly, it was coming again, that hot, sharp, spiraling pressure, the wetness, the shattering spasm of release.

Outside, a swift autumn squall had raced in over the mountain tops from the sea. The wind moaned. A hard rain pelted the windows like a shower of stones. The crimson moon rose. Inside, lost in a storm of their own making, Dan and Savannah surrendered to the darkness.

Afterwards, they lay together, in a tangle of arms and legs, cocooned as the rain streaked down the windows.

"Are we alive?" Savannah asked finally.

"I don't know." He touched his mouth to her breast, his lips warm against her cooling flesh. "Your heart's beating."

"That's a relief." She cuddled closer and did the same to him. "So's yours."

"Yeah." Dan skimmed a hand down her damp hair, all the way to her hip, then back up again. "I figure it should be back to a normal rate sometime in the next century. . . . Christ, you're unbelievable," he managed with what little breath he had left.

"I'm having a little trouble believing it myself."

He rolled over to face her, taking her with him, viewed the wonder in her still slightly unfocused gaze and felt a surge of chauvinistic male satisfaction for having put it there.

"I never felt that way before. I never realized it was possible to feel that way." She lifted a hand to his cheek.

"It's us," he said as he curled his fingers around her wrist and brought her hand to his lips. "You and I together."

He kissed each fingertip, one at a time, and watched the renewed desire warm those incredible green eyes. Dan was considering the possibilities of going for a personal best when his stomach growled, reminding him of other physical hungers.

"As much as I'd like to keep you in bed forever, I did promise you dinner."

"I suppose we should keep our strength up. Since I have a vested interest in your stamina."

"Sweetheart, the day you have to worry about my stamina where you're concerned is the day they stick me in the ground." He kissed her hard, savoring her taste in a way that almost had him deciding to forgo food.

He was given a tantalizing view of a sweetly curved bottom when she leaned down and retrieved her sweatshirt. "You won't be needing this." He plucked it from her hand and tossed it aside.

"Daniel!" she complained as the sweatshirt hit a chair across the room and slid back to the floor. "You can't expect me to eat dinner naked."

"Sure I do." He yanked on his jeans and a chambray shirt he didn't bother to button. "As a chef yourself, you undoubtedly know that dazzling scenery can improve any meal."

"I can't do it." He nearly laughed when she actually crossed her arms over her breasts. It was a little late for modesty, since he'd already seen—and tasted—just about every fragrant inch of that lush body. "I *won't* do it."

Dan had not a single doubt that if he pulled out his persuasive powers, he could change her mind, but reluctantly decided that the fantasy of Savannah perched naked across the table from him, looking like some mermaid who'd washed up on his beach, was yet one more thing to look forward to.

Which was why, minutes later, clad in the sweatshirt and a piece of lace too skimpy to be properly considered underwear, she was sitting on a kitchen stool, long legs crossed, sipping on the wine as she resumed reading Lucy's journal where they'd left off.

" 'Even after all this time, and all these miles,

the idea of what I'd done still seemed incredible,' " she read while Dan started a pot of rice steaming. " 'It was almost as if I'd been dreaming. But if I were, as I drank in the welcoming sight of the town that appeared to be as neat and tidy as a Swedish kitchen, I never wanted to awaken.

" 'Harlan was waiting on the platform, as promised. His photograph, while portraying a handsome man, had not begun to do him justice. He is tall, with shoulders the breadth of ax handles, and possesses a thick shock of dark hair. His jaw is firm, and the strong planes of his face appear to have been chiseled from granite. His size and strong features would give him a forbidding appearance were it not for his smile and his incredible eyes.' "

"I think she likes him," Dan said as he retrieved a white waxed-paper bundle of shrimp from the refrigerator.

"It seems so," Savannah agreed. "Which is fortunate, since it doesn't sound like turning around and going back home was an option." She turned the page and continued.

" 'How shall I even attempt to describe Harlan Hyatt's eyes? They reminded me of hot chocolate—warm and dark and smooth. As I stared up at him, two thoughts crossed my mind simultaneously. How could this man still be unmarried at the age of thirty? And what had I done right in my life to be gifted with such a husband?

" 'I know I'm no beauty. Hannah, who was gifted with our mother's looks and our father's manner of plain speaking, has certainly pointed out that unpalatable fact on more than one occasion. Yet, amazingly, Harlan seemed as mesmerized by my appearance, as rumpled and road weary as it admittedly was.

" 'For a long, suspended moment he stared down at me, his expressive dark eyes looking hard and deep, as if he could see all the way into my soul, and perhaps my heart, which was now pounding as furiously as a drum.' "

"Bingo." Dan began chopping mushrooms, scallions, and red bell pepper with a dexterity that, having firsthand experience of his clever hands, no longer surprised her. "Looks as if it's mutual."

"Yet just a few years later, she was supposedly running away on the day that she drowned." Savannah frowned as she took a sip of wine. "I wonder what happened."

"Keep reading and maybe we'll find out."

Savannah shook her head and sighed as she thought about lost dreams. " 'His first words were not poetic. Indeed, they were more than a little prosaic. "Welcome to Coldwater Cove," he said in a smooth, deep voice that wrapped around me like a velvet cape, embracing me in its warmth. On the spot, I decided that this man didn't need pretty words.

" ' "I'm pleased to finally be here," I responded with equal formality.

" 'We fell silent, studying each other. Finally, when my nerves were stretched as taut as a piano wire, I glanced down at the wildflowers he was holding in one huge fist and asked if they were for me.' "

Dan grinned over his shoulder at Savannah as he dumped the vegetables into a copper-bottomed pan with some grated ginger. "A man of excellent tastes."

Savannah smiled back, remembering the wildflowers he'd given her the night of the Sawdust Festival, then returned to Lucy's journal.

" 'He practically shoved them into my hand. I found the embarrassed flush rising from his collar immensely endearing and assured him that no bride could ever wish for a more beautiful bouquet.

" 'For some reason my words made him frown. "I'd hoped to marry you the moment you stepped off the train, but it seems that there's a problem," he said. The heavy regret in his tone caused my heart to take a steep and perilous dip.'

"Uh oh," Savannah murmured.

Dan topped off her wineglass. "Don't stop now."

Even knowing that they had married, Savannah was suddenly as tense as Lucy must have been at that moment.

" 'My mind spun with reasons for the frown darkening his face. I knew I'd never return home. There was no way I'd endure listening to Hannah saying "I told you so" for the rest of my life.' "

"Hannah sounds like a real gem." Dan tossed the shrimp into the pan and splashed in soy sauce.

"Not everyone is fortunate to have a sister like Raine." Savannah turned another page.

" ' "Unfortunately," he revealed, "the good citizens of Coldwater Cove won't allow it."

" ' "Oh?" I asked with very real trepidation. My heart had now sunk down to my toes.

" ' "We're a small, close community," he explained. "A wedding is a very special occasion, and the townspeople are not going to be denied their chance to give you a party." As if they'd been actors, awaiting their cue, the people who were gathered on the platform came forward.

" 'As Harlan introduced his many friends, I was greeted with such great enthusiasm that I found myself looking forward to the festivities and the wedding Harlan informed me would take place the following day at the lighthouse. But most of all, I looked forward to the rest of my life with my husband.'

"Damn," Savannah murmured as she turned the final page. "That's all there is."

"There's got to be at least another diary somewhere." The shrimp had turned pink. He stirred in some pineapple chunks, then spooned the mixture atop a mound of rice.

"Unless she stopped keeping a journal once she got married."

"I'm going to be really disappointed if she did. It's like a cliffhanger without the final reel."

They moved to the nearby table.

"I wonder, if Lucy had known how tragically her romance—and her life—would end, if she would have gotten on that train in Farmersburg," Savannah considered.

"From what we've read so far, I'd guess that

she wouldn't have hesitated. Love is always a gamble," Dan said. "Sometimes you get lucky and the reward turns out to be worth the risk."

From the way his expression had turned serious, Savannah had the uneasy feeling that Dan was no longer talking about Lucy and Harlan.

After dinner, Dan lit another fire in the downstairs grate and they settled back on the sofa.

"This truly is the most stunning place," she murmured.

The swift storm had already moved on toward Seattle. The rain had stopped, washing the star-spangled sky outside the glass wall as clear as crystal.

Savannah drew in a breath as a falling star crashed down to earth in a shimmering silver trail. "I think I could just stay here, like this, forever."

"Why don't you?" Dan's tone was casual; his question was not.

She looked up at him, her eyes wide and, he thought, more than a little wary in the firelight. "I didn't mean . . . just because we had sex—"

"We made love." Strange how saying the words out loud made Dan realize they were absolutely true. "It may not have been in the plans, but you can't deny that's what happened."

"It's not that easy."

She did not, he noticed, argue the major point—that they'd shared a helluva lot more than their bodies. "Perhaps you're making it more difficult than it is," he suggested mildly.

"I explained to you how I've spent a lifetime

watching my mother jump in and out of relationships. I've seen the harm it can cause to everyone."

"Granted. And while this isn't about Lilith, I can't see her leaving Cooper."

"No," Savannah allowed. She stared out into the well of darkness. "I believe her when she says that Cooper's her soul mate."

"So, extrapolating from that, a reasonable person might suggest that when a person finds the right partner—her soul mate—she ought to just grab her chance at happiness. Carpe diem, go for the gusto, so to speak."

"Now you sound just like a lawyer," she complained. "Quibbling every little point."

"I *am* a lawyer," Dan reminded her. "Arguing and negotiating—"

"Quibbling."

He gave her a mock stern look. *"Negotiating,"* he repeated, "is in our blood."

She stared back out the window for a long, silent time. Dan had always thought of himself as an even-tempered, patient man. Indeed, his prosecutorial work had demanded it. The law was seldom tidy. Nor was it swift.

But he'd discovered another side to his personality, an impulsive side that had him wanting to drag her upstairs, tie her to his bed, and make mad, passionate love to her until she finally acquiesced to stay here with him where she belonged.

"I rushed into love with Kevin," she murmured. "And that turned out to be a disaster."

"I don't think you were in love. Oh, I know you believed you were at the time," he said when she shot him an accusing look. "But you were a young, romantic girl far away from home who had the bad luck to run into a charming louse who knows how to pick his victims, Savannah. You weren't in love with the man; you were in love with being in love."

The same thing had occurred to her. "You may be right. But if I'd only taken the time to get to know him better—"

"We've spent more time together than either my parents or my grandparents before they got married," he cut her off with an impatient wave of his hand. "Besides, for the record, I'm not the weasel."

"No. You're definitely not, and I was wrong to make the comparison. But everything's so unsettled in my life right now, Dan. Whenever I think I'm beginning to get things under control, some new crisis pops up."

"Did you know that the Chinese use the same word for crisis and opportunity?"

"Perhaps I should have bought a damn lighthouse in China." She sighed again. "I'm sorry. I didn't mean to snap at you. It's just that I need to stay focused," she tried to explain. "If I'm going to open by Christmas, I can't afford any distractions."

Dan decided that he'd pushed enough. He'd planted the seed. Now, as John was always pointing out, he'd have to be patient while waiting for it to bloom.

"It's only because I'm wild about you that I'm going to overlook the fact that the woman I've fallen in love with just referred to me as a distraction."

He ran a slow fingertip along the ridge of her collarbone. "Since you seem to find this discussion not to your liking, I'll even change the subject." He drew her closer. "Do you realize how long it's been since I kissed you?"

"Fifteen minutes?"

"At least." His lips skimmed up her cheek. "Which is, in my book, about fourteen minutes and thirty seconds too long."

"At least," she agreed breathlessly as she placed her palms on either side of his face and brought his mouth to hers.

18

The call came just before dawn, the phone shattering the darkness. Dragged from an erotic dream in which he'd spent a long, pleasurable time spreading warmed honey all over Savannah's body and had just begun to lick it off, Dan extricated himself from her arms and snatched up the receiver.

"Yeah?"

"Dan, it's Raine. I need to talk to Savannah."

"Dan?" Savannah turned on the lamp. She sat up in bed, the tangled sheet down around her waist, her hair a wild mass of sleep and love-tousled curls. "What's wrong?"

"I don't know. It's your sister." Dan handed her the phone.

"Raine?" He watched her face go unnaturally pale, then twist with pain, as if someone had just shoved a sharp blade into her heart.

"Oh, no." She closed her eyes and sagged

against him. "How bad . . . I see. . . . Of course."
Her exhaled breath was a ragged, tortured
sound. "We'll be right there."

She looked up at him, her eyes bleak and terrified at the same time. "It's Ida. Henry found
her in the bathroom. She's had a stroke."

If Savannah had disliked the hospital the day
she'd spent waiting for Ida to have her tests, she
hated it now. At least in the examination areas
the mood had been orderly, and if impersonal,
at least efficient.

She prayed the emergency department was
equally efficient, but it was difficult to tell, with
all the people in white coats and different color
scrubs running around. They all had an air of
purpose, as if they knew where they were going,
she observed.

She, on the other hand, was lost the minute
she raced through the sliding doors beneath the
lighted red sign.

They were headed to the window where a
woman with impossibly red hair was seated at
a computer, when Raine appeared.

"We're in here," she said, taking Savannah's
arm and leading her across the central waiting
room. It crossed Savannah's numb mind that
there were a surprising number of people here
for this ungodly time in the morning. "Fortunately, Gram's name still pulls some weight. Mrs.
Kellstrom—she's the charge nurse—arranged for
us to have this private waiting room."

The walls of the small room had been covered in a blinding yellow burlap, which Savannah decided had been chosen in an attempt to lift spirits. It didn't.

"It's not much, but at least it has its own coffee maker, so we won't have to drink that toxic waste from the vending machine."

Trust Raine, even in the midst of a medical emergency, to have tracked down the person in charge and found coffee.

Lilith was sitting as stiff as a statue in a plastic avocado chair with chrome legs. Cooper was hovering over her and Jack was standing by the window, arms crossed, his face grim.

"How is Gram?" Savannah asked.

"The last we heard she's holding her own. They've still got her in the examining room."

"Can't we be with her?" Savannah shot a look at Jack. "You're the sheriff. Surely you can go wherever you want."

"We were with her for a few minutes," Raine revealed. "But when we seemed to be causing Gram more stress, Mrs. Kellstrom suggested it would be better if we waited in here."

"They've got her stabilized, and they're doing tests to determine how much damage the stroke has done," Cooper informed her.

"Oh, God." Torn between relief that her grandmother was still alive and fear for what state she might be in, Savannah sank into a pumpkin orange chair beside her mother and buried her face in her hands. She was vaguely aware, on some level, of Dan's comforting hand on her shoulder.

She'd get through this, she assured herself. It was just one more hurdle in what seemed to be a year of emotional Olympic trials. The important thing was that she stay strong. For Ida. And her mother.

She glanced over at Lilith. "How are *you?*" Her mother looked terrible, pale as glass and hollow faced.

"A bit like Mother." She managed a weak, feigned smile. "Holding my own." When she dragged a trembling hand through her silver hair, her husband caught it and held it tightly, reassuringly, between his. "Thank heavens Henry found her."

It should have been her, Savannah thought miserably.

"It's not even five o'clock," Raine argued when Savannah admitted to her guilty thought out loud. "Even if you *had* been at the house, you would have been sleeping."

"She didn't cry out or anything?"

"Actually, Henry said that she seemed irritated that he'd found her, which is much the same thing the paramedics said. It seems she was determined to just brush it off and get back to bed." Her laugh was flat and devoid of any humor. "That was pretty much impossible, since Henry said she was as weak as a kitten."

"Oh God," Savannah repeated. She glanced around the small room. "Where is Henry?"

"At home with Gwen and Amy. We couldn't leave Amy all alone out at the farm, and we didn't want to wait for a sitter to show up, so we just scooped her out of bed in her night-gown, wrapped her in a quilt, and drove her to the house. She never woke up."

"I never thought I'd be grateful Henry was staying there."

She also had never thought that she would have been grateful for the construction delays. Thank goodness the room she'd promised Henry at the keeper's house hadn't been ready.

Savannah sat there with the others, trying to remember everything the doctor had told them about strokes. She struggled to recall some-thing—anything—positive about her friend's ex-perience. But her mind was fogged with worry, fear, and, as the clock on the bright yellow wall slowly ticked off the passing time, fatigue.

There was nothing for any of them to do but to wait. Savannah had never felt more helpless.

And wasn't this just a fine kettle of cossacks? Ida lay on the gurney, growing more and more frustrated as the doctor kept asking her the same questions.

What was her name? Did she know where she was? Did she know what day of the week it was? Who was president? Over and over again. She answered him correctly every time—admit-tedly having to stop and think a minute before she realized that it must be early Wednesday morning—but for some reason she couldn't make the answers sink into his stubborn head.

What was wrong with him? Ida scowled up at the face that was swimming in and out of focus.

Was the idiot man deaf? She was tempted to just get up and walk out of here. The only problem with that idea was that she was strangely too exhausted to move. There was also the little matter of her right arm and leg feeling as if they'd turned to lead.

She'd just rest a bit, Ida decided. Since they seemed so damn determined to poke and prod at her, she'd let them have their fun. Then she'd leave.

"What are they doing in there?" Savannah leaned her forehead against the window, trying to keep herself from screaming. Beneath her initial fear, resentment began to rear its ugly head.

Dr. Ida Lindstrom had put herself through medical school, receiving her degree before the doctors and nurses working in the ER had even been born. She'd served the community of Coldwater Cove for more than five decades. She was a colleague of those very same people bustling around with a purpose they didn't seem inclined to share.

Her grandmother was lying somewhere out there in one of those dark blue curtained cubicles, perhaps hovering on the brink of death, and not a single person in this entire damn building cared enough to let her family know her condition.

Outside the hospital, the weather was as bleak as Savannah's mood. Another storm front had moved in over the mountains. A sky the color of bruises hung low over the town. A dreary drizzle streamed down the glass.

"She's going to be all right," Raine, who'd come to stand beside her, insisted for the umpteenth time since Savannah had arrived with Dan. Her nerves all in a tangle, Savannah turned to inform her sister that there were some things that even Xena the Warrior Lawyer couldn't control, when a distressed look came over Raine's face.

As she ran out of the room, Savannah shot a look toward Jack. His expression appeared sympathetic, but not overly concerned. The fact that he wasn't immediately on his wife's heels was explanation enough.

Savannah followed Raine down the hall to the restrooms and handed her a wet paper towel when she came out of the stall.

"Thank you." Raine wiped her face, balled the towel and tossed it into the waste bin, then washed her mouth out in the sink. "Christ, my timing stinks."

Savannah almost smiled at the self-reproach in her sister's voice. Trust Raine to believe that morning sickness was yet another event she could schedule into her Day-Timer.

"Actually, the news will undoubtedly be just the medicine Gram needs." She hugged Raine. "I'm so happy for you."

"I'm happy for me, too. Or at least I was before Gram decided to scare us all to death." Raine leaned back and gave Savannah a searching look. "Is this going to be a problem? After last fall?"

She'd gone to New York shortly after her miscarriage, seeking her big sister's comfort.

"Of course not. My miscarriage and your pregnancy have nothing to do with each other."

"That's a relief. I've been putting off telling you all week because I felt a little guilty. Since you're the one who always wanted a large family."

"I think it's fabulous," Savannah insisted. "Especially since I've recently discovered that I love being an aunt."

"Then you should really love being a godmother." Raine began digging around in her purse. "I hate morning sickness," she complained as she popped a breath mint into her mouth.

"It'll be gone by the second trimester. Meanwhile, the trick is to keep something in your stomach all the time and carry crackers with you."

"That's what all the books say." Raine pressed her palm against her still flat stomach. "Can I tell you something? Just between us?"

"Of course." Savannah was surprised she even had to ask.

"Ever since Henry called the farm with the bad news, I've been worried that this is my fault."

"Your fault?"

"You know, one of those life cycle things."

"Life cycle things?" Savannah stared at her. "Surely you don't believe that Gram might die because you're pregnant?" The ever practical, feet-on-the-ground Raine was the last person she would have expected to even come up with such an idea.

"Do you remember when Lilith was a Buddhist?"

"After she came back from filming that slasher movie in Hong Kong," Savannah remembered.

It had been a short-lived religious infatuation, triggered, she'd always secretly believed, by her mother's very public affair with her costar. Savannah had not been able to go into a supermarket for six weeks without seeing Lilith and her Chinese martial arts champion lover looking back at her from the covers of the tabloids at the checkout stand.

"She visited me for a few days during that time."

"She did?" Savannah was surprised. Until recently, Raine and their mother had not been close. In fact, their relationship could have been described as just short of estranged.

"She was in town for a publicity event." Raine shrugged. "I couldn't exactly refuse to see her. . . . Anyway, she was positive she'd found the key to the secret of life. Quite honestly, she was chattering away—you know how she does when she's in love—and I didn't listen to much she said. But something has stuck in my mind all these years. She told me that every breath we take stirs the universe and creates a reaction. That nothing happens in a vacuum."

"Are you talking about sort of a universal quid pro quo?"

"You're laughing at me." Which was, Savannah knew from childhood experience, something a person dared only at their own peril.

"No. I'm not laughing. Not really," she insisted when her sister looked on the verge of arguing. "I just think that perhaps these are runaway hormones talking. Because, no offense to the Buddhists, who I'm sure are very lovely people, but I don't believe life works that way.

"I also don't think that you would have believed it either, before this morning."

It seemed a little strange comforting her big sister. Strange, but nice, Savannah decided.

"Besides, knowing Mother, she probably got the concept wrong, anyway."

Raine managed a reluctant, self-conscious laugh just as the restroom door opened.

"The doctor's finally seen fit to talk to us," Lilith informed them. "He's in the waiting room."

Raine and Savannah exchanged a look. Then they followed their mother back down the hall.

Ida did not like being on the other end of the physician-patient relationship. She'd always known that there was no privacy in a hospital, but this was the first time she'd been the one lying naked beneath the impossibly thin pink blanket.

The ICU was annoyingly bright and as frigid as a meat locker. Someone should tell them to turn the heat up. Machines hummed, quietly monitoring vital signs. An IV bottle hung overhead, fluids dripping down the clear tube into the back of her hand.

"Let's check your reflexes and see how we're doing, dear," a chirpy voice said. A moment later Ida was blinded by a bright penlight. She knew the nurse only wanted to see how her pupils dilated, but Ida instinctively tried to close her eyes against the glare. Stubborn fingers held her lids open.

"Good girl," the voice said. "We're doing just dandy, Ida, dear."

As the nurse instructed her to push against her hand, Ida shoved as hard as she could—which, unfortunately, wasn't very hard when it came to her right hand—and struggled to read the woman's name tag. She wanted to tell this annoying female that she should give a person fair warning before she went shining lights into their eyes. She also had no right using a patient's first name unless invited to do so.

Unfortunately, her vision, made worse by the bright light, was still blurry. The nurse's pink face continued to fade in and out of focus.

She felt the pressure on her feet. Both feet, Ida realized. She knew that was a good thing, but couldn't remember why.

Still struggling with the answer that was hovering just out of reach in the foggy mists of her mind, Ida drifted back to sleep.

Just as when they'd first met with him, Dr. Burke didn't beat around the bush. "As you've all undoubtedly surmised, Dr. Lindstrom has had a stroke."

Somehow, hearing the diagnosis out loud from this white-coated man who was supposed to make things better, to make Ida better, hit Savannah as hard as Raine's original call. She struggled to focus on what the doctor was saying, but seemed only able to pick up the significant words. The frightening words.

"She suffered left brain damage, blah, blah, blah ... hemiplegia, blah ... weakness in her right side, blah, blah ... aphasia, blah ... apraxia, blah, blah, blah ... some relaxation of the muscles on the right side of her face, blah blah—"

"Wait a minute." Savannah held up a hand. "Would you mind going back to aphasia? And apraxia?"

"Of course. Apraxia is the inability to use the mouth and tongue muscles to formulate words."

"And Gram doesn't have that?"

"No. She's actually quite talkative for someone who's just suffered a brain insult."

He made it sound as if someone had hammered Ida with a sarcastic remark. Savannah glanced over at Raine, who rolled her eyes. Her expression also revealed that she was also thinking how difficult it was to keep Ida Lindstrom quiet when she had a point to make.

"The problem," he said, "is that her aphasia, which is the inability to express oneself in either spoken or written words, makes it somewhat difficult to diagnose whether she merely has expressive aphasia, or receptive aphasia as well."

"Which would be her ability to understand language?" Raine inquired.

"Exactly. For example, when she was first brought in, the admitting doctor asked her name, and she answered, 'Blood.' "

"Maybe she was trying to say something

about her blood pressure," Lilith said hopefully. "Perhaps she was afraid that's what had caused her stroke and she was telling them to check it."

"Her vital signs were being monitored at the time," the doctor said. "I understand that it's only natural to try to attribute some normalcy to what is, admittedly, an unnatural situation, but when Dr. Lindstrom was asked if she knew where she was, she responded with 'Brick' the first time."

"That's close," Savannah pointed out, like her mother, grasping at any straw she could reach. "This building is constructed of brick."

"The second time her response was, 'Dog.' The third time, 'Piano.'"

Language had always been so important to her grandmother. Her opinionated manner admittedly grated from time to time, but Savannah had always admired the way she'd never hesitated to speak her mind—a mind that now sounded hopelessly jumbled.

"When we tried some yes-or-no questions that she could nod to, she got most of them right," he said encouragingly. "This suggests she's able to understand a lot of what she's hearing."

"Yes-or-no questions couldn't be very complex," Raine pointed out.

"They are, by necessity, fairly simplistic," he allowed. "But it also indicates a stronger chance that she'll regain more of her comprehension and speech skills."

"Could you give us any sort of timetable for when this recovery might take place?" Lilith asked.

"Unfortunately, I can't. Every stroke is unique." He appeared to want to leave the room. "Well, if there are no more questions . . ." He was definitely inching toward the door. "The hospital Social Worker will want to meet with you regarding Dr. Lindstrom's rehabilitation team—"

"Team?" Savannah asked.

"Your grandmother will be assigned a number of specialists to help her achieve the best possible recovery. A physical therapist will determine the extent of the dysfunction in her weakened right side and help her work her muscles to allow maximum mobility."

"Will Mother be able to walk?" Lilith asked.

He frowned. "Again, every stroke victim is unique, but your mother's hemiplegia seems fairly mild. My educated guess is that her prognosis for walking—perhaps with the assistance of a cane—is quite good."

"That's very encouraging, Doctor." Lilith's faint smile was only a shadow of her usual dazzling one. "But I'm afraid you've made one grave error in treating my mother."

"Oh?" He lifted a brow.

"My mother may have had a stroke. But the one thing she's never been, and will never be, is a *victim*." At that moment, Savannah could actually see Ida in Lilith's dark blue eyes.

"Point taken, Mrs. Ryan," he murmured with a nod. "Getting back to the concept of your mother's team . . . unless anyone else has a question?" he asked.

"Fine," he said, outwardly relieved when

none of them spoke up. "Along with her physical therapist, Dr. Lindstrom will also be given speech and occupational therapists."

"My grandmother's retired, Doctor," Raine pointed out.

"I'm aware of that." There was a faint edge to his tone that suggested the Lindstrom women's continual questions were beginning to annoy him.

Tough, Savannah thought.

"An occupational therapist teaches stroke victims—"

"Patients," Lilith corrected.

"Patients," he agreed tightly. "As I was saying, this therapist will help Dr. Lindstrom with daily living skills, dressing, bathing, teaching her to feed herself, get around the house, relearn basic skills such as cooking—"

"We could probably skip that one," Savannah murmured. She'd meant to keep her comment to herself, but it had come out during a second of silence in the doctor's presentation and she knew she hadn't made points when the family all laughed.

The back and forth motion of his jaw suggested that he was grinding his teeth. "Of course, the family is one of the most important members of the team," he doggedly forged on even as he continued to move backwards. He was now standing in the open doorway.

"I'll arrange for you to see Dr. Lindstrom. She's been moved upstairs to ICU. At this time, I would suggest that you keep your visit down to ten minutes. And only the immediate family."

With that final instruction, he escaped.

"I think we're in trouble," Lilith said.

"What was your first clue, Mother?" Raine asked dryly.

"When the doctor brought up the team."

Savannah caught her mother's meaning right away. "You're right. Gram never has been a team player."

Although it wasn't very funny, they all shared another laugh because they needed one. And because, Savannah feared, what they were all facing wasn't going to offer many opportunities for humor.

19

Ida looked so small. So frail. It was all Savannah could do not to burst into tears as she stood beside her grandmother's bed, holding her hand.

"The doctor says you're going to be fine, Mother," Lilith soothed. She leaned over the bed railing and stroked damp strands of gray hair from Ida's forehead. Since her grandmother had worn her hair up in that untidy bun for as long as Savannah could remember, she'd never realized how long it was. If it had been brushed properly, it would have come nearly to her waist. "You just need a little rest."

Ida's eyes snapped. "Gorilla."

"I'm sorry." Obviously shaken by the terse non sequitur, Lilith bit her lip, avoiding her daughters' eyes, then squared her shoulders and tried again. "Are you trying to tell us something about Doctor Burke?"

Ida nodded.

"He has a very good reputation, Gram," Raine said reassuringly. "I did a background check on him when you had your first appointment," she revealed, surprising Savannah not at all. It was precisely what Raine would do. "His credentials are remarkable and he's worked at some of the top-flight research hospitals in the world, which, of course, made me wonder what he was doing here in Coldwater Cove."

"Not that you can't be a good doctor and a small-town doctor, too," Savannah said quickly.

Raine visibly cringed when she realized what she'd said. "Of course you can. You're proof of that, Gram."

Three of the four women in the room smiled brightly at that. Ida did not. Savannah couldn't tell if that was because she was insulted, or because she couldn't. The muscles on the right side of her face were lax, which caused that side of her lips to droop slightly.

"Anyway," Raine said briskly, as if wanting to move on to a safer topic, "it turns out that he's also an amateur mountain climber. Having conquered all of Colorado's major peaks, he's moved on to Washington. He's already done Baker and Rainier. Next spring he's doing Olympus. Then I suppose we'll be losing him, but of course, you'll be fully recovered by then, so it won't really matter."

Ida shook her head.

"Of course you will be, Gram," Savannah insisted. "We're all going to help you. And you're going to have a team of experts, as well, made up of all sorts of trained therapists. Which, of course, you already know about, being a doctor yourself."

Ida shook her head.

"Maybe she's forgotten," Lilith suggested quietly. "Dr. Burke says that you'll have a speech therapist." She raised her voice as if an increase in volume could facilitate understanding. "Along with a physical therapist, and—"

"Plane," Ida interrupted abruptly. She pointed her left hand toward the rain-streaked window.

"Rain," Savannah guessed.

Ida nodded. "Plane," she repeated.

"You want to go on a plane?" Raine asked.

Ida's head bobbed up and down.

"But you hate air travel," Lilith reminded her.

"Plane!" Ida slammed her hand on the bed. The angry pink hue darkening her ashen complexion would have been reassuring, were it not for a very real concern that she could work herself into a second stroke.

It took some more questioning to figure out that whatever distinguished between head shakes and nods had gone haywire in Ida's injured brain.

"You'd think that the doctor would have mentioned that a nod means *no,*" Raine muttered.

They tried again, everyone, including Ida— especially Ida, Savannah thought—becoming more and more frustrated with these early futile attempts at communication.

She jabbed the index finger of her good left hand toward the window again and again. "Plane," she kept repeating.

Realizing that the word itself was useless, Savannah focused instead on the message.

She went over to the glass and looked out over the town. Then she saw it. The house, overlooking the cove.

"Home!" she said. She spun back toward her grandmother. "You want to go home."

Ida energetically shook her head back and forth on the pillow. *Yes.* Tears streamed down her face.

"Of course you'll be coming home." Lilith took a tissue from the box beside the bed and began dabbing at the uncontrolled moisture. "As soon as you're just a little bit better."

"Dr. Burke says you should be released in ten days." Raine's words revealed that she'd absorbed more of what the doctor had been saying than Savannah had. "And then, of course you'll be coming home, Gram."

Ida seemed to accept that promise. She sank deeper into the sheets and closed her eyes. Tears continued to fall at a furious pace from beneath her lids, yet her lips—even the injured side—pulled into a lopsided smile.

Hers were not the only damp eyes in the room.

Determined to make the most of the time they were allowed, by mutual unspoken agreement Lilith, Raine, and Savannah remained beside Ida's bed, surreptitiously watching the monitor overhead. A line continued to move across a green screen in reassuring peaks and valleys.

Eventually a nurse wearing bright pink scrubs appeared in the doorway. "I'm sorry, but you'll have to leave. The speech therapist is here, and she needs to do some tests on Dr. Lindstrom."

"Dr. Lindstrom is sleeping," Raine hissed. "Can't she come back later?"

"She's here now," the nurse said in a stern, no-nonsense tone that brooked no argument. "The sooner she can determine your grandmother's condition, the faster Dr. Lindstrom can begin her recovery."

Those were, of course, the magic words. They left the room, pausing briefly to speak with the therapist, an attractive brunette in her early to mid thirties. Her hair was cut in a sleek bob she'd tucked behind both ears, and she was dressed in black jeans and black jacket brightened by a scarlet sweater.

"Dr. Lindstrom delivered both my parents," Kathi Montgomery informed the family. "Me, too. And she saved my social life when she treated my acne when I was fourteen."

That reference made Savannah recognize her. "You were Kathi Clifton." She'd been on the debating club, Savannah recalled. She'd also dated Dan O'Halloran.

"That was my maiden name. I'm thinking about going back to it now that I'm getting a divorce, but at this point, I'm just taking one step at a time. Your grandmother's my first client since I've come back to work."

"Oh?" Savannah worried about that.

Kathi smiled again. "You don't have to worry. I may have been sidetracked for a while, but

I'm very good at my job. I'll take good care of your grandmother."

"She looks so weak," Lilith worried.

"So would you, if you were in her shoes. She's had a rough few hours. But I was reading the admittance report, and I think she got off real lucky. Strokes are scary, foreign territory to most people." She assured them that they were not alone in their fears. "But no matter how bad things are in the beginning, they can get a lot better."

"Back to the way they were before the stroke?" Raine asked.

"Not always." Savannah admired Kathi Montgomery's honesty. "In fact, just about everyone will have some residual effects after a stroke. But people have amazing adjustment skills.

"We all want to believe that we can control our lives," she said. Since she was looking straight at Raine, Savannah added perception to the therapist's growing list of attributes. "But it's impossible not to run into surprises. Or detours.

"Right now, even though she's a doctor, all this is foreign territory to Dr. Lindstrom. Especially with her aphasia making it difficult to communicate. It's a bit as if she woke up this morning and discovered she was in Tibet."

Lilith sighed heavily. "Mother has always hated to travel."

At least feeling they were leaving Ida in good hands, they headed back to the ICU waiting room the family had moved to after Ida had been transferred from ER.

"Well, one thing's for certain," Savannah said as they walked past the nursing station.

Lilith glanced over at her. Savannah was relieved when she noticed that a little color had come back to her mother's cheeks. "What's that, dear?"

"Whatever her condition in ten days, she is definitely coming home. I don't care if she has another stroke after this one—a hundred strokes—she's not going to end up propped up in front of a television at Evergreen."

About this, they were in total agreement.

After Raine assured Jack that she'd be fine without him, and yes, she'd keep the saltines he'd brought her from the cafeteria close at hand, Jack left the hospital to check on Amy and reassure the little girl that her great-grandmother was going to be coming home soon.

The others stayed. All day, then long into the evening, going in to sit with Ida whenever the nurses allowed. As the hours passed, as the sun rose high above the cove, then set over the mountaintops, it began to sink in that this wasn't the type of life event that would be resolved any time soon.

Obviously, Savannah's planned holiday opening of the bed-and-breakfast would have to be put off. Despite having dedicated so many hours to the project, she didn't suffer so much as a twinge of ambivalence. She thought of what Dan had said about the Chinese word for crisis being the same as the word for opportunity. Her grandmother had always been there for her.

Now she was being given the opportunity to repay that debt.

In the grand scheme of things, Savannah supposed that her lighthouse, as much as it had come to mean to her, wasn't really all that important. Neither was Raine's Harvard law degree, Lilith's former theatrical career, or even Ida's medical practice.

Family was what mattered. Mother, grandmother, sisters. Amy, whom Raine adopted upon marrying Jack, and the unborn child they'd made together. Cooper and Jack, who'd married into the family but were no less a part of it, and Gwen, who had been welcomed in. Even, perhaps, baby Lily someday, if she chose.

That left Dan. He was, of course, technically family, since he was Jack's cousin. Savannah wasn't even going to begin to try to figure out the logistics, but that would make him her cousin-in-law. Or something like that.

But whenever she returned from the ICU and found him still in the waiting room, hour after hour, offering comfort, support, encouragement, and a tenderness she'd never known from any man, Savannah could no longer hide from the truth.

Despite her vow to hold her heart close, to avoid the risk of having it be wounded again, her feelings for Dan O'Halloran had gone far past cousinly.

Like most of the doctors she'd met over the years, Ida had never expected any of the illnesses she'd treated to ever happen to her. Logically, she knew that a medical degree didn't come with some invisible shield, but the simple fact was that she quite honestly had been of the belief that things like heart attacks, burst appendixes, cancer, and strokes happened to other people. They wouldn't happen to her.

Well, so much for that theory, she considered as she looked out the window at her little piece of sky and the small rectangular view that had been her entire world for the past eight days.

She knew she was fortunate that her motor skills weren't terribly impeded. The physical therapist, a huge black woman who could made Genghis Khan seem warm and fuzzy by comparison, but who Ida knew was sincerely dedicated to getting her back on her feet, had assured her that if she kept up the hard work she'd be out of her wheelchair in a month.

That prospect had been enough to keep Ida from slugging her this morning when it felt as if she'd jerked her shoulder out of its socket during her range-of-motion exercises.

She *was* getting damn frustrated at not being able to get her thoughts across. She'd tried communicating by writing on one of the yellow legal pads with a fat rollerball pen Raine had brought her, but while she thought she'd been forming the words just fine, all that the others could see was a squiggly black line that Ida reluctantly admitted looked as if it had been scribbled by a baboon.

Her speech therapist was a sweet little girl,

patient as a saint. Kathi Montgomery had suggested that she try to draw pictures, which, while she didn't have to worry about being acclaimed the next Grandma Moses anytime soon, did help get simple points across some of the time.

But Ida didn't like using the drawings because it was like admitting she might never speak again.

That wasn't an option.

That very first day, when the fog had cleared long enough for her to have figured out exactly what was happening to her, Ida had realized that she had two choices. She could just lie here, thinking that her life was over, that she was already a goner, so she might as well just die and free up the bed.

Or she could fight like hell.

This meant that there was really only one choice.

She was dozing when she became aware of someone else in the room, which wasn't all that surprising. This place was like Grand Central Station with the bright lights, people coming and going at all hours of the day and night, always poking and prodding and asking detailed questions about personal bodily functions that she'd always preferred to keep private.

She opened one eye, ready to snarl at that obnoxious nurse who continued to call her by her first name and talked baby talk to her, as if she were some drooling infant who couldn't understand proper English. After the penlight incident, Ida had vowed that she would not die.

She was going to get better. She was going to get strong.

Then she was going to kill that nurse.

But it wasn't her nemesis. It was Henry, standing there with a sunshine yellow plant in his hands, looking about as uncomfortable as she'd ever seen him.

"Didn't mean to wake you," he said gruffly. "I'll just leave this and go."

She shook her head. Once they'd explained to her that she had the head shaking and nodding mixed up, things had begun to get a bit easier. She lifted her hand—her right hand, which took an effort, but still felt more natural than her left—and waved him in.

"You're looking real good, Ida."

She pulled her lips tight, letting him know that her brain might have gotten a little scrambled, but she could still spot a lie when she heard one.

"Oh, you might not think you're looking quite up to snuff," he said when she shook her head. "But considering that you could have been lying on a slab down at Murphy's funeral home, you're looking damn fine."

Ida frowned. She'd never liked thinking about her own mortality. Recent events hadn't changed that.

He plunked the clay pot down on the table beside her bed.

She managed to lift her right brow. Or at least she thought she did. Sometimes it was hard to tell just how things were working.

"I figured it's past time I got you a thank you gift for letting me stay in your house."

She shook her head, pointing from herself to him. If it hadn't been for Henry finding her and his quick response in calling 911, she might have been a lot worse off.

He read her meaning and shrugged. "Guess we're even."

She nodded.

"Hope you like mums."

She nodded again. Emphatically this time.

"I was gonna get you some cut flowers, but the kid down at the Green Spot, that John Martin, said these would be better. They'll last longer."

Another nod. Ida was beginning to get a headache. Lord, it would be nice when she could talk again!

"I thought the color might sort of brighten the place up a bit. . . . You can quit shaking your head up and down," he suggested. "No point in rattlin' your brains more than they've already been rattled."

Vastly relieved, she drew a smiley face in the air. Ida had always hated smiley faces, but sometimes a woman had to make do.

He smiled back. Ida realized that her memory hadn't been all that good the past few months, but she was certain that she hadn't seen the man smile since he'd moved into her house.

"There's been some changes at the house," he revealed. "The family wanted to surprise you, and I don't want to ruin their fun when you come home tomorrow, but I've been thinkin' that perhaps you've had enough surprises lately and mebbe I ought to fill you in on the details."

She gestured again. This time toward the chair.

It was Henry's turn to nod. "I figured as much." He sat down and began to let her know what her daughter and granddaughters had been up to in her absence.

20

All the hours she'd spent working on the remodeling seemed almost like a vacation as Savannah ran back and forth between the hospital and the house, visiting Ida and preparing for her homecoming. Despite her grandmother's abbreviated vocabulary, Ida had made it clear that she didn't want either Raine or Savannah to sacrifice their own busy lives for her. They tried to convince her that taking care of her wasn't any sacrifice, but she'd been typically Ida-insistent.

Savannah called every rent-a-nurse agency in the phone book, but soon discovered that they weren't set up to provide the services her grandmother would need: driving her to therapy sessions, running errands, taking her out to lunch, shopping, anything to keep her from spending all day, every day, in the house. She'd always been an active woman; it was important that that not change.

Savannah had been at her wits' end when Lilith, who'd established a Coldwater Cove community theater group, had suggested a friend of hers. Martha Taylor was a widow who'd recently moved to town. Better yet, she was a former registered nurse, which, Lilith pointed out, could prove helpful. The fact that she'd won the Bette Davis part in the current production of *Whatever Happened to Baby Jane?* had worried Savannah just a bit until they'd met.

Martha seemed to be blessed with an unrelentingly optimistic attitude. She was cheery enough to lift Ida's spirits when they drooped, which they understandably did on occasion, and, having spent a two-year stint as a nurse in the King County jail, she had acquired enough toughness not to let Savannah's headstrong grandmother steamroller over her.

The two women had hit it off right away, and Martha, who'd confessed to having joined the theater group in the first place because she'd been so lonely after her husband's death, readily accepted Ida's invitation to move into the house.

Savannah felt her presence also helped provide a somewhat stable home for Gwen, who, thanks to Dan, was declared an emancipated minor, which effectively took her out of the clutches of Social Services. Despite all the recent stress, Savannah felt that the teenager seemed much less tense. More secure.

She only wished she could say the same for herself. Savannah couldn't remember when she'd been juggling so many balls. All of them breakable.

Fortunately, Raine was taking care of dealing with all the financial details. Accustomed to handling cases worth millions of dollars, even here in Coldwater Cove, since her software clients and businesses dealing in Asian Rim trade didn't care where her office was located, she found a mere insurance company and hospital billing department to be no match at all for her.

If her own grandmother hadn't been the subject of these turf wars, Savannah would almost have felt sorry for the clerk who'd tried—unsuccessfully—to deny Ida out-patient rehabilitation services.

During Ida's hospitalization, what seemed like the entire population of Coldwater Cove dropped by the house bearing casseroles, which Gwen and Henry were especially grateful for, since there were soon enough Pyrex dishes in the freezer to save them from meatloaf, in the event the occupational therapist managed to get Ida cooking again anytime soon.

The day before her grandmother was to be discharged, Savannah was in the front parlor, marking things off her checklist as activity hummed around her. For the past week the house had resembled a beehive: volunteer carpenters built ramps to the front porch and outside kitchen door, and removed moldings and widened doorways to accommodate the wheelchair Savannah hoped Ida would not need for very long.

Thresholds had been beveled, a safety rail was installed in the shower, and a second handrail had been put on the wall side of the stairs in anticipation of the day that her grandmother would be walking again.

Even the plumber who'd taken so long to install the Jacuzzi at her lighthouse showed up, accompanied by his wife, who was bearing a "Southwestern taco surprise" casserole. He took one look at the faucets in Ida's bathroom, went out to his truck, and returned with a single lever, which, he explained, would require less wrist and finger motion than the current round knobs.

"Put the same in my dad's bathroom when he had his stroke," the man informed Savannah cheerfully, as if he'd never received that stern lawyer letter Dan had written for her. "He said it made a world of difference."

He'd no sooner left when Dottie and Doris Anderson, twin owners of the Dancing Deer Dress Shoppe, showed up at the door.

"We know how Ida loves her jeans," Doris said as she took the lid off a box and revealed an olive green jogging outfit. "But this will be easier for her to get on and off."

"That's very thoughtful of you. Thank you."

"Mother Anderson had a stroke five years ago." Dottie pulled a scarlet garment from a shopping bag bearing the store's dancing deer logo. While the elderly twins dressed alike, Doris, the elder by ten minutes, preferred earth tones while her sister opted for brighter colors. "We found that putting on a terry cloth robe after her shower was often easier than toweling dry."

"I wouldn't have thought of that."

"It's a difficult time," Dottie said sympathetically. "But the important thing is that you're not alone, dear."

"That's nice to know." Savannah also knew from experience how difficult it was to break off a conversation with the Anderson twins, most notably the loquacious Dottie.

"You haven't been in the shop lately," Doris noted.

"I've been a little busy."

"Well, that's certainly understandable." Dottie patted Savannah's hand. "But you must steal a little time to drop in some day soon. We've opened up a bridal boutique since the last time you were in." Her round pink cheeks dimpled. "Our slogan is You Bring the Groom, We've Got the Gown."

"That's certainly catchy," Savannah said with a quick glance toward Raine, who'd just come from upstairs, where she'd been supervising the installation of the rented stair glide.

At first the plan had been to move Ida into the sunroom, which was on the first floor and was the cheeriest room in the house. But knowing how she valued her privacy, and wanting to keep things as normal as possible during this transitional time, the family had finally decided to put in the chairlift that would allow Ida to return to the bedroom she'd slept in for the past forty-five years.

"It was Doris who thought the slogan up,"

Dottie allowed. "Of course we don't really need any advertising these days, since your mother's and sister's wedding has gotten us business from all over the peninsula."

She skimmed a quick, professional gaze over Savannah that suggested she was taking mental measurements. "We've several models that would look lovely on you."

"I'm not really in the market for a wedding dress," Savannah murmured.

"Not yet, perhaps." Doris shot a pointed look out the front window toward Dan, who was walking up the front sidewalk.

Savannah was getting much too accustomed to seeing him at the end of the day. It wasn't just that the sight of him caused that little jolt to her heart. It was that it was beginning to feel so right.

"Do keep us in mind, dear," Dottie chirped.

The sisters left, pausing to exchange a few words with Dan.

The problem with a small town was, of course, that everyone knew everyone else's business. Then again, Savannah thought, as she watched Henry rubbing paste wax into the furniture and Martha washing the windows with vinegar and crumpled newspapers, people truly cared for one another.

Ida Lindstrom had always taken care of the people of Coldwater Cove. Now it was their turn to take care of her.

Dan knew every inch of Savannah's body intimately. He'd touched it, tasted it, dreamed of it. He could also tell, yesterday afternoon during a hurried coupling between her morning visit to the hospital and the afternoon courthouse appearance for Gwen, that there was less of it than when they'd first made love. Along with her obvious weight loss, there were deep shadows beneath her eyes and she was too pale. Dan still thought her beautiful.

"Good evening, Mrs. Ryan," he greeted Lilith cheerfully. "I've come to steal your lovely daughter."

Lilith glanced up from arranging issues of the AMA journal on a table next to her mother's favorite chair. "I do hope you mean Savannah, since I don't believe Jack would take well to his pregnant wife being kidnapped."

"If you kidnapped my mommy, Daddy would put you in jail, Uncle Dan," Amy said. She was sitting on the floor with a box of crayons, coloring a picture for her great-grandmother.

"Good point. Then it's a lucky thing for me that I've come for your aunt Savannah."

"Oh, Dan." Savannah's face fell. He recognized the look. He'd seen it a lot since she'd come back to town. More since Ida's stroke. "I'm sorry, but I've still got so much left to do."

"Oh, go with the man, darling," Lilith said. "We've got everything under control."

Knowing that he was taking unfair advantage, Dan drew Savannah into his arms. "I had this sudden yearning for fried chicken and potato salad. But it's no fun to go on a picnic alone."

"A picnic?" He could feel her softening, fitting her curves to his body.

"I have it on good authority that the Lindstrom women are suckers for picnics." He shot a grin over the top of Savannah's head toward Raine, who, amazingly for a woman who entered a courtroom looking as if she had ice water in her veins, actually blushed.

"My husband and I are going to have to have a little chat about sharing when I get home," she murmured.

"Jack never said a thing," Dan assured her. But he remembered the look on his cousin's face the day after his spring picnic with Raine in the woods. It was the first time Dan had realized that it was possible for a guy to look poleaxed and smug at the same time.

He turned his attention back to Savannah. "So, how about it? I also happen to have picked up a Bordeaux at the mercantile, which Olivia Brown assures me is voluptuous without being too bold, and nicely complex while remaining user friendly." He grinned. "Sort of like someone I know."

When he felt her wavering, he coaxed her out the front door onto the porch to escape their audience. "I just want to steal a little time alone with you, sweetheart. Before Ida comes home and things get really hectic."

"We were alone yesterday."

"I enjoyed every minute of our little tryst parked out on the skid road," he assured her. "But I have to admit that I'd just as soon tumble you without having to keep an eye out for logging trucks."

"I'm disappointed." He watched a bit of laughter spark beneath the fatigue in her eyes. "Here I thought you were a man who enjoyed adventure."

"You're all the adventure I need." It was the absolute truth. He rubbed his palms over her shoulders, soothing muscles that were as rigid as boulders. "Have pity on me, Savannah. I've spent all day thinking about you." He moved his stroking fingers up her neck.

"I've thought about you, too." She practically purred as the tension slowly slid away.

"Then come with me." He touched his mouth to hers and felt her lips soften. Yield.

She lifted her arms and linked her fingers behind his neck. "How can we have a picnic? It's going to be dark soon. And cold."

"I'll keep you warm," he promised.

"You keep me hot," she corrected as she brushed a kiss against his jaw. "All I have to do is think about you and it's as if I'm burning up with fever." He felt her soft sigh against his cheek and was encouraged again when she didn't pull away.

"I know the feeling. Very well." He touched a fingertip to her chin and brought her lips to his. The kiss was light and brief, but still, as always, packed a helluva punch. "As for the dark part, I've got that covered. You just have to trust me."

She leaned her head back and looked up at him, her eyes more sober than he'd ever seen them. Even more sober than that night on the Ferris wheel when she'd told him about her failed marriage.

"I do."

"That's a good start." Deluged by feelings, by her, he pulled her tight. "We can work from there."

Dan had known women who made him ache. Women who'd made him burn. Even women who could, on a particularly satisfying occasion, make him tremble. But Savannah was the first woman who had him willing to crawl.

If he thought that might do the trick, if there was even a chance that it would tear down that last defensive barrier she'd constructed around her heart, he'd do just that, without a second thought, on his hands and knees across shattered glass. Through burning flames. Through hell.

Through no fault of her own, Ida had thrown a monkey wrench into all their lives. Into his plans. Understandably, the aftermath of her stroke was taking up a great deal of Savannah's attention. He'd just have to be patient a while longer.

As she walked with him back down the sidewalk to the SUV, he decided to have John order some greenery. A holiday wedding at the lighthouse would be a nice touch. Christmas was a little more than a month away. Plenty of time, Dan decided with a renewed burst of optimism.

"When did you do all this?" Savannah stared around the lantern room.

"I got some of it done this morning before I went into the office."

He'd unearthed the blue and white blanket spread over the hardwood floor at the bottom of the linen closet his mother had filled when he'd first come back to town. She had been appalled to find her only son living, in her words, "like a hobo." He'd tried to tell her that he'd bought the house for the view and that the sleeping bag he'd thrown on the bed was sufficient for the time being, but that hadn't stopped her from showing up at his door with more sheets and towels than he'd figured he'd use in this lifetime.

"A little more during lunch."

The clay pots of buttery yellow flowers surrounding the blanket had been John's suggestion, as had the blue spruce, which had been a bitch to haul up the stairs. But his nephew had assured him that they could decorate it for Christmas, then plant it outside in the spring. Dan liked the idea of planting a tree with Savannah, watching it grow each year, along with their kids.

"And I did the shopping after court recessed this afternoon, before I dropped by your grandmother's house."

When she'd begun ringing up the mercantile's entire stock of candles, Olivia had asked him if he was expecting a power outage. Then she'd gotten to the wine and Johnny Mathis CD. From the knowing look she'd given him while they waited for Fred to do a price check on the wine, Dan had realized that by tomorrow everyone in Coldwater Cove would know he'd been setting up a romantic tryst with Ida Lindstrom's granddaughter.

It might have been worse, he'd thought at the time. Fortunately, he'd planned ahead and stocked up on condoms at the busy, impersonal Walgreen in Port Angeles.

"It's wonderful for you to have gone to so much trouble." She toed her sneakers off and sat down on the blanket. "I'm already starting to relax."

"That's the idea." He hit the remote for the stereo he'd hidden behind the tree.

"All this and Johnny Mathis, too?" she asked with a smile as the seductive light baritone sounds of Mathis getting "Misty" drifted from the hidden speakers.

"Hey, my dad swears by him." Dan decided it might blow the mood if he shared the fact that according to his mother, who should know, he'd been conceived to Mathis.

"Better we use your father's music than mine," she decided.

Since, from what he'd always been able to tell, Reggie Townsend screamed his lyrics rather than sing them, Dan concurred.

Using Mathis to set the mood might be a cliché, but as he'd told himself while standing in line at the mercantile, the entire picnic idea was pretty much a cliché. But maybe that's because it worked. Because it was romantic.

The funny thing was, he considered as he went around the room lighting the candles that had seemed to so amuse Olivia Brown, he'd never been the sort of guy who went in for grand gestures. Of course, he'd never met a woman who made him want to go that extra distance. Until Savannah.

He suspected she could have cooked the

chicken a lot better than the extra crispy pieces he'd picked up at the mercantile deli, but she seemed to enjoy it, which was all that mattered. The potato salad and cole slaw were pretty much standard deli fare, but this evening wasn't about food. They both agreed that the wine, as promised, was excellent.

During dinner they talked about the additions to the house, about Henry's surprising decision not to move out until Ida was back on her feet, about Gwen's new independence and the fact that she was trying for early admission at Dan's alma mater. The Stanford recruiter had been encouraging and had assured her that scholarships and work-study programs should cover her costs.

Life wasn't perfect.

"But it's getting better," Savannah said. With obvious satisfaction, she glanced around the room that was lacking only furniture. "Now that Lilith's found Martha, I'm still hoping to move in here before Thanksgiving, even though I probably won't be able to open for business until after the first of the year."

"Some things are worth waiting for."

She looked into his eyes. "True."

Dan placed a hand against the small of her back, drawing her closer. He did his best to show Savannah, with every kiss, every touch, how much he loved her. Emotions he'd never felt, never realized he possessed until recently, came pouring forth from him into her. Until Savannah, Dan hadn't known that it was possible to feel so much, so deeply, and still want more.

He undressed her slowly, tenderly. With trembling hands she did the same to him. Then they looked at each other and found each other wonderful.

Skin dampened, hearts thundered, bodies entwined. She moved under him without inhibition, touched him in all the secret places he was touching her without hesitation.

Dan breathed in the scent of her—soft talc, the peach shampoo she'd used that morning, the floral perfume that lingered in his mind all day—all night—long.

He tasted her, the sweet, intoxicating flavor of her lips, the hot, tangy essence of her skin. She tasted like sex and sin and temptation. He could have drunk from her succulent lips forever.

He watched her, the mysterious, seductive darkening of her eyes, the way her hair spread over her bare shoulders and breasts like tongues of flame. Looking at her bathed in the flickering warm candlelight, her flesh gleaming like molten gold, Dan fully understood why ancient man had made sacrifices to pagan goddesses.

"Oh God," she moaned on a ragged laugh as they rolled over the blanket, "I have this terrible problem."

"Let me fix it."

"That's the problem." Her mouth, wild and willful, clung to his. "I think I've become a sex addict."

"So, what's the problem?" The taste of her flooded into him, through him.

"All day long, while I was dealing with plumbers and Dottie and Doris and a thousand other people and problems, I kept thinking about how much I love the way you make me feel. How you can drive me mad."

She rubbed her breasts against his chest in a way designed to create sparks. "And how I wanted to do the same thing to you." She sprawled over him, her firm tanned thighs draped over his legs.

"So far, you're succeeding." When she began to move against him, the blood surged from his brain to other, more vital organs. "Now that," he muttered on a breath as sharp and ragged as broken glass, "is definitely overachieving."

"Trust me, I've just begun." Savannah went up onto her knees, straddling his burning body, rubbing against him like a provocative cat as her mouth blazed a hot, wet trail down his chest. "Have I mentioned how much I absolutely adore your body?"

"It's all yours." Somewhere Mathis was singing about a thousand violins playing. "At least until you kill me." And that, Dan considered, would not be such a bad way to go.

Her hair draped over his thighs while her tongue swirled sensually around him, pulling him into a deep, swirling maelstrom. Like a drowning man, he struggled to fill his lungs with air.

Dan had thought he'd experienced passion. Believed he'd experienced pain. But Savannah was proving him vastly wrong on both counts.

On the brink of losing what minuscule control he still possessed, he grasped her waist, lifted her up and lowered her body onto his.

"Now," he panted.

Her knees were pressed against his thighs, her soft, yielding body a hot sheathe for his power.

"Now," she agreed on a breath as labored as his.

Dan surged upward. She met him thrust for thrust, hot flesh against hot flesh. All the time Dan never took his eyes from hers.

He watched them darken, then widen, as they rode up the tumultuous peak, watched her lips part in passion and stunned pleasure as they came crashing down the other side.

Their bodies were slick with perspiration. Savannah was sprawled atop his chest and Dan was still inside her, loathe to leave when the sky outside the lantern room lit up with a flare of red, white, and blue fireworks. A booming sound like cannon fire rattled the glass while Mathis declared everything wonderful, wonderful.

"Oh, my God." He felt her laughter. "We'll *never* be able to top this."

"It's Friday night. The Coldwater Cove Loggers are playing the Richland Bombers at the high school." He rolled them over, draping one leg over her hip so he could keep her close. "Obviously the Loggers just scored."

"They're not the only ones."

He chuckled at that. He dipped his head, circled the rosy tip of her breast with his tongue and felt her heart, which had begun to slow to something resembling a normal beat, quicken again. "Want to see if we can make the earth move next?"

"On one condition." She bucked when his teeth tugged on her nipple, then trembled as his hand slipped between their bodies to cup her.

"Name it." She was slick, hot, and his.

"Before you take me back to the house, we try for a tidal wave."

"A hat trick," he said approvingly as he began to move his hips in a slow, deep rhythm she immediately met. "I like it."

21

"Good morning, Ida." The nurse she'd come to dislike more with each passing day breezed into the hospital room. The family was already two minutes late picking her up, and Ida was already not in the best of moods. "So, today's the big day, isn't it, dear? I'll bet we're so-o-o excited to be going home."

"If you're coming with me, I'll just throw myself out of this wheelchair in front of an ambulance on the way out of this place. Dear." Ida answered mentally. Since she knew she wouldn't be able to string all those words together just yet, she shot the woman her most blistering scowl instead.

Blithely ignoring it, the nurse began pushing the chair toward the door. If she could have dragged her feet to stop the forward progress, Ida would have. As it was, the most she could do was make a futile grab for the door frame with her good left hand as she was wheeled through it.

"Where?" Thanks to Kathi Montgomery, she now had a vocabulary of about twenty-five words. Unfortunately, none of them were curse words, which she could have used about now.

"Oh, it's a surprise." They were headed down the hall. Ida looked around, frustrated further when she saw no sight of her daughter or granddaughters.

She could understand Lilith not being there. While her daughter seemed to have become much more responsible since her marriage, Ida supposed a little backsliding was inevitable. Savannah was usually more dependable, but it was possible she'd had to drive out to the lighthouse for some reason and had gotten sidetracked with more construction problems.

But that didn't explain why Raine wasn't here. Her elder granddaughter was as punctual as a Swiss clock. It wasn't like her to be late for anything. That thought had Ida's irritation turning to fear. What if there'd been an accident? What if something had happened to them on the drive here? What if Gwen had borrowed Savannah's little red car and skidded out of control on the rain-slick road and driven into the cove? Or perhaps Amy had fallen out of that swing Jack had hung in the tree behind the farmhouse and broken her arm? Or worse.

Perhaps that sweet child was in the ER right now, barely hanging on to life, while she was fussing because they were a few minutes late.

Ida had never been a worrier. But that was before experiencing the mental and physical equivalents of a car wreck. As a doctor, she understood that her uncharacteristic dread of the unknown was attributable to normal post-stroke depression. But that medical knowledge didn't keep her rebellious, damaged mind from spinning up the bloodiest, most unlikely scenarios, most of which starred members of her family.

Perhaps, she thought as she cast a hopeful glance toward the bank of elevators they were racing by, once she was totally recovered, she'd try her hand at writing horror stories.

A mental image of the baby-talking nurse being eaten alive by a land shark who'd crawled out of Coldwater Cove almost made Ida smile.

"Surprise!" The cheers greeted her as she was wheeled into the solarium. Bright, helium-filled balloons hugged a ceiling draped with streamers of autumn-hued crepe paper. On the wall, next to a cardboard cutout of a turkey that had gone up a few days earlier, was a huge, hand-painted sign that read Good Luck Dr. Lindstrom. It seemed to Ida that the entire hospital staff had crowded into the room, even Dr. Burke, who'd made himself as scarce as hen's feet lately.

Ida didn't begrudge the neurologist his obvious discomfort with her condition. She understood professional pride; stroke patients tended to burst the little fantasy bubble of physician omnipotence. It was, after all, difficult to pretend to be God when you couldn't heal a medical problem with either drugs or surgery. She had the feeling he would have been much happier if she'd had a brain tumor he could have carved out of her head.

"Surprise!" The way everyone was shouting didn't help the headache Ida had awoken with, but the outpouring of goodwill more than made up for it.

She felt a rush of relief when she saw Lilith, Raine, and Savannah standing beside a table that held a sheet cake with Good Luck written in red icing. As her eyes filled, Ida decided that just maybe she'd let her baby-talking nemesis live after all.

Thanksgiving morning dawned bright and clear. Having given Gwen and Henry instructions on how to start roasting the turkey, Savannah, who'd moved into the lighthouse two days earlier, was driving to her grandmother's house with a trio of pumpkin pies when one of her father's songs came on the car radio.

Reggie Townsend was a rock legend. Born in Great Britain, he had attended Liverpool's Quarry Bank High School—the very same school that had given the world Beatles Paul McCartney and John Lennon. Although the singer-songwriter had just celebrated his fifty-second birthday, his glittering star continued to rise after three decades in the music business. Savannah's father had been described by critics and fans alike as cheeky, irreverent, outrageously sexy, irresistible, and brilliant.

Right before his sixth marriage, he'd appeared on the cover of the December *Rolling*

Stone magazine, looking like a biker Peter Pan in a pair of sprayed-on black leather pants, studded vest, and silver-toed cowboy boots. It had been his wedding suit, Savannah had read.

In a masterful bit of cross-promotion, Reggie's new bride, Britta, had had her own centerfold layout the same month in *Playboy*. She'd been dressed—or mostly undressed—in the froths of satin and lace intended for her honeymoon.

"That was *Unholy Matrimony,*" the DJ announced after the heavy-metal sound screeched to an end, "the song Townsend ended his Portland concert with last night. According to Portland police, the teens arrested during the short-lived melee have all been released into their parents' custody and there were no serious injuries.

"One baby was reported born during the excitement; her parents, students at OSU, announced that they've named the little girl Regina. We're told that Reggie dropped by the hospital after the concert disguised in scrubs, visited with the family, and had his photograph taken with his namesake."

Savannah smiled at the idea of her father donning surgical scrubs to sneak into a hospital. A perpetual child himself, he'd always liked kids, which, she supposed, was one of the reasons his fans ranged from teenagers who admired his rebellious reputation to older baby boomers who'd grown up with him.

While she had no intention of following in her father's marital footsteps, the one important lesson Reggie had taught Savannah was to follow her dreams, using his own brilliant career as proof that any goal could be accomplished if you only worked hard enough. Cared enough. While work might not be the first thing people thought of when they heard the name Reggie Townsend, Savannah knew he expended vast amounts of his seemingly endless trove of energy on his career.

A ticket to one of his live concerts was not inexpensive, but even his most vocal critics couldn't say that his fans didn't get their money's worth.

Even though she was accustomed to sharing her larger-than-life father with his adoring fans, Savannah was not ready for the crowd that had gathered in front of her grandmother's house.

They were uniformly clad in black Dark Dreams—The Danger Tour T-shirts. Reggie's road crew traveled with hundreds, perhaps thousands of these shirts, which he'd throw into the crowds during performances.

She parked behind a stretch limo that looked as if it could easily house a family of ten.

The crowd, for some reason that escaped her, began screaming when she got out of her car. Savannah was never as glad to see Dan as she was when his Tahoe pulled up behind her and he and John shepherded her past the fans.

"Can you believe this?" Raine greeted her sister with a hug as Dan practically shoved her in the front door and closed and locked it behind them. "I used to wish my father would at least want to meet me. I even had a fantasy of us someday practicing law together. Whenever

Reggie shows up, I remember that sometimes *not* having a father can be a good thing."

Savannah grinned. "Dad may be a bit over the top—"

"A bit?"

"Okay. He's Rock's Bad Boy. But he can be a lot of fun. In small doses."

She recalled a wonderful trip to New York when she'd been twelve. He'd taken her to a grown-up lunch at the Plaza's Pool Room, a matinee of *Cats*, and afterwards a Knicks game. Savannah wasn't much of a basketball fan, but she had been excited about being with her father, even if they were constantly interrupted by autograph seekers. And to top off a perfect day, the Knicks had won in overtime.

Of course, afterwards, while she'd been upstairs sleeping in their gilded suite, Reggie had gotten busted by security for frolicking in the Pulitzer fountain outside the hotel with two of the Knicks cheerleaders.

"Is that my luv?" the signature deep, gravelly voice called out from the living room. "Come in here and give your old man a kiss."

She hugged the man dressed in black jeans and a ribbed black shirt that hugged a washboard stomach she knew came from working out on the tour bus. "What a surprise."

"We just did a gig in Portland last night, and since we were so close, we wanted to come see how Ida's doing."

Savannah could remember a lot of things

Reggie had said about Ida over the years, none of them flattering.

He laughed at her openly skeptical look. "I know I wasn't exactly head of your grandmother's fan club. But I've always admired her spunk. Besides, it's time you met your new stepmother. She was a little nervous about crashing a family party, but I told her that it wasn't right for her to be eating her first American Thanksgiving dinner in a restaurant. Not when the best chef in the country, who just happens to be my own daughter, is doing the cooking."

As he introduced the tall blond woman towering over him, Savannah fully understood the term *supermodel*. Britta Townsend was a good six inches taller than her husband, even before you added the platform sneakers. The canary yellow diamond ring on her left hand was Texas size. Having never quite gotten over the poverty of his youth, Reggie liked surrounding himself with the trappings of wealth.

They definitely had a full house. Not only had the entire family gathered for the holiday dinner, along with Henry and Martha, but as soon as Lilith had discovered that Kathi Montgomery was going to spend Thanksgiving alone, she'd insisted Ida's speech therapist join them as well.

Amy was sitting on the living room floor beside Ida's wheelchair. They were watching the Macy's parade—a departure from *Sesame Street*, which Savannah's grandmother watched every morning, afternoon, and evening. Kathi had explained that since the stroke had wiped out the

part of Ida's brain that knew how to turn letters
into words, she'd have to relearn her alphabet.
With that end in mind, Kathi had recorded
hours of the PBS program.

The parade segued to a football game, which
had Savannah wishing for Big Bird. There was a
bit of muttering when she turned the television
off during the third quarter for dinner, but she
ignored it and soon everyone had squeezed into
the dining room, which John had decorated
with copper and gold mums and garlands of autumn leaves.

Conversation flowed easily. Savannah was a
little surprised by Reggie's new wife. She may
be young enough to be his daughter, yet she
seemed far more self-possessed than most people of her years, which Savannah thought may
be due to the fact that she'd gotten her first
modeling job—for a disposable diaper company—when she'd been six months old.

"I fell in love with Britta when she showed
up at the studio to star in one of my videos,"
Reggie announced with a cocky grin toward the
blond who, even seated, towered over him.
"Asked her to marry me that first day."

"Now why doesn't that surprise me?" Lilith
murmured.

"I've always been impulsive," he agreed easily.
"But this is different. Britta keeps me in line."

"Really?" Lilith skimmed her gaze over the
tight jeans and sweater. "Where on earth do you
hide your whip and your chair in that outfit,
dear?"

Britta looked a bit confused by the question, but Reggie just laughed. "She has her own ways of persuasion, luv. My darlin' wife's into positive reinforcement."

"Well, I'm truly happy for you," Lilith said, sounding as if she meant it.

"I'm happy for me, too. I'm even happy for you, Lilith, luv." Reggie grinned over at Cooper. "You've got yourself a fine woman, Coop, old man. Just practice your ducking skills. Lilith has lethal aim with the Waterford."

"Cooper doesn't give me any reason to throw vases at him," Lilith said with a toss of her head.

"Good for him. Man must have the patience of Job, since you're not exactly the easiest of women to get along with, luv."

"I've been thinking about something," Savannah said quickly as temper flared in Lilith's eyes.

"What's that?" Raine asked just as quickly, obviously appreciating her sister's sidetracking what could well be the beginning of World War III.

"You know how difficult it was, running back and forth between the hospital and work—not that we minded, of course, Gram."

Ida, sitting at the end of the long table in her wheelchair, just waved Savannah's words away with an impatient hand. "Go on," she said.

Savannah was suddenly a little nervous at the way everyone at the table was looking at her so expectantly, waiting to hear what had seemed like a good idea while she was driving back to the lighthouse last night after stopping by the house to have supper with her grandmother and watch a tribute to the letter *E*.

She'd been planning to discuss it with Dan, after she'd finished making the pies, but then he'd started kissing her and she'd decided the subject could wait until the entire family was gathered together today.

"I was talking to these people I met in the cafeteria, the Simpsons—"

"They're that nice couple from outside Forks," Raine remembered.

"Doesn't Mr. Simpson own a hardware store?" Lilith asked. "And they both work in it?"

"That's them. Mrs. Simpson's mother's was an oncology patient, in the late stages of lung cancer. They were telling me how difficult it was to afford a motel room every time she had to be hospitalized. This last bout, the nurses managed to find a bed for Mrs. Simpson, but whenever her husband visited, he had to sleep on either the floor or the waiting room couch."

"I saw him there one night." Lilith frowned. "Poor man looked exhausted. I was almost wishing I could just take him home with me."

"That's my idea." Savannah smiled, pleased that someone else had thought the same thing. Of course, that someone was Lilith, who'd never been known for her practicality. "That's what I want to do."

"Bring more people into this house?" Raine asked.

"No, of course not," Savannah said, shooting a reassuring gaze at Ida who'd furrowed her brow. Her grandmother had always been a generous person, but there were limits. Especially these days. "But *I* have the room."

"Which you intend to use for a bed-and-breakfast after the new year," Lilith reminded her.

"I'm still going to do that. But *I'm* living in the lighthouse and the keeper's house has a lot of bedrooms, since it was designed for a large family. . . ." Her voice dropped off as she recalled the reason Lucy's house hadn't been filled with children.

"It's okay," Henry said gruffly. "It's no secret how my mother died. I'm just glad to know my folks had some good years." Savannah had given him the journals and was pleased when they seemed to have brought him some comfort.

"My point is that in the event all the rooms in the keeper's cottage get booked, and I go ahead with my plan of adding a dinner menu, as well, I'll probably have about as much business as I can handle without having to hire more people, which I don't really want to do at this point. And that makes the assistant keeper's house superfluous."

"But it was going to be the honeymoon cottage," Lilith said.

"It would have made a lovely one," Savannah agreed. "But it should also make a lovely cottage for out-of-town guests whose families are stuck in the hospital."

"Are you thinking along the lines of the Ronald McDonald houses?" Dan asked.

"Exactly." Dan's ability to understand precisely

what she was thinking may have made her a little uneasy in the beginning, but she'd come to be pleased at how easy it was to share ideas with him. "Since the whole idea is to give the families someplace to relax and get away from the hospital atmosphere without putting themselves in debt with motel bills, I'd want them to be able to stay free. Unfortunately, even with your generosity in agreeing to carry back some of the mortgage, Henry," she said with a smile his way, "I can't afford to just give the cottage away."

"You'll need to set up a nonprofit foundation," Dan said.

"I was hoping you and Raine could take care of that."

He exchanged a look across the table with Savannah's sister, who nodded thoughtfully. "Sure. The paperwork won't be difficult to set up at all. But you're still going to need some funds to administer."

"I had a thought about that, too." Savannah turned to her mother. "I was hoping perhaps we could have a film festival of all your old slasher movies at the Orca Theater."

"Really?" Lilith's smile flashed like a newborn star. "Do you think anyone would actually want to come to a Lilith Lindstrom film festival?"

"False modesty doesn't suit you, luv," Reggie said. "Your films have reached cult status. I'll bet you'd fill all the ferries in Seattle with fans flocking to see them. Especially when they found out we were going to get together on stage for old times' sake."

"You?" Savannah stared at him. "Are you talking about giving a benefit concert?"

Reggie's grin was as bright as his former wife's. "Now, you didn't think I was going to let your mother have all the fun?"

Tears of gratitude and love burned at the back of her lids. Savannah couldn't recall the last time her mother and father had been together in a room without vases and curses flying, and she thought back to what Raine had suggested about every breath stirring the universe.

Their grandmother's stroke had been a terrible thing. Yet it hadn't happened in a vacuum. Henry had definitely become more thoughtful; Coldwater Cove had lived up to its slogan as The Friendliest Town on the Peninsula; thanks to her parents' cooperation, families with ill loved ones would be helped; and wonder of wonders, Lilith and Reggie actually seemed to be burying old hatchets. And not in each other.

That made Savannah wonder if perhaps the Buddhists might just be on to something, after all.

22

After the last touchdown had been scored and pie served, after Ida had ridden her glider upstairs for her evening nap and a drowsy Amy had been tucked into the same bed her mother had once slept in, Reggie took Dan aside and suggested they go out on to the back porch where they could have a little private chat.

The evening was cool but clear. A few resolute fans still waited in front of the house for Reggie's departure, but so far there'd been no problems. Dan suspected that one reason for their good behavior was Jack's Olympic County Sheriff's Department Suburban parked in Ida's driveway.

Reggie pulled a gold case from one of the zippered pockets of his metal-studded black leather jacket, offered a cigarette to Dan, who refused, then lit one for himself.

"Britta doesn't like me to smoke," he revealed

conversationally on a plume of blue smoke. "She's a health fanatic."

If tobacco was the only thing Reggie was smoking these days, Dan figured Britta may already have moderated her husband's behavior.

Reggie tugged on an earlobe, where a diamond stud glittered in the moonlight. "So, what are your intentions concerning my baby girl?"

"I like a man who comes straight to the point," Dan murmured.

"There's not much I haven't done, some of it I've regretted, most I haven't. But every so often, I actually learn from my mistakes," Reggie said. "Not saying anything when Savannah showed up in London with her new husband is one of the few I regret."

"She was already married. What could you have done, realistically?"

"What I should have done. Ripped out the bugger's heart and had one of my roadies toss him into the Thames."

From the dangerous edge to his tone, Dan had the feeling that Reggie wasn't kidding. Or exaggerating.

"That sounds like a warning."

"You're a perceptive bloke. I'll give you that."

"I'm also in love with your daughter."

"Loving Savannah's not hard to do." The tip of the cigarette glowed red as he inhaled. "It's what you're planning to do about it that interests me."

Dan knew he could end this conversation by telling Reggie that his relationship with Savannah was none of his business. Especially, since from what Dan had heard, Reggie had never been in the running for Father of the Year. But having been thinking a lot about family and children lately, he could understand Savannah's father's concern. He could also understand Jack's often stated desire to lock Amy in a convent closet until she turned thirty.

"I'm going to marry her."

"Does she know this?"

"I haven't said anything, but I suspect she's picked up on the signs. I'm also not certain she's real thrilled with the idea. Yet."

"Wouldn't think she would be," Reggie agreed as he looked out into the deep shadows of evergreens at the edge of the yard. "Her mum and I didn't set a real good example."

Dan wasn't about to argue with that.

"Never met anyone who could drive in a point like a barrister, though. Most of them are stubborn blokes." He slanted Dan a look. "Guess you are, too."

"When it's something—someone—I want."

"And you want my Savannah."

"Absolutely. Forever." The idea had admittedly come as a surprise. The more Dan had thought about it these past months, the more he couldn't imagine how he'd ever thought of a future without Savannah in it.

"Now there's an idea," Reggie murmured. "I envy a man who can feel that commitment for one woman. You might be almost good enough for Savannah. . . .

"I wasn't the best dad," he volunteered, proving again that Reggie Townsend also had a major talent for understatement. "But I like the idea of being a grandfather."

The wide grin that had graced the cover of *Rolling Stone* innumerable times over the past three decades flashed brilliantly in the spreading yellow glow of the porch light.

"I'll get the little nipper a set of drums. He can come on the road with his old gramps during school holidays. Another generation of Townsends makin' his mark."

"Another generation of O'Hallorans," Dan corrected mildly as he imagined a miniature Reggie, clad in black leather, hammering away at a snare drum in the living room. When the mental image made him smile instead of cringe, Dan decided that just went to show how flat-out nuts he was about Savannah.

"What were you and Reggie talking about earlier?"

They were at the lighthouse, in the lantern room Savannah had turned into a bedroom, sprawled in the lacy white iron fairy-tale bed she'd found at an estate sale in Gray's Harbor. She was playing with his hair while Dan nuzzled his face between her breasts.

"Just guy stuff." He frowned as he viewed the bruise, touched his lips against marred, fragrant flesh. "I was too rough with you."

She lifted her head from the pillow and looked down at the bluish brand. "You could never be too rough. Besides, it was mutual."

Her smile reminded him of a satisfied Siamese as she skimmed her fingertips over his cooling skin. "Wait until you see your back."

Ruled by the ravenous hunger that had been building all day during the family Thanksgiving dinner, they'd fallen on each other the moment they'd entered the lighthouse, hands bruising, mouths feasting, hearts pounding. He'd taken her like a conqueror; she'd ridden him like a witch.

They'd left clothes scattered across the floor, and he was going to have to go shopping to replace the skimpy scarlet-as-sin silk and lace that she'd been wearing beneath her sweater and that was now lying torn somewhere on the stairs.

The idea of wandering around like a bull elk lost in a frou-frou potpourri-scented lingerie shop wasn't exactly his idea of a fun time. Maybe he could just make a quick sweep through the place, buy one of everything, then bring the haul back here for her to try on. Dan imagined Savannah putting on a private fashion show for him right here in the lantern room. Now that would be a great time.

"What kind of guy stuff?" she asked.

His lips moved lazily, lingeringly down her torso. "You know. Football—"

"Reggie doesn't believe Americans play football," she reminded him.

"Basketball, then. Baseball. Fishing."

"I cannot imagine my father drowning nightcrawlers."

He felt her chuckle against his mouth as he

tasted his way down her stomach. "Okay. We mostly talked about you."

"I was afraid of that." She sighed. "When he called last month, I made the mistake of mentioning your name. Just in passing, but he latched onto it and started drilling me like he was some Victorian earl determined to keep his daughter chaste until he could marry her off."

"I think that's undoubtedly a universal feeling among fathers of daughters."

"I hope he didn't come on too strong."

"Nah. He just wanted to be certain that I was planning to make an honest woman of you."

"What?" She bucked as he dipped his tongue into her navel.

"We got along like gangbusters once I assured him that I'm not just amusing myself with your luscious body. That I intend to marry you."

Dan had decided, somewhere between the pumpkin pie and ripping her clothes off, that there was no point in wasting any more time. The lighthouse was nearly ready for its grand opening, Ida was recovering by leaps and bounds, and except for the new little detail of the charitable foundation Savannah wanted to establish, which should be a snap to set up, there really wasn't anything keeping them from making this arrangement permanent.

"Marry?" A chill raced over her skin. She stiffened beneath him.

"I guess that wasn't tonight's secret word." He sighed heavily as she pulled away. "You can't tell me that it comes as a surprise, Savannah. I've been up front all along about how I feel."

"I knew you wanted me."

"Wanting's easy. I want my bank statement to balance, a cold beer when I'm fishing, and to decimate my opponent in court.

"I *love* you." In contrast to his earlier passion-driven caresses, he trailed a feather-light touch over her breast. Splayed his fingers over her heart.

"Maybe you just love the sex."

"There's no maybe about it. I'm wild about the sex. It's world class, triple-A blow-your-brains-out sex, and if we could figure out a way to bottle it, we'd make a fortune.

"However, whatever crazy ideas you might have picked up from the weasel, great sex and marriage are not necessarily an oxymoron."

Dan knew things were going downhill when she pushed away his hand and pulled the rumpled sheet that carried the scent of their lovemaking up over her bare breasts, nearly to her chin.

"Know that from personal experience with Amanda, do you?"

"No." He heard the edge to her tone and assured himself that a jealous woman was not an indifferent one. "I know that from personal experience with *you*. With us together. If you weren't so focused on the past, you'd realize that you know it, too."

An anger born of frustration began to claw at him; Dan ruthlessly banked it. "What we've got going here isn't any short-term, no-strings, convenient affair that satisfies a temporary physical itch. I'm still going to want to rip your clothes off when I'm ninety. I'm still going to get hard as a boulder when I think about doing this."

He caught her chin between his fingers and kissed her, hard and deep and long until he'd drawn a ragged moan from her throat.

"And this." She was already going lax, her bones turning to water as he reached beneath the sheet with his other hand and stabbed his fingers into her. Her hips moved with him, the hot, slick moisture making a sucking sound as he unrelentingly drove her to yet another shuddering climax.

"Tell me you won't still want me sixty years from now, Savannah. Try telling me that you won't want me to want you."

"You know I can't tell you that." Her swollen, ravished lips trembled. "Of course I want you. I need you. But I don't *want* to need you, damn it."

It was the despair in her voice that slashed at him. Made him back away when he knew that if he pressed his case, he could win. But at what cost?

"I know you don't." He ran a hand down her tousled hair, feeling as if she'd taken a dagger to his heart when she visibly flinched. "But we can deal with it. Together."

"I have to deal with it on my own." Her eyes glistened, but her mouth had firmed. Along with, he sensed, her resolve. "I have to be clear, in my own mind, that I'm not just using you."

"Darlin', you're welcome to use me any time your sweet little heart desires."

His attempt at humor fell as flat as a heavy stone thrown into the cove. "This isn't funny."

"On that we agree." He reluctantly pushed himself out of her bed. "Not that I want to put any pressure on you, but how much longer do you think this journey of self-discovery might take?"

"I don't know." She was looking down at the sheet she was smoothing with nervous hands. "If we could just keep things the way they are, perhaps—"

"Nope. That's not an option."

"Why not? We're doing so well. Why risk ruining what we have?"

He'd watched the color drain from her face, turning her complexion as white as the cold sickle of moon hanging in the sky outside the windows. Then he admired the way she gathered up the composure that had momentarily scattered.

Her back stiffened; he resisted, just barely, the urge to stroke it. Part of him wanted to shake her, to make her see what was so clear to him; another, stronger part wanted to kiss her silly.

"I've reached a point in my life where I'm not all that interested in an affair. There's just no challenge in it. It's too easy to find someone to sleep with you, someone who doesn't want to hang around and try to make morning conversation afterwards when all you really have in common is lust.

"I want the whole ball of wax. And I want it

with you. Marriage, kids, even some furry mutt that'll chew up our shoes and dig up all John's carefully planted tulip bulbs. How about a golden retriever? They seem sort of like a family-type dog, don't you think?"

She blew out a breath. "I think you've gone crazy."

"Crazy about you," he said agreeably. Since the warm, fuzzy mental family image was pleasing him when their discussion was not, he decided to concentrate on it as he yanked on the briefs that had been dropped on the floor halfway between the door and the bed.

"I can't be a mother right now. I have a career."

"So does Terri Stevenson," he reminded her. "And Raine. But I understand that a new enterprise takes more time. So, I'm willing to wait a while for the kids."

"Crazy," she muttered because she couldn't argue against the two examples of working mothers he'd presented.

He tried again. "I can understand how, after all the storms you survived growing up, you'd be tempted to find a nice, pretty little harbor, drop anchor, and stay safe and sound. But sometimes those harbors aren't as safe or pretty as you might originally believe.

"Change is always a little scary, Savannah. But it's also good. Dumping the weasel and escaping your bad marriage was good. Moving home was very good. What you've done with this place is spectacularly good.

"And, at the risk of sounding immodest,

falling in love with me was one of the best and smartest changes you've ever made."

"I don't . . ." She slammed her mouth shut before the lie could come out.

The fact that she couldn't tell him that she didn't love him was enough, Dan decided. For now. He'd let her stew for a while, then he'd marry her.

"Tell you what, why don't you spend some time thinking the situation over and give me a call when you've made up your mind."

"Give you a call?" A temper she didn't show often snapped in her eyes.

"You said you wanted to sort things out on your own. So, I'll just leave and give you the space you need." He could tell this was not what she'd expected.

"Jack gave Raine all the time she needed to make up *her* mind," she reminded him on a flare of frustrated heat he enjoyed a helluva lot more than her earlier chill.

"I'm not Jack," he reminded her back. "Besides, their situation was different. She had to choose between Coldwater Cove and New York and the clock was ticking. Right now, where we're concerned, you're anchored in that safe little harbor bobbing contentedly on calm waters. There's nothing to prevent you from toying with my affections until doomsday."

"Toying with your affections?" She dragged her hands through her hair. The frustrated gesture caused her breasts to bounce in a way that had him almost reconsidering this strategy. The trouble with ultimatums was that they didn't leave you a lot of wiggle room.

"Hey, contrary to popular belief, we guys have feelings, too."

He scooped his shirt from the lacy iron pillar of the bed. "Let me know when you've made up your mind."

Dan dropped a kiss on her tightly set lips, flashed her the boyish grin that had, over the years, worked on females of all ages. Then, though it was one of the hardest things he'd ever done in his life, nearly as hard as coming home to bury his sister and claim her son, Dan walked out of the lantern room, leaving Savannah alone in bed.

With his resolve hanging by a thread, he did not allow himself to look back.

Savannah hadn't really believed Dan. Oh, she knew he loved her. But she didn't really believe that he intended to break things off entirely. Until he disappeared.

"I can't believe he didn't tell you where he was going," she complained to Raine. They were in their grandmother's kitchen drinking tea. Martha had taken the ferry to Seattle to do some Christmas shopping, so they'd spent the morning taking turns reading to Ida.

She'd always loved murder mysteries, the bloodier the better. She might not be able to tackle them herself quite yet, but Kathi, who Savannah had decided was an angel masquerading as a speech therapist, had predicted it would be only a few more weeks.

"I'm truly sorry," Raine said. "But he refused to tell me."

"He must have told Jack where he was going, since John's staying with you. What if something happened to him?"

"Jack probably does know. But he's not talking. You know how those O'Hallorans stick together."

"It's emotional blackmail," Savannah muttered darkly.

"Is it working?"

"Of course it is. Which is ironic, since he told me that he was leaving to let me make up my own mind." Savannah glared into her teacup as if she could read the answer to her dilemma in the swirl of black leaves at the bottom. "As if he isn't trying to manipulate things with this Houdini act. I'm surprised he hasn't rented one of those planes that make smoke messages to fly over town and write 'Surrender Savannah' in the sky."

"I used to think of marriage as a form of surrender, too," Raine revealed. "I spent so many years working hard for my independence, if I hadn't been so madly in love, I might have ended up resenting any man who'd ask me to give it up. But Jack never asked."

"Neither has Dan," Savannah admitted.

"I wouldn't think he would. He's confident enough that a strong woman isn't going to intimidate him, or prick his male ego."

"Do you think I'm too complacent?" she asked. Raine didn't immediately respond. "I believe," she said, choosing her words carefully, "that we both developed our own defense mechanisms. Our coping skills. My instinct is to fight like a tiger when I feel threatened."

"While I dive for the foxhole," Savannah said with self-disgust.

"You're being too hard on yourself. You've just always preferred to find a compromise."

"I compromised in my marriage, and look how that turned out." She threw up her hands. "Don't say it. I know. There's no comparison between Dan and Kevin."

"From what I can tell, sitting on the sidelines, Dan has never asked you to compromise yourself or your dreams or goals. All he wants is for you to love him, the way he loves you."

"I do."

"Then surely you, of all people, can find a compromise between your desire for autonomy and his desire to spend the rest of his life with you."

Raine leaned forward and covered Savannah's hand with hers. Her woven gold wedding band gleamed like a promise in the light from the copper lamp that hung over the table.

"While you're making your decision, you might want to keep in mind that since my marriage, my life is fuller than I ever could have imagined possible."

"You're lucky."

"Blessed," Raine corrected with a slow smile. "I suspect you could have that with Dan."

Savannah absorbed Raine's statement. "It's not that easy."

Raine sighed. Her eyes filled with sympathy. "I wonder if it ever is."

He'd made his point.

By the time he'd been gone a week, Savannah couldn't think. How was she supposed to think about booking reservations and what flowers to put in what room when all she could do was wonder where the hell he was? And if he was thinking about her.

She couldn't eat. The rest of the family had jumped at the chance to try out possible menu items and assured her that her praline butter Belgian waffles were a gastronomical delight and her braided blueberry loaf topped with vanilla icing was a taste of paradise. But she could have been eating dried ashes. Her own taste of frustration spiced with regret was too strong.

Worst of all, she couldn't sleep. The lacy white iron Victorian wonder of a bed, which she'd fallen in love with at first sight, the bed that she'd actually seen in her dreams since childhood, now seemed to be as wide and desolate as the Sahara Desert.

She didn't need him. Not really, she told herself over and over again. She was a strong woman with her own budding career and a loving, supportive family. She didn't need a man to make her feel complete. She didn't need him to make her world complete. The little corner of the universe she'd created for herself was still safe. Still secure. And lonely.

23

![ornament]

"Savannah?"

Savannah glanced up from the computer, which she'd been using to pay bills, and saw John standing in the doorway.

"Hi." She was tempted, as she had been each day this past week, to ask him if he knew where his uncle was. But knowing how it felt to have your openness taken advantage of, she'd managed to restrain herself. "I'm glad you're here. I couldn't believe it when I came home last night and saw all the greenery you'd hung. I wanted to thank you for all the trouble you obviously went to."

"I'm glad you like it. The boughs in the lantern room were Uncle Dan's idea."

"Well. Isn't that nice." She wondered if he'd mentioned it to John before leaving, or if the two of them had been in contact.

She had to stop this, Savannah instructed

herself. She was not going to let him make her crazy.

"I was just putting the poinsettias from the greenhouse in all the rooms, like you asked, and I thought you might want me to take a couple over to your grandmother."

"That's a wonderful idea." She shut down the computer. "Give me two minutes to button things up here and I'll drive you."

"You don't have to do that. It's a nice day and I've got the baskets on the back of my bike."

Savannah looked out the windows at the clouds stippled with the last light of the day. "It'll be getting dark soon."

"I've got a bike light. Uncle Dan lets me ride at night," he reminded her. "As long as it isn't raining and the streets aren't slick."

Just because his heart was as open as a child's was no reason to treat him like one. He was, she reminded herself, on the Special Olympics bicycle team. Still, she worried.

"Ida loves poinsettias. Why don't I drive by in a while and pick you up so you don't have to ride all the way to the farm?"

"I'm not going to the farm tonight."

Okay. She had to ask. "You're not?"

"No. Uncle Dan called Jack. He's coming back home tonight because he has to be in court in the morning."

"I see." So how long would he have stayed away if he hadn't had a court case scheduled, she wondered.

"Oh. I forgot something." He reached into an

inside pocket of his parka and pulled out a small book she recognized right away. It was another of Lucy's journals.

"Where did you find it?"

"I was putting the wheelbarrow away in the crawlspace and I had to move some stuff to fit it in."

While she didn't spend any more time than necessary down there, she'd inspected the crawlspace when she'd bought the property. It ran nearly the entire length of the keeper's house, had a packed dirt floor and a ceiling about six feet high, which made it large enough to use for outdoor storage.

"There was this old, rusted box beneath a broken wagon wheel," he revealed. "The book was inside it."

When he handed it to her, a spark of electricity arced from his fingers to hers. Savannah told herself that it was only static electricity. And that was strange, because they were both wearing sneakers planted firmly on the wood floor. Seeming not to notice, John wished her a nice evening, then left.

Savannah stood at the window and watched him pedal away with a cardboard box in each of the wire baskets on either side of his rear wheel. She looked out toward Dan's house and wondered if he was home yet.

Then she shook her head with self-disgust, sat down on the Victorian lady's fainting couch she'd had recovered, and studied the embossed leather cover of the journal. There'd been a time when she would have tried to convince herself that she was only imagining the warmth emanating from the slender volume. But there had been enough odd moments that defined explanation to convince Savannah that the stories were true. Lucy's spirit did live on in this lighthouse.

She opened to the first page and began to read.

The letter came by mail packet this morning. I was, at the same time, both shocked and saddened to learn that Hannah, of all people, could have been hiding such a secret for so long. To think that her husband would have taken to beating her these past years that I've been away is unimaginable. I do remember his temper, on those occasions when he'd overindulge in liquor, as being exceedingly hot. But it always flared out quickly, and afterwards, while a palpable tension might linger for a time, outwardly things returned to normal and such lapses were never spoken of. At least within my hearing.

I'd always believed such strains and occasional storms were part of being married. Now, of course, after nearly seven years with Harlan, I know differently. My husband is as incredibly passionate as I'd always dreamed. Indeed, I believe my darling Henry was conceived that first time we made love, on our wedding night here at the Far Harbor lighthouse.

Yet he's also a gentle man. A caring man. Having watched the way he shows his love for our son, I can as easily picture him holding this new child I'm carrying beneath my heart as I can imagine him rowing his dory out into storm-tossed seas to rescue some poor sailor who's fallen overboard.

One thing Harlan did not exaggerate was this piece of water's reputation as a "ship killer." I could not count the number of ships that have nearly wrecked on the rocks below the cliff and shudder to think what might have happened if this light, and Harlan, had not been here.

I do find myself on the horns of a dilemma. Hannah writes that she ran out of her escape funds upon reaching San Francisco. My first thought was to send her the necessary money immediately, but she then writes, in a hand so shaky that she could not be exaggerating, that she's taken ill. If I don't come to rescue her, she and the children could well be thrown out in the street.

I know I should discuss this with my husband, but Harlan is in Portland, receiving training on new shipwreck rescue techniques, and I don't expect him back for another five days. The schedule he keeps in his desk reveals that the Annabelle Lee is sailing out of Seattle tomorrow morning.

After much thought, I've decided to leave Henry in the care of the assistant lighthouse keeper's wife, take the ferry to Seattle, and book passage to San Francisco. Clouds are gathering in the western sky, which disturbs me since I've never been a good sailor. But Harlan, who points out the new ships as they pass our lighthouse, has told me the Annabelle Lee is one of the most stable ships in the passenger fleet. I only hope that turns out to be true, since I won't be much help to my sister if I arrive in San Francisco as ill as she.

I plan to write Harlan a letter explaining my unexpected departure. Then I will find hiding places for my journals. As much as I love my sister, I have never welcomed her unfortunate habit of invading my privacy in her apparent need to know the most minuscule details of my life. Now that I know the secret life she's been forced to live, I suppose I can understand her need for control.

There is little I would not do for my older sister. But I refuse to share the intimate secrets of my love for Harlan, and his for me. That is not only secret, it is sacred.

As she closed the journal, Savannah once again compared her situation to Lucy's. Both had left behind a former life to come to Coldwater Cove. Both women had found the lighthouse a source of comfort and fulfillment.

Both had found men they loved. Men who

loved them. Men who wanted to have families with them.

The difference was that Lucy had been brave enough to risk everything for Harlan Hyatt. Tragically, their time together had been cut short, but the journal entries assured Savannah that even if Lucy had been able to look into a crystal ball and see what lay in store for them, she still would have chosen those seven happy years over a life without him.

"This is what you wanted me to know, isn't it, Lucy?" Savannah murmured into the silence. "You weren't running away. You didn't desert your husband and son."

She felt a zephyr waft over her, stirring her hair. That was, of course, impossible, since it was December, and no windows were open.

Savannah reminded herself that the light-house was a hundred years old. It was bound to be drafty.

She almost had herself believing that logical explanation—until the electric candles she'd placed in the windows suddenly turned on.

A week after he'd left Savannah in bed at the lighthouse, Dan walked into his cousin's office.

"Hey, the prodigal returns." Jack was sitting back in his chair, his feet up on the scarred desk that had belonged to his father, working his way through one of Oley's Timberburgers with all the trimmings and an order of French fries.

"I've got a court date tomorrow." Dan snagged a fry and sat down on the other side of the desk. "Kathi Montgomery's divorce."

"How's she doing?" Jack shoved half the burger on its yellow waxed-paper wrapper across the desk.

"A lot better." Dan bit into the juicy flame-broiled burger. "As you know, she's gone back to work—"

"Yeah, Raine says Ida gets better every day."

"That's undoubtedly partly due to Ida's un-sinkable spirit," Dan allowed. "Anyway, Kathi's moved out of the shelter into an apartment, and by this time tomorrow she should be a free woman."

"I'm a little surprised her husband hasn't caused any more problems."

"Me, too. Maybe the idea that he can't keep her married to him by force finally sank in."

"Maybe." Jack didn't sound as hopeful. Then again, Dan considered, if he had spent all those years as a big-city cop, he'd probably expect domestic violence cases to go from bad to worse, too.

He leaned over the desk to grab some more fries and was amused by the title of the book next to Jack's boots: *Everything the Expectant Father Should Know, But Is Afraid to Ask.*

"How does it feel to be facing fatherhood for the second time?"

"Terrific." Jack took a drink of root beer. "And terrifying. I'd also forgotten that pregnant women tend to go insane from time to time.

Raine actually cried at a tire commercial last night. You know, the one with the babies?"

"That sounds a bit extreme. But she seems pretty sane at the office. Or at least she was when I left."

Jack mumbled something around a mouthful of fries that Dan couldn't quite make out.

"Besides, it could be worse," he suggested. "*You* could be pregnant."

"That's what Raine keeps reminding me. She also suggested that it's easy for me to stay calm since I'm not the one who's going to have to pass something the size of a basketball through a small opening in my body."

Dan grimaced. "Good point."

"She's also got me reading all these damn books." He nudged the thick book with the toe of his boot.

"Never hurts to be informed."

"Yeah. But you know Raine when she sets her mind to something." He took another noisy slurp of root beer. "Christ, I keep expecting to come home to a pop quiz."

"Sorry pal, you're not going to get any sympathy from me."

During the week he'd forced himself to stay away, far from temptation at his cousin Caine's fishing cabin in British Columbia, Dan had not stopped thinking about Savannah. One of the more appealing fantasies, after the hot sex ones that had him waking up as horny as a two-peckered billy goat, was the image of her ripe and round with his child.

"You're damn lucky."

"I know." Jack glanced over at the framed photograph of his wife and daughter. "I could put up with the tears and the stacks of books she keeps bringing home. I could even handle the Mexican food we've been having every night for dinner for the past two weeks because she has a craving for hot sauce. But you want to know the kicker?"

"I'm not sure."

"You may have noticed that the Boob Fairy has paid us a visit."

"This may come as a surprise, but I don't spend a lot of time checking out your wife's breasts."

"Well, if you did, you'd have noticed that they're suddenly spectacular. Playmate quality."

"Congratulations," Dan said dryly.

"The trouble is"—Jack plowed his hand through his hair—"I'm not allowed to touch."

Dan laughed at the exasperation on his cousin's face. "That *is* a bummer."

"It's not funny." Jack took a huge bite of burger, as if attempting to crave his sexual hunger with ground beef. "She told me they're for the baby. For Christ's sake, we're talking another five months before the kid's born. . . . Remember back when we were in high school, all we could think about was how to score with a girl?"

"Sure."

"Well, second base has never looked so good."

Dan laughed as the intercom from the outer office buzzed. Still muttering about injustice, Jack scooped up the receiver.

"What's up?" Something hard Dan had never seen before moved across his face. "Goddamn it." It was fury, Dan realized. Ruthlessly, rigidly controlled. "Any word on injuries? What about people inside the house? Did you call it in to the State Police? Okay. I'm on my way. . . . Montgomery just went ape-shit and shot his wife when she came out of Ida's."

Dan shot to his feet. "How is she? Is anyone else hurt?" Had Savannah been at the house? The possibility sent a chill racing through his blood.

"Kathi's still alive, but I don't know her condition. According to Gwen, who called it in, the bastard was hiding in the bushes, shot her once, then took off. The family's shaken but, thank God, safe."

He grabbed his Stetson from its wall hook and was out the office door, Dan right behind him.

"Wait." Iris Johansson held up a hand as they passed her desk. "Another call's coming in. . . . There's been an accident. The subject hit a bicyclist while fleeing the scene of the shooting. . . . The hit-and-run victim is reported to be John Martin."

"What?" Dan spun back toward her.

"Just a minute." She tilted her head, obviously listening to the voice in her headset earphone. Her eyes, as they slid from Jack to Dan, darkened with sympathy. "The suspect is in State Police custody after running off the road on the old highway and hitting a tree. . . . The deputy on the first accident scene is reporting that the victim doesn't show any vital signs."

"Tell him to look harder," Dan shot back.

"The paramedics have arrived at the scene," she continued passing on what was coming into her ear. But the information was directed at Dan's back as he and Jack tore out of the office.

Jack hit the siren before they'd slammed the doors on the Suburban. "Fasten your seat belt," he barked at his cousin. "The one thing we don't need is another O'Halloran landing in the ER."

There'd been a mistake, Dan told himself over and over again as they raced down Harbor street. They had the wrong victim. Or the deputy didn't know how to check for a pulse.

John couldn't die now. Not like this. Not after all he'd already survived in his young life. Dan wouldn't let him.

"He isn't dead, damn it," Dan repeated again and again. His words were half curse, half prayer.

Savannah found Dan pacing the floor of the same small room where they'd all spent too many hours waiting for news of Ida.

"Raine called me." She wrapped her arms around him, held him tight.

"Thank God." He buried his face in her hair. "I need you."

"I need you, too." Strange how those words had ceased to cause that knee-jerk fear. Savannah realized that when your world went spinning out of control, it was a relief—and, as Raine had pointed out, a blessing—to have someone to hold on to. "But we can talk about all that later."

Dan was trembling. It broke her heart. "What have they told you?" she asked gently.

He took a huge breath and lifted his head so he could meet her gaze. His handsome face was haggard and gray. His flat blue eyes had that thousand-yard stare that a soldier's might acquire after a horrendous battle.

"Not much. The cop couldn't find any vitals, but the EMTs brought him back on the way, then lost him again." He dragged in another gulp of air on a ragged moan. "Since no one's come in to tell me any different, I'm going to assume he's alive."

"Of course he is." She couldn't imagine otherwise. "You need to sit down." She urged him toward one of the orange chairs. "Before you fall down and break that pretty face." She framed the face, which was anything but pretty at the moment, between her palms.

"I hate this," he muttered. But as docile as a lamb, he sank onto the chair.

Savannah sat down beside him, his cold hand tight between both of hers. "I know."

"Christ. If forcing people to wait for news was an Olympic sport, this place would win a goddamn gold medal."

"I know," she repeated. "But as you said, in this case, no news is probably good news." She looked up as Jack came into the room. "Hi."

"Hi." His tone was as flat as hers. "They've still got John in the crash room. I managed to get a look at him surrounded by people, but one of the nurses kicked me out before I could get a handle on how he was doing. I was thinking about using my badge to pull rank, then decided that if I hung around, I'd just be in the way."

"That's good news that they're still working on him," Savannah said, her positive tone meant to assure them all. Especially Dan, who was looking like death warmed over himself.

"That's what I figured," Jack said.

Dan merely grunted. Then dragged the hand Savannah wasn't holding down his face.

"Kathi's going to be all right," Jack volunteered into the silence that had settled over the room like thick, dreary winter fog. "Fortunately Montgomery was a lousy shot. There was a lot of blood on the scene, but the wound turned out to be superficial. They're going to keep her overnight, then probably release her in the morning."

"That's something," Dan said. "What about Montgomery?"

"He was thrown out of the car. Broke his neck on impact and was DOA."

Dan nodded, satisfied at least about this. "Good."

No one spoke for another long time. Finally, a nurse appeared in the doorway. Dan jerked when he viewed Mrs. Kellstrom's blood-stained scrubs. Knowing that it was John's blood made

Savannah want to burst into tears. But she was determined to remain strong for Dan.

"The doctor asked that I talk with you, since he's on the way to surgery. He wanted you to know that we've got John stabilized." Her steady brown eyes didn't reveal a thing. "It was touch and go when he first came in. We almost lost him twice, but Dr. Hawthorne refused to let him go. The entire time he was doing CPR, he kept muttering about plastic flowers."

The name, coupled with the mention of plastic flowers, rang a bell. "His mother has Alzheimer's," Savannah said. "John planted a plastic garden for her so she'll always have flowers."

"That's what Dr. Hawthorne said," the nurse agreed. "I wasn't surprised, knowing how good John's been to my Cindy." She smiled encouragingly at Dan. "He's a wonderful boy. He's bound to have built up a lot of credits in heaven."

"Just so long as he doesn't end up there anytime soon," Dan countered. "Why's he going to surgery?"

"Dr. Hawthorne believes his blood pressure crash was due to internal bleeding. John has multisystem injuries—a broken arm and nose and several fractured ribs. There was no sign of it on the x-ray, but the doctors were worried about a torn lung, so we put in a chest tube.

"Since John kept lapsing in and out of consciousness, Dr. Burke was called for a consult, but the CAT scan didn't reveal any brain damage, other than some swelling that's fairly routine in traumas like this."

"Nothing about this is routine."

"Of course it's not to you," Mrs. Kellstrom agreed with Dan's gritty assessment. "Dr. Hawthorne suspects that the internal bleeding may be coming from a ruptured spleen," she continued her report.

"Jesus." Dan turned from gray to green.

"I wish I had better news. But the doctor's an excellent surgeon," she assured them all. "So long as he can stop the bleeding, John's chances of a full recovery are excellent."

She skimmed a professional look over Dan's face, apparently not liking what she saw. "John will probably be in surgery well into the night. Why don't you go home and get some rest and—"

"No." Dan shook his head. "I'm not going anywhere."

"Neither am I," Savannah said.

Jack folded his arms. "Me neither."

The nurse didn't look at all surprised. "I'll have the cafeteria send up three dinner trays."

Savannah suspected that neither Dan nor Jack had any more appetite than she did. But it seemed easier not to argue.

With nothing to do but wait, they hunkered down for the duration.

24

⁓

They were still there in the morning when Dr. Hawthorne finally showed up in the waiting room. His scrubs bore dark blood stains, just as Mrs. Kellstrom's had last night. His face and eyes looked weary, but not, Dan determined, defeated.

"It was touch and go for a while," he told them. "But, barring complications, John's going to be fine. We didn't have to remove his spleen, his lungs are fine, and at his age, bones heal fast."

The breath came out of Dan in a slow, relieved whoosh.

"When can I see him?"

"He's in recovery now. Give him some time to come around, then you'll probably be able to visit him in the ICU in"—he glanced at his watch—"about an hour."

"Thank you." Dan could have kissed him, then decided against embarrassing the man who'd literally brought his nephew back from the dead.

"It was my pleasure." The doctor, who looked as if he needed sleep as much as the rest of them, managed a smile. "I owed the kid a huge favor for what he did for my mother. I was grateful for the opportunity to pay him back."

"You sure did that," Dan said. "In spades."

"Well," Jack unfolded himself from the hard plastic chair and stretched. "Now that we've survived this latest crisis, I think I'll go home to my wife and daughter."

"Good idea." He hadn't kissed the doctor, but Dan hugged his cousin. "Thanks for sticking around."

"John's family," Jack said simply, as if that explained everything. Which, Dan thought, it did. "So are you." Jack bent and kissed Savannah's cheek. Then left them alone.

Savannah turned toward Dan. "I missed you."

"I missed you, too."

His eyes were exhausted, but the life, the warmth, was back. So was his color. The stubble of beard was sexy, Savannah decided. Actually, everything about Dan was sexy. That was only one of the many reasons she'd fallen in love with him.

"*You're* the one who went away." Now that things were looking up, Savannah allowed herself a slight sulk about that.

"And thought of you every damn minute. Besides, you're the one who said you needed some time alone," he reminded her. "The one who equated loving me with weakness."

"I was wrong." It irked a little. But she'd get over it. They'd get over it together. "So sue me."

"I'd rather kiss you."

He skimmed his palms over her shoulders, down her arms. When his fingers encircled her wrists she viewed the flash of male satisfaction in his eyes and suspected he'd felt her pulse rate jump.

"I'd rather you kiss me, too."

The kiss was long and sweet and satisfying.

"That was nice." She rubbed her cheek against his roughened jaw.

"I can do better," he promised. "Later."

"I'm going to hold you to it." She tilted her head back and smiled. "Later."

Savannah wanted to tell him all about Lucy, about the journal and the candles, but that could wait. After all, they were going to have a lifetime together.

"My grandmother's always had a saying I've been thinking a lot about lately," she revealed. "Carpe diem. . . . Seize the carp."

He smiled back. "Wise woman, your grand-mother."

"I've always thought so. I've also come to re-alize how there are no guarantees in life. That we can lose the ones we love in the blink of an eye."

"I've noticed the same thing."

"So, in the interest of not wasting any more time, do you still want to marry me?"

His smile widened to that bold, buccaneer's grin Savannah knew would always have the power to thrill her. "Sweetheart, I thought you'd never ask."

The Far Harbor lighthouse stood atop the cliff, looking like a dowager dressed in her best jewels. A rare snow had fallen the night before, spreading a white cloak over the ground that sparkled like diamond-studded velvet in the winter sunshine.

The fragrant evergreen boughs John had draped across the top of the lantern room windows added an even more festive note to this special day.

They'd decided that since Dan's house was larger and had more room for the growing family they planned, they'd live there. Savannah would continue to use the first floor of the lighthouse as her office. They'd also agreed that the lantern room she'd loved from the first would be a perfect romantic hideaway.

Dan had grumbled a bit, but had helped her temporarily move the bed out to allow for the gathering of O'Hallorans and Lindstroms who'd come together to celebrate the forging of another link between the families.

John, his grin broad in his still bruised face, seemed to revel in his role as his uncle's best man. Despite having been released from the hospital only two days earlier, he'd insisted on creating Savannah's bouquet. The arrangement of white roses and holly was more precious to her than emeralds.

Ida had arrived on Henry's arm, leaning on her Christmas gift—a polished wooden cane on which he'd carved the universal symbol of her profession, the coiled snakes of a caduceus.

As she exchanged vows with Dan, Savannah thought how Lucy had pledged the same promise right here in the Far Harbor lighthouse. She hadn't felt the ghost's presence since the day she'd read the last journal entry; she and Dan had decided that, having succeeded in revealing the truth about her death, Lucy's spirit had finally been freed to join with that of her beloved husband's.

Savannah had also been relieved when Doris Anderson, president of the Coldwater Cove historical society, had contacted a fellow history buff in San Francisco who'd unearthed a newspaper article revealing that Hannah had remarried a prosperous local banker. She had more children and lived a long and apparently happy life.

Proving again, Savannah had thought, the power of hope over experience.

The words they'd chosen were simple. Traditional. Timeless.

To love. To honor. To cherish.

When her lips touched Dan's in their first kiss as man and wife, Savannah knew that her heart—and the Far Harbor lighthouse—had led her to exactly where she belonged.

Here, among her family, with the man she would love until the end of forever, Savannah was finally home.

POCKET BOOKS
PROUDLY PRESENTS

NO SAFE PLACE

JoAnn Ross

Available in March 2007 from
POCKET BOOKS

Read on for a preview of
No Safe Place. . . .

SHEETS OF LIGHTNING TREMBLED AGAINST a vermilion sky curtained with rain.

Kate Delaney stood at the apartment window in the French Quarter, looking down on a writhing tangle of tropical plants. A crumbling stone statue stood in the center of the overgrown courtyard; Kate found the trio of satyrs chasing the comely nymph through the algae-choked green water a perfect metaphor for this sin-drenched city.

"She wouldn't have committed suicide."

"You said it's been fifteen years since you've seen your sister." Nick Broussard was leaning against the doorframe, hands in the front pockets of his dark suit trousers. "People change."

"Now there's a pithy observation." The smoky neon sign from the strip club next door flashed pink and green shimmers onto the rain-slick cobblestones below. Underlying the burned-wax scent of votive candles in red glass, another vaguely unpleasant odor hung in air thick enough to drink. "Maybe you should embroider it onto a pillow."

"Dubois was sure enough right about you having a smart mouth on you, *chère*."

Kate hated the humor she heard in the detective's voice. To her mind there was nothing humorous about murder. "It goes along with my smart head," she said as thunder rumbled in from the Gulf. "Unlike Detective Dubois, who undoubtedly found his shield in a box of Cracker Jacks, there's no way, given the condition of this room when he and his jerk-off partner arrived on the scene, any cop with half a brain could've called this a suicide."

Crime scene photos revealed Tara had stacked all the bedroom furniture against the door before jumping—or being thrown—out the window. "She was trying to keep someone out of here."

"Wouldn't be the first working girl to suffer from drug-induced paranoia."

Kate wished she could have been surprised to learn that her twin had grown up to be a prostitute. If only . . .

No! She could give in to the dark emotions battering her and wallow in guilt later. Right now the objective was to put her sister's killer behind bars. With or without the help of the local cops, who were dragging their damn feet.

"I want her book." If she could only get her hands on Tara's client list, she could begin narrowing down the suspects.

"The police are looking for that," Broussard said with exaggerated patience that grated on Kate's last nerve. "But being a murder cop yourself, *chère*—"

"It's detective," she corrected.

"Being a murder cop yourself, *Detective chère*," he said, his drawled Cajun patois as rich as whiskey-drenched bread pudding, "you oughta know police investigations take time to do right."

Kate snorted. "What you mean is the cops are giving any city hotshots who may have paid my sister for sex time to cover their collective asses."

He sighed heavily. Pushed himself away from the door and crossed the room to smooth his large hands over her shoulders.

"Hey, darlin'. This is New Orleans. Folks have a certain way of doing things here."

"The Big Easy."

"That's what we call it, all right," he agreed.

"The movie." She shrugged off his touch. "Dennis Quaid says it to Ellen Barkin."

He brightened at that, his smile a bold flash of white that Kate suspected had charmed more than its share of bayou belles into slipping out of their lace panties for him. "You like that movie, *chère*?"

"I *hate* any movie that glamorizes crooked cops."

He shook his dark head. "You're a hard woman, Detective Delaney."

"Like you said, I'm a murder cop." Rational. Logical. Tough-minded. Where others saw shades of gray, Kate's world consisted of black and white. Cops and killers. Good versus evil.

As a gust of wind rattled the green leaves of the banana tree in the courtyard, Kate sensed a movement just beyond the lacy iron fence.

A man, clad all in black, and wearing a brimmed hat that shielded his face, was standing on the sidewalk beneath an oak tree dripping with silvery moss. The tree's thick, twisted roots had cracked the cobblestone sidewalk; the limbs Tara had crashed through on her fatal fall to the ground clawed at the window, leafy branches scratching against the glass.

"The landlord said other women had been killed in this building."

"That was before my time." Broussard was standing close enough behind her that she could feel the heat emanating from his body, along with a musky male sweat and the tang of lemon, which would've seemed incongruous on a man who reeked of testosterone if Kate hadn't known the cop trick of using lemon shampoo to wash the smell of death out of your hair. "The way the story goes, a young slave was found in the formal parlor, her dark throat slit from one pretty ear to the other."

His hands were on her again, long, dark fingers massaging the boulderlike knots at the base of her neck. "Later the police discovered eight other bodies buried in the garden. They'd all been raped. Brutalized. All had a *gad* cut into their breasts."

He paused, waiting for her to ask.

The silence stretched between them, broken only by the sound of the wind, moaning like lost souls outside the window.

"So, what the hell is a *gad*?" she finally asked on a frustrated breath.

"It's a tattoo designed to protect the wearer from evil spirits. The guy who built this place was a *bokor*. A priest who specializes in the dark arts, what voodoo practitioners call the left-hand way. They're not all that common, though we've got a handful of 'em living here in the city."

"Sounds as if the tattoos weren't all that much protection." Having had a mother who staged fake séances, Kate didn't believe in magic, either white or black. Or any other woo-woo things that went bump in the night.

He shrugged. "Hard to stop a man with killin' on his mind."

She could not argue with him about that.

"Your sister had one."

"One what?" The rusty gate squeaked.

"A *gad*."

She glanced up at him. "The report didn't mention that."

"The autopsy's scheduled for tomorrow morning. It'll probably show up in the coroner's report."

"Dubois still should've put it in."

"Like you said, Dubois isn't the sharpest knife in the drawer."

The man was now in the courtyard, staring up at the window. A lightning bolt forked across the sky, illuminating the malevolence in eyes, which blazed like turquoise fire in a midnight-dark face. Kate, who'd always prided herself on her control, tensed.

"What's wrong, *chère*?" Broussard's fingers tightened on her neck.

"That guy in the courtyard." White spots, like paper-winged moths, danced in front of her eyes. She blinked to clear them away. "He's—"

Gone. Kate stared down at the thorny tangle of scarlet bougainvillea and night-blooming jasmine.

He'd vanished. As quickly and silently as smoke.

Read on for a preview of

IMPULSE

JoAnn Ross

Available now from
POCKET STAR BOOKS

SEVENTEEN HUNDRED MILES FROM THE Savannah waterfront where he'd been shot three months earlier, Will was dragged from the nightmare, drenched in sweat, his out-of-control heart pounding so fast and so hard it could have been about to go into cardiac arrest.

The first time he'd felt this way, although he'd growled like a wounded grizzly, Gray had rushed him to Memorial Health University Medical Center, where an ER doctor who didn't look old enough to legally drive had stopped the wild heartbeat by massaging his carotid artery while a sadistic nurse slapped a wet towel onto his face.

"Have you experienced any stress lately?" the doctor had asked.

"Who hasn't these days?" he'd muttered from beneath the icy cloth. Working undercover Vice wasn't for sissies. Especially after you'd been dragged back from the jaws of death right here in MHUMC's trauma unit.

"Well, from your symptoms, and your positive response to treatment, my best guess would be you've got paroxysmal atrial tachycardia."

Will had ripped the rag away before he lost his nose to frostbite. "Any chance you could try saying that in English, Doc?"

"In layman's terms, the stress you've been under is causing your brain to send glitched electrical impulses to your heart. Which in turn, created an overload, which, in turn, caused it to lose its natural rhythm."

His encouraging smile was faked, as if he were auditioning for a role on *ER*. "It's really not that uncommon. And certainly not fatal."

He'd scribbled something onto Will's chart and handed it to the nurse. "I'm going to order an EEG, just in case. And I suggest you learn to be a little easier on yourself. Maybe take up yoga. Or meditation."

That'd be the day.

The wind, which had been battering the town ever since he'd arrived six weeks ago, had stopped. Moonlight was slipping between the slats of the blinds as he went into the kitchen, dumped a handful of ice cubes into a mixing bowl, and filled it nearly to the brim with water.

He took a deep breath.

Shut his eyes.

Then stuck his face into the bowl.

The icy water slammed into his system, instantly resetting his glitchy heart's rhythm. It might not be the most enjoyable way to start his day. But it was a helluva lot preferable to twisting his body into yoga pretzels.

Cursing himself for not being able to fight off the anxiety that had caused him to walk away from a job he'd loved and had been good at, and knowing from past experience that there'd be no more sleep tonight, he turned on the kitchen radio and spooned some Folgers (another thing that Doogie Howser clone had warned against) into the Mr. Coffee.

"Can you believe this night?" the all-too-familiar voice on the radio asked. "I've been here a year and this is probably only the third time the wind's stopped. Who knew Wyoming could be so silent?"

Who knew that the woman he'd shared those kisses with atop the Ferris wheel three years ago would show up in Hazard, Wyoming, of all places.

What the hell were the odds?

But, like Han Solo had said in *The Empire Strikes Back,* "Never tell me the odds!"

The woman currently calling herself Faith Prescott had the perfect voice for nighttime radio—dark and smooth, like rich cream over warm cognac. It slipped beneath your skin on lonely winter nights, encouraging hot midnight memories of her in his bed, those sultry, dulcet tones talking dirty in his ear.

"It's the kind of night you don't want to be alone." Her husky purr echoed his own thoughts.

Although she'd been in town a year, she continued to dominate breakfast conversation among ranchers who'd congregate every morning to clog their arteries with cholesterol-drenched eggs, hash browns, and country smoked ham and down gallons of coffee.

According to the scuttlebutt, the fact that she hadn't taken up with any of the locals had the members of the breakfast club wondering if she might be a lesbian.

Which would be, all agreed, if it was true, a crying shame.

She may not have given any of the males in town a tumble, but Will knew, firsthand, that Faith was no lesbian.

Despite Hazard's being a one stoplight town, so far they'd managed to avoid each other since he'd returned. Which was just as well, given that his life, which had always been exactly how he liked it before that damn shooting, had become impossibly complicated. He had no time for a woman with tiger eyes and a sinfully alluring mouth.

But that didn't stop him from fantasizing lying with her on that bearskin rug at the Red Wolf Lodge.

The night-chilled air thickened with the scent of musk. In his fantasy, they were both naked, her fragrant body gleaming in the flickering orange glow from a fireplace large enough to stand in.

He'd just run his fingertips up the silken skin of her inner thigh and was planning to follow the path with his tongue, when the wall phone had the image shattering like splintered ice.

He scooped it up. "Yeah?" His unusually harsh voice was roughened with pent-up sexual need.

"Sheriff?"

Inner alarms began blaring. "What's happened?"

Sam Charbonneaux, Hazard's chief deputy, was one

of the most capable cops Will had ever worked with. He never would've risked waking his boss up in the middle of the night for anything minor.

"It's bad, Sheriff." The deputy's voice sounded clogged. "Real bad." There was the sound of a ragged intake of breath. "It's that skater."

"Skater?"

"You know, the kid from those soup commercials. Erin Gallagher." He paused to drag in another deep breath. "She's dead."

Damn. Erin Gallagher had been America's best hope for a gold medal in this year's Winter Olympics before she'd turned her back and walked away from figure skating. While Will wasn't up on celebrity news, Josh subscribed to *Sports Illustrated* and he remembered the teenage skater appearing on the cover.

He was vaguely aware that she'd moved to Hazard in September to attend college, but since she hadn't gotten into any trouble, their paths hadn't crossed.

Until now.

After a brief conversation, he determined that Sam wasn't exaggerating. Instructing the deputy to secure the crime scene, Will hung up and immediately called the coroner, who sounded less than thrilled at getting dragged out of bed in the middle of a freezing winter's night.

After pouring the now brewed coffee into a stainless steel thermos, Will trudged back to the bedroom to throw on some clothes. Five minutes later, he'd written a note, letting his father—with whom he'd moved in with after returning to Wyoming—know that he'd been called out and had no idea when he'd be back.

He was at the door of the mudroom, about to head out to Silver Lake, when he turned back. After all that had happened, he didn't want to leave without saying good-bye to Josh. Because you just never knew when you might not be coming back.

The room was typical teenage messy, clothes thrown over the chair, strewn over the floor; skis, a Christmas gift still unused, propped up against the wall; a set of dumbbells beneath the window; a can of Coke sitting abandoned on the night table.

The screen saver on the laptop computer showed a sun-drenched beach fringed by palm trees; Will knew his sixteen-year-old son missed the freedom of his former unsupervised days in L.A., resented all the changes in his life since his mother's death, one of which was being handed over to a cop father who had a shitload of problems of his own.

Josh was also not adjusting well to life in this isolated high-range town where the wind blew nearly nonstop, snow stayed on the ground from October to June, and nothing much ever happened.

Remembering his own rocky teenage years, which, if it hadn't been for his father's influence, would've landed him in juvie more than once, and feeling a surge of fatherly fondness for this son he'd never known existed until that attorney had shown up in his hospital room in Savannah, Will stepped over the flotsam of teenage life to the side of his son's bed.

He wouldn't wake him. Just touch him. A hand to his hair, as Will had been denied the ability to do back when Josh was a baby and probably wouldn't have shied away from every paternal touch.

When his fingertips skimmed the empty pillow, Will belatedly realized he hadn't heard any breathing.

He turned on the bedside lamp, blinking against the sudden glare of the light flooding the room.

Shit. The bed was empty. Since Josh wasn't real good about making it each morning, Will couldn't tell if it had been slept in.

Frustration, mixed with ice-cold fear, threatened to trigger another attack.

With his damn glitchy heart hammering against his ribs, Will hissed out a breath and yanked up the shade. Dark eyes, a legacy from his Arapaho grandmother, scanned the vast, endless white landscape outside the window.

Where the hell was his son?